GREKS

by

SHAWN P B ROBINSON

BrainSwell Publishing
Ingersoll, Ontario

ISBN 978-1-989296-78-3

Cover design and artwork copyright © Shawn Robinson
Interior Page Dividers designed from images downloaded from Freepick.com.

BrainSwell Publishing
Ingersoll, ON

Dedication and Thanks

This book is dedicated to all those who feel that so much in life often falls apart, but yet still hold onto the hope of a better, brighter future.

This book is a work of fiction.
Characters and places and such are fictional. Now,
I would think this would be obvious information
and therefore unnecessary to include in this book,
but even so, I am putting this statement in here. I
guess it's possible that there may be someone,
somewhere who might think this story is based on
a true experience of an alien invasion.
If, by chance, this is you—you happen to be the
one who believes the stories on these pages are
true, and we have been invaded—then I encourage
you to do this:
Look outside and evaluate. Are all buildings across
the planet destroyed and do you see towering alien
creatures walking the earth?
If so… I'm sorry. It's all true.
If not, then… it's fiction.
Simple?

Special note on the allegorical aspects of this story:
Personally, I believe nearly all stories have, by their very
nature, an allegorical aspect to them of pointing towards the
condition of the human heart and a hope for a better future.
This story holds true to this shared desire held by people
down through the ages.

Preface

This book came about through a discussion with a friend about what a story which drives a video game could look like. How would it flow? What would it convey? How does it grip the gamer beyond gameplay, and how does it create a beautiful allegory of hope?

A challenge, of course, is the problem of violence, as I'm not an author who enjoys writing violent stories. Another challenge when creating a story that points to the condition of the human heart is how to convey that story in a manner that comes across as neither preachy nor dorky.

In response to this, this story is not only about the events in these pages, but the heart of Xavier in his struggle to be more than a soldier and more than a survivor, which I think is beautiful, since all of us long to rise above the rubble, the destruction, and the ashes that we often see around us and not only *find* but also *be* something more.

Shawn P. B. Robinson

CHECK OUT THESE BOOKS BY
Shawn P. B. Robinson

Adult Fiction (Sci-fi & Fantasy)

The Ridge Series (3 books)
ADA: An Anthology of Short Stories
The Grek Invasion (3 books)
Modder's Run (Coming Soon)

YA Fiction (Fantasy)

The Sevordine Chronicles (5 Books)

Books for Younger Readers

Annalynn the Canadian Spy Series (6 Books)
Jerry the Squirrel (5 Books)
Arestana Series (3 Books)
Activity Books (2 Books)

www.shawnpbrobinson.com/books

Table of Contents

PROLOGUE

Tuesday, 12:04pm

The burgers sizzle on the grill, and a smile slowly stretches across my face.

Doesn't get much better than this.

Three weeks of leave, and the best weather of the season expected in the days ahead. Alliah and Aaron seem to be getting along… I think. Can't always tell with those two. But Connie's easy to read from the huge grin on her face.

I flip the burgers and smile again. I could get used to this, but I ship out again in… no. Not shipping out. I'm flipping burgers. This is what I'm doing right now.

I smile again.

"Hey," Connie says as she comes up beside me.

I put my arm around my wife, and she nestles in close. I've been gone too long. "Hey."

"Did you get the emergency alert?"

I laugh. "Emergency? No, I left my phone in the bedroom. I'm not even sure it's charged. I don't want any calls or texts or emergency alerts or anything but this." I give her another squeeze.

She smiles but can't seem to take her focus on her phone. "This one's weird, though. It says 'Emergency. Remain indoors. More information to follow'."

She holds up her phone, and I glance at it, not overly interested. "Maybe it's just a…"

A loud BOOM knocks us to our knees, and the sun turns red as a huge meteorite tears across the sky.

Wednesday, 9:28am

"Down here!" Connie hollers.

Alliah turns and follows without a second's hesitation, but Aaron's a little off. I grab the back of his jacket and yank him off his feet, not dropping him down again until he's facing the right way. We can't afford a lack of concentration right now. If one of us doesn't listen, we'll lose that one in the panicking crowd in seconds.

We squeeze into the small alley Connie's found while we catch our breath, letting the people race by out in the street. I'm good to go, no need for a break, but Connie's never run much, and Aaron's always been a bookworm. He'd rather read than run and play. Alliah's not having much trouble. Track and field champion every year since she was seven. She's not as fast as me in a brief run, but she could outrun me any day over a distance.

But right now, it doesn't matter who's a bookworm and who's a runner; I need them all to outrun me. I don't know how else to keep them alive.

I check them over, one by one. They don't even ask what I'm doing anymore as I check for cuts, for injuries, they just answer any questions like, "Does anything hurt?" or "How did you get this rip in your shirt?" My singular focus is to keep these three healthy and alive.

"Did you see it?" Aaron asks in a whisper as I check him over, inspecting the cut on his belly he got yesterday.

"See what?" I ask, barely paying attention. The bandage needs to be replaced. It's not a serious cut, small enough the tape will hold it together. I've had worse many times in the field, but he'll need antibiotics.

"The… thing. The thing they call a Grek."

I stop and look at him. Alliah and Connie have gone silent as well. "You saw one? When? Where?"

"Behind us. It had… in its mouth… or… on its back… or… it had…"

His eyes are glassy, unfocused, and I put my hand on his cheek. "Look at me, buddy." It takes him a moment, but he focuses, and I smile. "We've got each other, right?"

He nods.

"And we love each other, right?"

He nods again.

"Do you want to tell us what you saw, or do you want to tell us later?"

He stares at me for a moment, then whispers, "Later…" but as I pull away, I hear him quietly say, "Never…"

Coming back, I give him a hug. He'll need to talk about it, but maybe not now. For now, we run.

I herd the family back toward the crowd racing down the street, and we join the flood of people, all running as hard as they can from what they don't understand. And none of us even know where we're running to.

But for now, all we can do is run.

Saturday, 3:09pm

"Head into the open!" a man hollers at the crowd.
We've been running.

Well… running isn't the right word. At this point, even Alliah can only put one foot in front of the other.

"Why the open? They'll get us!" a woman shouts back.

Somehow, while running for our lives with thousands of others, we ended up splitting away from the masses along with about fifty people. Don't know where the thousands of other people are now, which is strange, but we're with these people at the moment.

The guy in plaid's name is Geoff, and he fancies himself as a leader. He might be okay at it… if he had any sense.

"They're not interested in us!" he explains between breaths. "Look at them! They just ignore us. All they want to do is tear stuff down. If we get away from the buildings, they won't bother us. They'll grow bored when everything's destroyed, and they'll leave!"

Connie looks at me, and I shake my head. "Doubt it," I say.

"You have something to add?" Geoff growls at me.

He must have noticed my reaction. "Geoff," I say, coming to a halt. The rest of the crowd slows down and stops around us. This isn't the first time Geoff and I have butted heads, but I suspect it might be the last.

I turn slowly around, scanning the area. From this spot on the road, I can see six Greks, the closest at least seven or eight hundred yards away. Tall. Four legs. Hairy, thick body, tentacles on top. Hideous creatures!

Geoff's right about one thing: they're not interested in us. For the moment, anyway. "You see the lack of military?"

"Yeah!" he says with a sneer. "I gather they're fighting them all over the place."

"It's possible," I say. "It's also possible the Greks took out every military installation on day one."

His face turns beet red in a second, and he clenches his fists. "We don't know that!" he screams. "You don't know what you're talking about!"

Geoff turns and walks away, but I take another stab at it. The people seem to gravitate towards him. Not sure why, but they hang on his every word. "If the army still existed, they'd be fighting. Even if they weren't fighting here, we'd see signs. We'd hear gunfire, see the Airforce flying over our heads, and more. We'd at least hear the jets, if nothing else. Here's my take on it, Geoff, based on years in the Navy. Once these Greks took out the military and likely most of our infrastructure, preventing food and supplies from reaching us, they turned their attention to destroying buildings. Either they like destroying buildings, or they're removing every place we can hide. This… attack… that's what it is, Geoff, an attack. It's an operation. It's strategic. It's not chaos. Not random. It's…"

"You don't know what you're talking about!" Geoff shouts again as he waves for everyone to follow.

Connie, the kids, and I remain where we are while the crowd moves along, giving me dirty looks and coaxing Connie and my kids to go with them. One lady even whispers to Alliah, "You don't have to listen to him. Come with us. We'll keep you safe."

I want to scream at the lady, but I know my daughter. She frowns at the woman and crosses her arms. My girl isn't fooled that easily.

Before they get too far from us, I wave for my family to crouch, and we move along the edge of an enormous pile of rubble, turning down an alley, and weaving our way through the ruins.

"Where are we going?" Connie asks.

"I saw a pile of rubble back there that looks like it had some places to hide. I think we need to wait this one out. More's going on here than Geoff or the others think."

In another twenty minutes, we find our hiding spot. It's near a destroyed market, and I take a run over to the ruins, finding some cans of food amongst the broken beams, bricks, and mortar.

That'll get us through a couple more days, at least. Then I hope to know more about what's going on.

Thursday, Time unknown. Late at night.

"I hate that you were right," Connie whispers to me as we sit in a crevice between two piles of rubble. I can barely see her in the dark.

We've moved three times since we left Geoff's group. I'm glad none of the others saw what happened, but I did, out scavenging for food a few days ago. Once the Greks finished tearing down every building, the creatures converged on anyone out in the open.

Nowhere to hide out there.

And now… people… *humans*… they…

I saw Geoff when they took him, beating his fists against the large body of the Grek, its four legs thudding along the ground, moving off to the north. Most of the others fought just as hard, but no one had any chance against those beasts once those tentacles wrapped around them.

A few hours later, the Greks returned, carrying the same people they'd left with. Geoff, as much as I despised the man… I didn't want this for him. His eyes are now just like the Greks, glowing green eyes most of the time, yellow when they think they have someone to find… just like the aliens.

And all the people… the *humans*… they've somehow joined the Greks.

"I hate it too," I say, genuinely wishing I'd been wrong. "But it is what it is."

"You think we're the only ones left?" she asks, still in a whisper.

I glance back at the kids. I can't see them in the dark, but I hear their breathing. They sound asleep to me. Turning back to Connie, I say quietly, "I hope not. I truly hope not."

PART I

CHILDREN

Weeks later…

The small boy picked his way through the rubble, all that was left of his school. He thought he might be standing where his grade one class had been, but he couldn't be sure. The occasional wall rose a foot or two above the piles of bricks and concrete and steel bars, possibly offering some cover if he pulled some plaster over himself, but he also had plenty of desks to hide under, if needed. And it would be needed. He knew that better than he knew where he was or where his next meal might come from.

Part of the chalkboard remained on the wall jutting up before him. Not much, just enough to see that it was, in fact, a chalkboard. The faded writing only remained because half a cabinet had fallen over, covering up what lay beneath.

Checking first to see if it would be a good hiding place—he had learned to look for that kind of thing first—and satisfied that it would do just fine, he crouched down and examined the chalkboard. The writing, faint as it was, showed names. His teacher always wrote names on that corner of the board, names of kids who had done well, a way to thank those who had worked hard, or smiled a lot.

Aaron had often got the smile award in class most days, along with Chloe. She smiled a lot, too. The two of them had been friends.

And they had a lot to smile about.

Aaron tried to get his lips to move into that position, that smile. It seemed so long ago. Only weeks, from what his mom had told him, but he didn't think that could be true. His mom wasn't a liar, never, but he thought she might be this time. It felt more like he'd spent his entire life running, hiding.

He squinted at the first letter of the name on the board. In the early morning light, along with the faded chalk, it was impossible to make out the letter. He thought the second letter could be an "H" or it could be an "A". The top of the letter was smudged too much. The third letter, though… that was clear. It was definitely an "L". Aaron's teacher had a fun way of writing an "L" when she put a name on that list. She always wrote it with a little curve. Chloe. The name… it's Chloe.

He nodded. Chloe had been smiling a lot that day. He could no longer remember why. She had told him, but the memories of that day were fuzzy.

That last day.

Aaron knew where he was. Definitely his classroom.

Chloe never smiled anymore, at least not when Aaron saw her. No one taken by the Greks smiled anymore. No one at all.

Well, that wasn't really true. They smiled, but Aaron didn't like their smiles. The smiles weren't safe smiles. They weren't happy smiles. They were smiles that told you that you were about to be caught.

Thud… thud… thud… thud…

Aaron's heart dropped in his chest. The Greks were on the hunt.

He quickly slipped between the cabinet and the wall, his heart racing, the sweat breaking out along his forehead and running down his back.

"Calm your breathing, Aaron…"

That's what his dad always said. Somehow, his dad and his mom stayed strong when he and Alliah could barely keep from crying all the time. Well, Aaron didn't cry, but Alliah still did. Aaron couldn't find tears anymore. They just wouldn't come. He hadn't cried in weeks? months? years? That seemed to scare his mom more than the crying did. She wanted tears. Or, at least, she wanted him able to.

But he didn't think the tears would ever come again.

No more tears. Only fear.

He slipped inside what was left of the cabinet. The spiders didn't bother him anymore. They seemed friendly compared to the Greks. And the *human* Greks.

Thud…

Thud…

Thud…

Thud… thud… thud… thud…

Slow steps, then fast steps. Aaron's dad said that was the way they searched. A few slow steps, then fast. As long as they don't make that noise… that *Grek* sound… the sound they got their name from… the sound they made when they see someone…

When they made that sound, dad said to run. Don't look back, just run.

Thud…

Thud…

Thud…

Thud… thud… thud… thud…

Aaron closed his eyes and tried to calm his breathing. A moment later, he opened them again, and checked over his entire body, doing his best to make sure no part of him stuck out. He was sure they couldn't see him, but he pulled himself back further inside the cabinet just to be sure.

As he moved his foot, a stone moved with it, then rolled down onto one of the few spots where he could see the floor tiles of his former grade one class. The stone clacked against the tile, not loud, but maybe too loud.

The thuds came to a halt, and he waited. One-one thousand… two-one thousand… three-one thousand…

Aaron nearly screamed when he heard the dreaded sound.

"GRRREHHHHK!"

Scrambling out the far side of what remained of the crumbling wall and cabinet, he ran as hard as he could over broken concrete and bricks. He got through the standing arch of the doorway, and out into the hall connecting the classrooms, then through the rubble of the grade two class and up and over the bricks of the outside wall. When he reached the bottom of the pile of bricks and hit open ground, Aaron ran. Hard. As hard as he'd ever run in his life.

He raced across the playground, angling toward the gate leading into the neighborhood behind the school, back where his house used to be. Not many houses still stood, but a few walls here and there and the occasional house rose up somewhat intact.

But not his own home. It was nothing more than a pile.

Aaron didn't look back as he ran. His dad always said, "Just run. Forget everything else. Run and hide."

He'd learned to obey, for the most part, and as he ran, he wished he'd obeyed this time as well.

Thud… thud… thud… thud…

GRRREHHHHK!

Thud… thud… thud… thud…

Running as hard as he could, he reached the far side of the schoolyard. Maybe they hadn't seen him yet. He hoped he might be far enough away.

The tears seemed to have come back suddenly. A bad time for it. Made it hard to see as he ran for his life.

He reached the gate, but didn't make the turn in time, slamming into the fencing and stumbling off to the side. The moment he regained his balance, he took off to his right until the fencing opened into the empty street.

He had his escape route already down. His mom and dad had drilled it into him so many times he knew where to go wherever he was in the city—what was left of it, anyway.

He turned into the street and risked a glance back. Two of them. The big ones, the full Greks. Large, four legs—hard like a crab's—with a hairy spider-like body. No wonder the little spiders never bothered him anymore.

The *human* Greks were probably back there somewhere. He figured Chloe might even be with them. She was around a lot. She'd always been fast and small. Aaron thought they used her a lot for that alone.

He raced up the street past the piles of rubble from all the homes and turned sharply to the left toward a house, hoping to lose his pursuers. Crouched low enough he couldn't see the Greks past the debris left from the ruined buildings, Aaron rushed along a mostly clear path laying between two destroyed houses. He moved along a wall still somewhat remaining, standing just above his own height, and then made his way toward a hole he could see ahead.

"GRRREHHHHK!"

He broke into an all-out run, but barely made it two steps before something slammed into his chest and yanked him right off his feet. Spinning around through the air, he struggled, but then crashed down next to the wall he had just passed. A moment later, a large hand covered his mouth before everything went dark.

"Calm your breathing, Aaron…"

The hand came away, and Aaron wanted to shout and wrap his arms around his dad's neck, but he dared not move or make a sound. His dad had covered the two of them in one of those silver blankets, the one he thought would hide them from the Greks.

"Will it work?" Aaron asked.

"This will be a good test. We'll know in a few minutes."

"Should we try to make it into that hole? I saw one just up ahead."

"No," his dad replied, so quiet Aaron could barely hear. "They're too close. Don't make a sound."

They waited, remaining still, listening to the crashing sounds all around as the Greks tore along the streets, looking for them.

No, not *them*. Looking for Aaron. The Greks didn't know about his dad.

"Maybe I should go out there. Then you can get away. They're not looking for you, dad."

He felt his dad tense for a moment, but then his dad lowered his head and rested his cheek on top of Aaron's head. "My brave boy, always willing to sacrifice for others. Don't you worry. We'll get out of this. Together."

They settled in, waiting for what felt like hours, the searching Greks stomping along the streets and through the rubble. In time, the sounds changed. No more quick thuds. No more screeches.

Thud...

Thud...

Thud...

Thud...

"They've calmed down," Aaron's dad whispered. "They're back to their normal search pattern. We can leave soon."

"Do you have a way out?"

His dad chuckled. "About four of them. We won't know which one we want until we take a peek."

They waited a little longer before his dad carefully pulled back the silver blanket. Aaron couldn't see anything out there, other than the blue sky above, but when his dad finally dropped the sheet, the Greks were out of sight. Only the faint sounds of their feet on the ground far off gave any threat of danger.

"This way."

Aaron followed carefully, mimicking his dad's movements exactly, just as his dad had taught him. They moved along, crouching as low as they could, sometimes even crawling on their knees, until they reached a dip in the ground. Moving down into it, Aaron felt some of the stress leave his shoulders. It always felt best when they were down out of sight.

At the bottom of the dip, a small stream flowed freely, the level slightly higher than yesterday after last night's rain. The grassy bank grew thick with overgrown grass and weeds, and they took the time to stop and have a drink. It wasn't clean, but it was the cleanest they got those days. The water tower itself had come down the first day of the attack, so any tap they found did nothing at all.

"Come along," his dad whispered once they'd had plenty to drink and filled their canteens. "Your mom and sister are worried sick about you."

His dad didn't say it, but Aaron knew he'd messed up. He had just wanted to see his school again. He'd hated school—every second of it—but he'd give anything to be back there now with Chloe and everyone else. Even the bullies. They were easy to deal with compared to this life.

Crawling along the bank of the stream, they reached a culvert running under a road. Most were too small for Aaron's dad, which meant a quick run up and over the road, risking exposure, but this one stood tall enough Aaron could walk and his dad could move along with only hunching his shoulders and neck.

They never spoke in a culvert or tunnel of any kind. Sound moved strangely in tunnels, and the risk of giving away their location was too great.

On the far side, they paused. The culvert came out in a small forest running alongside the stream. No Greks could make it through the trees—at least not without tearing the trees down—but the *human* Greks… they were harder to see, didn't make as much noise, and could call the Greks in seconds. And they could go anywhere Aaron and his dad could.

The two waited patiently, slowly surveying the area, ensuring no eyes, no searching eyes, could see them. Aaron scanned the area as carefully as his dad, his heart racing. The forest… it was exactly the kind of place the *human* Greks hid. That and some of the few remaining buildings.

The only thing that made it easier, although it added to the terror, were the eyes. The *human* Greks' eyes glowed like the big Greks. Green was regular, normal searching. Yellow, his dad thought, was aggressive searching and attack. And white, they'd only seen that once before, but Aaron's mom thought it might be caution, fear.

"I think we're good," Aaron's dad hissed. "Gotta move."

Aaron followed quickly. He still wasn't sure it was clear, that the Greks really were gone, but he wouldn't lag behind. He didn't want to lose his dad.

They ran along the bank of the stream, pushing their way through thick bushes, around trees, over fallen logs, and even crossing the shallow stream a few times, back and forth, just for easier travel.

When they reached home, Aaron collapsed right into his mother's arms. His sister, Alliah, frowned and shook her head, but before she could say anything, Aaron whispered, "I'm sorry. I shouldn't have gone."

"You're lucky we figured out where you were," his dad whispered. No one spoke loudly anymore. Their home, just a black tarp over an open area with sticks and leaves covering the entire outside to camouflage their presence, would never keep the sound in.

Without another word, they settled in for breakfast. Aaron had left before the sun had risen, hoping to get back before his family noticed, but, like every day, the busy schedule started early.

Alliah wanted to yell at her brother, but she knew she couldn't. The sound would betray them all, and it wouldn't do any good. Aaron wasn't the same boy he'd been a few weeks ago. He still cared for others, in a way, well… at times, but he'd grown hard, cold… angry… not at all the kind boy she'd known ever since he'd come home from the hospital with her mom. At least not kind toward her.

Her mom and dad wouldn't do anything about it, either. They never did. They didn't seem to do anything about anything anymore. Well, nothing other than hunt for food. Their only focus seemed to be to stay safe and stay fed.

When they finished eating their breakfast, Alliah and her family left their little hole in the ground, stepping out into the early morning light. On the way out, they carefully covered up the opening before circling the area to make sure nothing of the tarp showed at all. Once her parents were satisfied, they split up. Today, she went with dad. She didn't know who she liked to go with more, but she liked that her dad moved fast. Her mom spent more time in each place. Aaron liked to do that too, so it was probably better that the two of them traveled together.

"Let's find our food for today," her dad said with a smile. He always smiled at her and Aaron. Alliah didn't know what there was to smile about anymore, but her dad said getting through these first few weeks with all four of them alive was enough reason to smile.

Alliah thought she agreed, but wasn't sure.

By early afternoon, they'd found a house with food. Alliah assumed most houses had food in them, but digging through the rubble was too difficult, especially since it had to be done quietly while keeping an eye out for movement. What they did instead was scan the surface of the ruins for any signs of anything they could eat.

More than a week had passed since Alliah had seen anyone else, other than the Greks and *human* Greks. Although her parents disagreed, she figured no one else had survived. Maybe the four of them were the only free humans.

The day turned out to be a good day for hunting. They found cans and even some freeze-dried food, enough for three, maybe four days. When her dad told her they could go back to their home, it was sometime around five or six in the evening, based on the height of the sun above the horizon.

They reached home or, *the cave* as Alliah called it and found mom and Aaron had a good day too. With everything collected, Alliah guessed they had close to a week's worth of food. She hoped that meant they could take it easy for a few days, but her dad wouldn't hear of it. "Every day!" he told her. She wondered if he feared they'd one day find nothing—ever again.

They ate cold peas and cold stew that night, and even Aaron liked it. Alliah suspected he was just happy they wouldn't have to eat stewed tomatoes a fourth day in a row.

When they settled down for the night, Alliah pulled herself deep into her little corner. Her dad didn't come to kiss her goodnight, nor did her mom. She ground her teeth and felt the anger grow. They never did anymore. Not since the Greks came. She lay there thinking to herself that they never really had time for her now.

Maybe they never would again.

The minutes dragged on as Alliah lay there, right next to her little brother. She hated the feeling of bugs crawling on her. Not much she could do about it, though, so she tried to brush them off. No matter how hard she tried, she'd never get them all.

Squeezing her eyes tight, she tried to block out the bugs, to block out everything, but something caught her attention. A sound. Nothing too loud. Not a Grek sound, but something else. Something that broke through the wall she'd built around her heart.

A sniff.

She rolled over quietly and listened. There it was again. Her mom. Her mom was like a rock. Nothing shook her.

Her dad turned his head and looked back at Alliah, then over at Aaron. In the darkness, he'd never see Alliah's eyes looking back at him, but whatever he could see, he seemed satisfied. They whispered, her mom and dad. Whatever they talked about, it couldn't be good. Maybe they'd have to move. In one sense, that would be nice, but then again, the next place could be worse. Even their secret meeting places, the places they'd marked out to meet if they got separated, none of those places even kept the rain off, let alone the bugs out.

Alliah pushed back her damp blanket and crept closer. She'd learned quickly how to move silently, and she kept to the edges of the little cave they called home. Even if her dad looked back again, he might not see her. She could barely see them in the darkness.

"…could have lost him today, Xavier! We'll never get him back if they take him. We'll just have to watch him wander around like all the others, looking for us. I can't bear to see our kids living out their lives as… those things!"

"I know, Connie. I know. But we got him back. That's the important thing."

"I know… and I'm glad. I really am, but…"

"But what?"

"I need something from you."

"Connie, I can't predict when one kid is going to run off. Nor can I stay up all night long and guard the door. I'm barely on my feet as it is!"

Alliah wrapped her arms around herself to keep herself from shivering, despite the heat. She hadn't realized how tired her dad was, or how upset her mom was.

"No, I don't mean that. I mean…"

Her mom paused for long enough that Alliah thought maybe the conversation was over, and she'd just missed the end. She was about to crawl back to her bed when she heard her mom whisper, "I want a promise."

"What promise?" her dad asked.

"Promise me you'll…" She took a deep breath and said, "the kids are what's important. More important than you or me."

"I agree," her dad said, without hesitation.

"Then I want us to promise each other that we'll protect the kids first—even if it costs each of us our lives."

Alliah's mouth dropped open, and she nearly spoke up, but stopped when her dad chuckled quietly. "I'd give my life for Alliah or Aaron in an instant. I wouldn't even hesitate! You know that. I know you'd do that same."

"I know. That's not what I'm asking."

"What are you asking?" His voice had grown serious again, and Alliah's heart raced. What could her mom be talking about?

"I mean… I mean, if it comes down to me or them, Xavier… save them."

Alliah's mouth dropped open again, and she forgot to breathe for a few seconds. *We don't do that kind of thing! It's all or nothing with us. That's the way it's been. That's the way it'll always be. My dad will tell her. He should yell at her! How dare she! How could she even think this? He'll remind her!*

She waited for her dad to tell her mom off for saying something so wicked, but his voice grew even quieter. "And you'll do the same for me? The kids first?"

"Yes."

In the darkness, Alliah couldn't be sure, but she thought he nodded. "I promise."

"I promise too. The kids first."

She backed away as her parents hugged, her heart racing and confused. In the night's silence, she fell asleep to the sound of her parents weeping.

They ran along an alley between two destroyed buildings, the one on the left all concrete, tiles, and beams, the one on the right, bricks, beams, plaster, and books. Alliah thought for sure it must have been a library, but she didn't know this area. They were far from their home. Her dad had told her what city they were in, had been in for the last week or so, but she hadn't listened. She didn't care. All that mattered was staying away from the Greks.

For another day.

Another week, maybe.

Maybe even a month.

The Greks had smashed the structures on either side inward, like many of the buildings in this city, leaving the alley just perfect for running and hiding, but what lay ahead was the real problem. They never knew where their steps would lead them.

Reaching the street, they stopped and checked the area. No one said a word. They'd done this too many times, over and over, to wonder how to act. Her dad gave the signal, and they raced across the street, down another alley, then came to a startled halt.

"Wha…?" Aaron asked, his voice barely heard above the sound of everyone's breathing.

Alliah's mouth moved, but no sound came out. Ahead sat… buildings. Somewhat unbroken buildings. Windows smashed, of course—the Greks liked to break things—but most of the walls stood intact. A school, a few houses, a store. For each structure, only about half the building still stood, but that was far more than most. She wondered if people had survived! They'd seen no one other than *human* Greks in weeks. Or months. She couldn't remember how long it had been.

But none of that mattered. All that mattered at that moment was how they responded to their mom's command. "RUN!"

They took off across the street.

RUN had become a sacred word, spoken only when Greks spotted them. *Move* meant they had to run fast and stay hidden. *Sneak* meant move slow and stay hidden. But *RUN*… that meant Greks had their eyes on them. That meant the Grek eyes had turned yellow.

Alliah had the lead. She was the fastest out of all of them. Her dad next. Then Aaron. Then her mom. Because of Alliah's speed, she chose the path, unless her dad or mom shouted a different order, a different direction.

She led them across the street, directly into the school. The doors stood open… or torn off, but the hallways lay clear of debris. A perfect escape, or a perfect trap. They'd know soon.

She pushed the second possibility out of her mind. That risk was the same with every situation, every time the Greks saw them. In every place, they could always find themselves trapped.

She turned down a hallway and ran through the dark. Despite how difficult it was to see, she raced on, her dad's heavy breathing not far behind, and Aaron and her mom's footsteps echoing along the walls, reminding her she wasn't alone.

Thud… thud… thud… thud… thud… thud… thud… thud…

The big Greks had arrived, and Alliah turned down a hallway, brighter than the rest. It led out into the open. She thought that was the last place they wanted to be right then, but they had to check. Always check. Always find out where the danger lay.

They ran out into the sunlight, Alliah shielding her eyes from the sun to give herself the best chance of seeing where to go next.

Thud… thud… thud…

She skidded to a halt, and her dad crashed into her, grabbing her and picking her right up to keep the two of them from sliding into the leg of the Grek that had stepped out right in front of her. They turned to go back into the school, just as a Grek came up beside them, knocking a wall right over. Alliah and her dad stood frozen, his fingers digging into her arms as they watched the brick wall collapse right on Alliah's mom.

Alliah screamed, and Aaron joined in. Her dad rushed to her mom's side, the top half of her body somehow managed not to be covered. Alliah's heart filled with relief when her mom turned her head up to look at her dad.

Alliah's mom focused on her dad for just a second, then let her eyes flick briefly to Alliah, then to Aaron, then back to her dad. She ground her teeth before she growled. "This is it, Xavier. YOU PROMISED!"

It had all happened in a moment, all so fast. Alliah couldn't quite remember the promise, but she knew it wasn't good. She turned to Aaron just as a tentacle came down and wrenched him into the air. Alliah lunged toward him, to get him back, but something yanked her back so hard it nearly ripped the shirt off her, and a moment later, she found herself carried back into the school over her dad's shoulder. The last sight of her mom was of her struggling to get out from under the wall as two large Greks circled around.

No sign of Aaron. Her brother was gone.

She thought at first the screams were her mom's. A tortured sound, a scream of rage, horror, the sound of a heart breaking. But as she beat her fists against her dad's back, she knew it all came from her, her screams blocking out the faint sounds of her dad's moans.

As he carried her, he turned, then again, then again, and she found herself whipped around through the air. When she came to a halt, her face was less than an inch from her dad's, his hands firmly on each side of her head.

"STOP!" he ordered, and Alliah immediately snapped her mouth shut. There was never time for grief or fear. Only time to follow orders. The ones who followed orders survived.

"What about mom and Aaron?"

"Listen closely, Alliah. There's a small window here. I'm going to drop you out of it. It's just a few feet to the ground. It won't hurt. Make your way to our secret spot. Hide there until I return. I'm going to see if I can get Aaron and mom back. Do you understand?"

Alliah nodded, unsure if she could do it, but her dad waited for nothing else. Her body spun around, and a moment later, she dangled out the window for just a heartbeat before he let go. A short drop to the ground, and she looked up to see her dad's desperate eyes for the last time.

She turned to go but ducked quickly behind a bush as the terrifying *thud* sound announced the coming of a Grek. Knowing the bush might not hide her, she scanned the area for a way out, but all she could see was a small hole in the brick, leading back into the school, right into a classroom similar to the one she'd been in with her dad a moment before. She scrambled through the hole and behind the teacher's desk as three *human* Greks raced past the door in the hallway. *Human* Greks never spoke, but their eyes... yellow... that was all she needed to know.

"I need to help," she thought quietly to herself, then made her decision. She'd follow her dad and see if she could help get her brother back.

2

LOSS

I race through the school, turning down the corridors. The Greks won't come in here, not the building. They like to destroy any structure they find, but they don't do it if someone's inside. They want the people.

But they won't get me.

And I'm going to do everything I can to make sure they don't keep my son and wife.

I slow, then come to a halt outside a doorway. Seeing what I'm after, I race into the room. On the far wall, a large hole leads out into the side yard of the school. I reach it and stick my head out, scanning the area. No Greks. No *human* Greks.

Slipping out, careful to be as quiet as I can, I focus hard on Connie and Aaron, doing my best to push Alliah out of my mind. If I'm not careful, the fear that the Greks will catch her will keep me from my mission. Just have to trust Alliah to keep herself safe. Right now, my only focus is to get Connie and Aaron back.

I run hard across the schoolyard. I always kept in shape over the years but focused more on muscle. Running was never my thing. But the last few months… it feels like that's all I do. Now, as long as we can find enough food and water, running comes easy. And it's a good thing, too. The Greks who have my wife and son have quite a lead on me.

And they're fast. The only good news is, carrying someone slows them down.

On the other side of the yard, I climb past a broken fence and run down a street, mostly clear of debris. I'm risking a lot to run like this in the open, but I have to get Connie and Aaron!

I catch sight of the Greks ahead. They're tall, standing above the wreckage of the buildings. They face forward, their eyes ahead, away from me, following behind. I'm safe for now, as long as nothing else sees me.

Ahead, the street turns. The buildings before me are all torn down, but climbing the pile of debris will slow me down too much. I turn to the left, then race to the next street heading the direction I want, only half a block away. When I reach it, I turn to the right and see a dead end ahead, but this dead end leads right into an open field. I get to it and push through the thick, tall grass and weeds. This kind of running is dangerous. Never know what holes might lie before me. A broken foot will not only end my chance to rescue my wife and son, but it might also stop me from reaching Alliah again.

Just to the right is a bit of a hill, and I run up the side of it, crouching down when I get near the peak. I need a better view of where we're going. When I reach the top, I come to a halt. The Greks… there are hundreds of them ahead. I've never seen anything quite like this.

There's some kind of… spaceship, I guess. It's massive. It sits down in a bit of a valley; the valley explains why I'd never seen this before.

But that's not important. Not to me. All I can really see are the two Greks carrying my wife's battered body and my son's struggling frame into a large doorway, into some kind of structure, leading deep into the earth.

I collapse on the ground. Hidden by the tall grass and weeds, I lay there and weep while my world slides away.

I don't know how long I lay there, but it's dark by the time I get up. My heart races as I scold myself for wasting so much time when I could find Alliah. I can protect her, at least. The secret place we'd picked isn't far, but it'll be slow going in the dark. Greks' eyes are the only thing that stands out in the dark, but they close them nearly to slits at night, hiding themselves well. Occasionally, though, we've found them asleep.

By the time I reach our spot, the place we'd picked in this area to meet up if we got separated, the sky is just beginning to lighten. It's not much, but it's enough that I can see the place well.

From the outside, it looks just like any other ruined building, but right up in the center, near a collapsed piano, a small hole leads into a dark area, just large enough for the four of us. Not dry, but big enough for us to sleep.

Well, plenty big enough for the two of us, now.

I scan the area for any signs of Greks. I don't want to lead them to my daughter.

Following the rules I laid out for the family, I sit… and wait. Watch… and wait. Wait until I'm sure it's safe.

As the sun makes its way to the horizon, I see more clearly, but still I wait, hoping she's in there, safe and sound.

When I'm just about to go to her, I see movement and freeze where I'm at. I crouch low and pull a sheet of camouflage netting from my pack. We'd found enough for all of us, and I'd spread it out among the family, each of us with a piece in our pack big enough for our bodies.

The form moving along in the early morning light takes shape, and I see it's a person. Human or *human* Grek, I'm not sure, but there's no reason to risk anything yet.

Small. I think it's a girl. My heart races, and I want to call out for her, but I still don't know if it's Alliah or someone else. She steps out from a shadow and makes her way toward our hiding spot, and I catch sight of the light brown jacket she wears and the dirty khakis.

A smile breaks out on my face. It's my girl.

I'm about to step out, but something still holds me back. I'm not sure at first what causes me to hesitate, but then I see it. More movement.

She looks back toward the shadows moving behind her. Whoever is with her doesn't scare her. Maybe she found another survivor.

When he steps out, I nearly laugh with joy. The dark green jacket. The rough, torn jeans. It's Aaron! She found him! Somehow, she found him!

I move my foot, and the gravel under the sole of my shoe scratches against the stone and rubble. At the sound, both Alliah and Aaron whip their heads around toward me, giving me the first look of their faces since they arrived. They look strong. They look healthy. They look ready, with their glowing, yellow eyes scanning the area.

My heart drops in my chest, and I want to scream and run and smash anything I can find that's still left to be smashed!

My children are gone!

Now, whatever has them is searching for me.

3

ALONE

I sit there, leaning back against the broken section of cinder blocks, all alone. Don't know what to do. Don't know where to go.

Part of me wants to run. Part of me wants to grab my kids and take them somewhere else, try to get them away.

And part of me… I hate to admit it… wants to stand up right now and let my little girl and my little boy catch me, call the Greks, and take me away. Maybe it'll be easier. Easier than being the only one left.

I put my hand on a large piece of rebar, jutting out of the rubble to my left. Deciding to go with the easiest option, I use the bar to pull myself up, and I bring myself to my full height, facing away from my kids. I don't think I can stand to see their eyes. Perhaps it won't bother me once I'm one of them.

Turning around, I force myself to look.

They haven't seen me yet. Aaron's looking down into the hole leading into our secret hiding spot. They must remember at least some things. Maybe I'll remember that I love my wife and kids once I'm taken. That'll be enough, I think.

Alliah's out of sight. I gather she's in the hole looking for me. No actual Greks around. I guess they thought just sending the kids would be fine.

My boy… he looks so small. Memories flood my mind of coming home to see him, playing with his toys on the floor, or flipping through one of his many books. Even before he could read, he made up stories to go with the pictures.

All that… lost, but…

I hesitate. They're looking in the hole. They remember some of what we had together. Maybe… just maybe… they're still in there! If that's true… I can get them back!

I'm not what, but something I did must have made some noise. Aaron's head whips around again, but this time, his eyes land on me. No expression fills his face, but I hear Alliah scrambling up. A moment later, her head is out of the hole, and she sees me too.

If I'm to get my kids back, I can't give up! And today is not the day to go with them.

I turn and bolt out of there.

I can't hear them over the sound of my feet on the gravel and shattered plaster and bricks under me and over the steady sound of my breathing, but I know they're after me. Aaron won't be a problem to outrun, but Alliah…

She can outrun me any day. Her weakness was she could never learn the terrain.

I zigzag through the area, taking one of my many escape routes. After a few minutes, I risk a look back. No sign of my girl.

Thud… thud… thud… thud…

GRRREHHHHK!

Thud… thud… thud… thud…

The Greks have joined the hunt. They have the advantage of height and speed, but they can't manage with small areas, and they're not the best in the rubble, despite the fact that they're responsible for it.

Taking off down a small alley leading between two destroyed buildings, I slip behind a massive broken pile of bricks. I'd guess this was an old store, judging from what I can see of the smashed walls, windows, and more. As I climb, I come across a shoebox with some wet, mildewy shoes sticking out the side.

Connie had a pair of shoes like that. She wore them on…

No! *Focus, Soldier!*

When I get to the top of the pile, I peer over. A quick count gives me a dozen or more Greks, some popping in and out of sight. All looking for me. They won't allow even a single person to escape them.

But they aren't what worries me. They're all looking in the wrong places. What worries me most are the people—the *human* Greks. There has to be a few hundred of them, perhaps more. They walk in a line, shoulder to shoulder, stretching off to my left and right. Separated from each other by only six or seven feet, they're making their way toward me. They're slow, taking their time, but there's no way I can escape that if I let them catch up to me.

Now and then I see one of them disappear out of sight for a moment before they climb back up and join the line. They must be thoroughly searching any holes or crevices they find.

I slide and climb back down the rubble and reach the bottom. Gotta get out of here, but I have to stay low. They won't give up easily. My only hope, from what I've learned over the last couple months, is to stay ahead of them for the next four or five hours, at least. They won't give up before then. Maybe not even then.

I rush out of the alley, keeping my head down. The great thing about destroyed buildings is not only is it hard for any *human* Greks to hide in them, but most of the piles give me a bit of cover if I don't stand up straight.

Running along a street for as long as I dare, I keep glancing back to see if any Greks or *human* Greks—*HGs*—come into view. The *HGs* are the biggest threat. I've noticed the Greks themselves, despite their height and speed, have limited vision. I've walked right out in front of one or two, and the creature walked right by me, when my clothes matched the

coloring of the buildings behind me. Although, sometimes…
only sometimes… they seem to see by heat. Nothing's entirely
consistent with them, just that they can't always see that well.

The *HGs*, on the other hand, their vision is perfect.

Looking back, I see the tops of the Grek's heads above
the rubble, and I turn down a side street, zigzagging and
working my way through the city. I'm not entirely sure where
to go, but if I have to stand and fight, I won't do it without
weapons, nor am I going to do it when I'm facing more than a
dozen Greks and hundreds of *HGs*, two of whom could be my
own children.

I come around a building and find the road ends,
leading into a field. Fields are dangerous. The grass and weeds
after a summer of neglect have overgrown to hide holes and
dips.

Dropping to my knees, then to my hands, I scramble
through the thick, overgrown grass. Moving like this, no one's
likely to see me, and hopefully I can keep myself from dropping
into a groundhog hole or something. The field itself looks to
have been a park before the Greks arrived. I see broken bars
that might have been play equipment, and there's a backstop
not far from me.

I make my way behind the backstop and stand up just
a little, knowing the fence will disguise me enough that a quick
peek won't hurt. Sure enough, the *HGs* are nearly at the edge
of the field. Not sure how they're keeping up with me, but
there's enough of them I'll likely need a break before they do.

I scramble out the other side of the field and onto a
road leading right and left. An old cement mixer sits near the
curb, and I make my way to it to use as cover while I cross the
street and disappear behind two wrecked houses. The backyard
of the one looks a lot like my old home.

But… those days are gone.

I push on, pulling out some food and water on the run
to give me the energy I need to stay ahead, all the while working

on my plan to get my kids back. Or, at least, trying to come up with any plan that doesn't sound like suicide.

The Grek hasn't moved for the last hour. That's not unusual. They often stand still, sometimes for days. I've seen the *HGs* do that as well, but not for as long. They collapse if they stand for too many hours in the sun. It's no wonder. Most *HGs* I see are malnourished. They must be feeding them something, but certainly not enough to keep them strong.

My dummy's ready, along with my escape route. I need to know how to get past the Greks. I've had enough experience slipping past regular humans, just some proper camo, and I'm good to go. But the Greks and *HGs* are a different matter.

The dummy's packed full of dried grass and old clothing, with a shirt and pants holding it together and a mannequin's head on top. I tried using a full mannequin, but the thing fell apart with too much manipulation. With this grass-stuff dummy, I'm able to tie it all tight enough it holds together.

Swinging the dummy up into the air on the wooden pole I have it strapped to, I watch closely to see the Grek's reaction. At first, I'm thrilled to see it spin around, eyes focusing on my little creation. The mirror I look through to keep myself fully hidden gives me a good view. The Grek takes a step forward, then stops, eyes still on the dummy.

So, general movement and shape aren't enough. I wait for a few moments, but nothing more happens, so I move on to Stage Two.

I use a thin rod connected to the dummy's wrist, and raise up its arm, moving it back and forth, waving at the Grek. That movement earns another step forward, but the creature stops again.

Movement, shape, and specific human actions aren't enough.

Good to know.

———•——•———⬤———•——•———

My new dummy sits ready. This one's a lot heavier and certainly more awkward. I came across an intact waterbed bladder earlier this week. At first, I just passed it by, but then when yesterday's dummy didn't get enough of a reaction from the Grek, I thought of a use for it.

I tied it up in a rough—very rough—human shape and then heated some water. Fires are dangerous as they draw attention, but I managed a fire long enough to heat enough water for my needs and now I have a human-shaped dummy made out of a waterbed bladder.

There's no way for me to know how close to body temperature it is, but it'll have to do.

Checking the mirror to make sure the Grek is in place, I swing the dummy up in the air and watch.

The Grek spins around as expected, but this time, it bolts forward. I slip around out of sight and watch from behind a large stone slab. The Grek stops inches from the dummy—pausing, examining. I think it might even be sniffing, but I'm not sure. The mirror I'm using here is quite small. I don't want to give myself away through an errant reflection.

The Grek doesn't touch the dummy. If that were a human, the Grek would have it up on its back already, held in place by the small claws up there. But with the shape and the heat, it doesn't seem to know what to do with it. After a few moments, it circles around the dummy, still not touching anything.

After another two, maybe three minutes, the Grek abruptly loses interest and wanders off.

I think I have enough information. They're attracted to movement, but heat draws them in. And they can tell the difference between human and human shape. Maybe it's the size, maybe it's the lack of continued movement. Not sure, but that confirms that I need to hide my body heat. If I can do that, then perhaps if I'm surrounded by Greks, I can simply remain still until I'm safe.

4

OTHERS

I roll off to the side, hoping to get out of sight before I'm seen, and roll right over a rock the size of my fist. Keeping the grunt inside, I stagger to my feet and hide behind a small section of the remaining wall. An *HG* is not far away. Too big for one of my kids. Haven't seen Connie at all. Not sure what they do with injured humans. My mind keeps going to the worst, but I have to control my fears.

I peek around the edge just enough to scan the area and see no sign of the *HG*. They can hide as well as I can at times, so they're much easier to stumble upon than the big Greks. That's what happened this time. I came around a corner and nearly ran into an *HG's* back.

Judging from the shoulders and build, I'm guessing a man. I reach down and pull a small length of rebar off the ground. It's a solid weapon. I doubt he'll survive.

Scurrying off to the side, away from where I saw the *HG*, I try to make my way south. Every day of my life now is just a matter of moving and trying to stay alive. Still no plan on how to get my kids back. Can't get through to them. I know that because I once saw someone plead with her husband after he'd been taken. She might as well have been speaking to the rocks on the ground for all she got through to him.

I think I'm just about out when I hear the crunch of shattered bricks under a boot and spin around, rebar in hand, to see an *HG* standing above me, his yellow, piercing gaze freezing me in place for a second. What keeps me there, however, is not his gaze, but recognition as I see his face clearly for the first time.

"Geoff?"

My heart fills with rage at the sight of that man. Obnoxious. Pushy. Ignorant. Arrogant. His short-sightedness got all those people captured. Now, he's truly the enemy, and I nearly rush up the pile of debris and drive the rebar into his heart!

…but I hesitate.

He's… it's out of his control. Whatever is controlling him is the issue here. I can't kill him.

I spin around and take off at a run. The bad news is this *HG* has likely alerted the big Greks. As if on cue, I hear the distant *thud, thud, thud, thud* of a Grek's approach. The good news, however, is I know this area well after spending the last few hours in it, and Geoff is anything but a fit man. He'll never catch me. I just have to get away before his big friends arrive.

Thud…thud…thud…thud…

GRRREHHHHK!

Thud…thud…thud…thud…

Pushing hard, I race off to the south, down an open street, then zigzag between all that's left of the houses in this area. At one point, I catch sight of Geoff, far enough away that he's no longer a threat to me, but he has his eyes on me.

Others are with him now. A young woman with wild hair, maybe nineteen, twenty years old. A woman about Connie's age runs with her, holding the hand of a young boy. Mother and son, I assume.

Ducking between some piles of rubble and an overturned truck, I turn east and make my way along. By the time I need a break, I'm far enough away that I no longer hear the Grek's footsteps, but I can still make out the alien creature in the distance, searching the area where I'd be now if I'd kept along the path I was on.

If I'd been wearing my new suit, the one I'd made to block out my body heat, I might have been able to hide a little easier. But then again, the reason it's not on my back is because the heat can't escape through its thick lining. It's hot enough out here in the sun that I'd bake. Better to throw it on when I need it or at night when the temperature drops a bit.

My new suit works well for the *HGs* too as I wrapped the outside in camo netting. I've had two *HGs* walk right by me in the last day or so while wearing it.

On that note, they're definitely on the hunt right now. *HGs* scouring the area, running through open fields, hiding, waiting… they're looking for something, and I suspect it's me.

"Uh… uh… Sir?"

I spin around, the short length of rebar still in my hand, and raise my weapon high.

The man… boy… cowers before me, hands up in the air, eyes nearly bulging out of his thin face. "No, NO… no…!" he hisses, trying his best to keep his voice quiet. "I'm a friend. A… a friend!"

I stare at the boy, still gripping the rebar as if I'm about to use it on him. He's… maybe he's not a boy anymore. He's small, thin, looks really young. But…

"We've been watching you," he whispers. "And…"

"Watching me?" I growl. "How? And why?"

"Uh… I mean…" he stutters and swallows once, then again. "I mean… it's nothing weird. We just set up a camera. Or a bunch of them. One's up in that tree over there." He points, and I let my eyes flick in that direction for just a moment. "We just wanted to keep an eye on what's going on out here. We haven't seen anyone for a long time. I mean… until you… right?"

The boy's eyes drift off to the side for a second, and his hand briefly moves toward his right ear. A second later, his eyes fill with panic, and he spins around, looking in every direction. "They're coming!" he says quickly, backing away from me. "Three of them, coming from the south."

I turn in that direction, and the boy follows my gaze, obviously not aware of which direction is which. I don't see anyone, but I believe him. Must be others with this guy.

"Look," he says, turning back to me. "You can do what you want, but if you're comin' with me, you gotta come now."

Taking one more glance off to the south, he nods at me and slips around a large pile of rubble and then stops in front of a board, laying up against the crushed bricks, mortar, moldy insulation, and soggy drywall. Sliding it aside, he motions for me to squeeze through a newly revealed hole.

I shake my head and crouch down. Not sure what I'm doing here, but it can't be worse than what I've been doing all along. I grunt and struggle my way through the opening. It's barely high enough for me, but once I step through, my foot drops down, and I have enough height to get through. The problem, however, is the width. Even once I pull off my pack, I still struggle to get my bulk through. Once I finally do, I stand there in the darkness while my eyes adjust and see my new "friend" easily slide through behind me, pulling the board back over the opening.

In the dim light, I watch him pull out a flashlight, and when he turns it on, I notice he's covered the lens with some kind of thin paper to dampen the light. "That way," he whispers, pointing ahead of me.

We move along the thin corridor for only a few steps. I've been in places like this, hiding from the Greks. They're not typically all that stable, but I think this guy has tried to reinforce the area. At this point, he can squeeze around me, and he grabs a rough-looking tarp, swings it aside, and I nearly gasp. In front of us sits a solid steel door, but that's not what's shocked me. On the right side is a working keypad and palm scanner!

I've seen no electricity in months!

The young guy punches in a code, and the door clicks open. As we step through, he awkwardly explains they never put his palm into the system, so he still has to use his code every time.

On the other side of the door is a short platform leading to steps. Above me, fluorescent lights buzz just slightly, although one out of three lights is burned out. The walls are a light gray and, aside from the floor, the place looks brand new.

The door closes and locks securely behind me, and I nearly raise the rebar again. I'm not used to being in places I can't get out of.

"Down here," he says nervously, but stops one step down and awkwardly reaches out his hand to me. "I… I'm Logan. I… I guess I didn't say that before." He then laughs, but a strange laugh. Not a laugh that makes me suspect him, more of one to let me know this guy has been nothing but awkward his entire life.

I shake his hand, and he looks at my arms. "You're… do you work out? I… I mean I do. I work out. Every day. I…" He raises his arm and flexes for me.

I stop myself before I tell him that my eleven-year-old daughter has bigger muscles than he does. This guy's awkwardness feels contagious. Instead, I just flex for him, and his mouth drops open.

"Okay, then… I guess I have a ways to go." He grimaces at me and adds, "Well, can't keep the baby waiting."

I shake my head as I follow him down. I'd be out of here if this wasn't the first non-*HG* I've seen in weeks, ever since… I push those thoughts down. I have to get them back, but I don't have to focus on what I've lost.

When we reach the bottom of the stairs, there are only two options: a door that leads to a set of stairs leading down, and an elevator. Logan just steps onto the open elevator, and I cautiously follow him. He hits a button marked "M" and then pushes the button to close the doors.

"Nothing's automatic here, not really, anyway," he says, shifting on his feet. As strange as it seems, I think he's trying to impress me. "Gerb could fix it so it just opens and closes and stuff, but he's pretty busy."

"Gerb?"

"You'll meet him in a moment."

The elevator slows and then jolts before the doors open. I'm half expecting to see all sorts of activity, but it's just another hallway. When we step out, everything's clean and all, but just like above, a few lights are out here or there. I'm guessing that whatever this is, it's not a fully staffed base.

As we walk down the hall, I glance through small windows into rooms. Some are dark, but others are lit up, and I see workstations. "This a lab?"

"It is," Logan tells me. "Gerb and I work here. Or, we did. Well, we still do."

I glance through another window and come to a halt. Grabbing the door handle, I give a pull, but it's locked tight.

"Oh, yeah, you can't get in any of the doors without one of these things," he says, holding up a small keycard tied to a belt loop on his waist. "We can get you one, if you're stayin'."

Turning back to the window, I stare into a large room of shelves. Every shelf is full—FULL—of cans of food and packages and boxes. Without a doubt, these guys have it made.

"You have a lot of food," I say before I realize how dumb that sounds.

"You have no idea," Logan says. "We have four rooms like that. Dr. Terrance, the lady who ran this lab, wanted the base to be self-sufficient. Well, at least for a few years. That's about how much food we have stored up. Maybe more, since there's only four of us. I… uh… mean… if you stay."

"That's how many are here? Three plus me?"

He nods. "Come on. Let's meet the baby."

I shake my head but follow. I had wondered if I'd gone a little squirrelly, living all by myself, but this guy makes me feel normal.

The lab he leads me to lies at the end of the long hallway. It's hard to believe someone's built this place all underground. A few steps back, I passed a map of the facility. It's four floors, all underground, and each one is bigger than the one above it. Must have cost a fortune to put this thing together. And now, to house only four people…

Logan swipes his keycard on the pad and swings open the door. When I step inside, I find my mouth drops open. The room we're in is large, maybe sixty feet by sixty feet. There's everything in here from workstations complete with Bunsen burners and beakers to a kitchen with fridge, stove, and cupboards, to a couch and a massive tv. Off to the far right is a set of bunk beds.

Aside from a few things like toilets and showers, I'm not sure what else these guys would need from day to day. But the strangest sight is the guy stepping around one of the workstations. He's… oddly proportioned. Average height, heavyset, with a too-large round head, almost too round to be real, a large torso, short legs, and long arms. If I didn't know better, I'd say he's an adult-sized…

"I'm Gerb," the round-faced boy says.

"Yeah, everyone calls him that 'cause he looks like an oversized baby!" Logan adds.

He's right. I'm not sure how else to describe the guy, but he certainly is built like an adult-sized infant.

"Good to meet you," I say, then add, "My name's Xavier. I hear you've been watching me."

Gerb gives a rapid nod and smiles. "We have! Just for the last day or so, when you've been around the base."

"How long have you guys been down here?"

"Ever since it all happened," Logan explains. "We used to work in this lab, before… you know… everything. Then when it did, while everyone was running for their lives, we came here, and Dr. Terrance was the only one around."

"Is she the fourth?"

"The fourth?" Gerb asks.

"Yeah, Logan said there's four here now. You two, me, who's the fourth?"

"Oh," Gerb says, "that's Fred. No, Dr. Terrance left. Said she had to meet with some people she called the 'higher-ups' and left with a pile of papers under her arms. We haven't seen her since."

"So, who's Fred?"

A crash sounds to my right, and I spin around, ready for an attack, only to find Logan with a sheepish look on his face, staring at a broken plate on the floor. "Oops. I… uh… sorry. I just… didn't see it there on the counter. But… Oh, Fred! Yeah. Right. He's like our janitor. He's around here somewhere. Probably be surprised to see you. He fixes stuff and cleans up messes. There are some leaks on the bottom level, and he's been down there most of the last month or so. Just comes up to eat and watch us race."

"Race?"

Logan laughs and points at the tv and couch. "When we're not working, we usually play. Got some good racing games. And hockey. Gerb likes hockey. I'm more an FPS kind of guy, though."

I'm not really sure what they're talking about, but I figure I'll learn in time. "What do you guys do here? When you're working."

The two glance at each other, and Gerb's eyes drop to the ground for a moment before he looks back up at me and smiles. "I'm a chemist. Loge's a biologist."

I look at Gerb, then at Logan, then back to Gerb. "Level with me."

"Uh, well," Gerb says, "we were working in the lab as assistants. We're students."

"What year?"

"Third year chemistry," Gerb tells me.

When I turn to Logan, he says, "Third year biology."

"So, both of you have a bunch of general science courses down, but you haven't specialized yet?"

They shake their heads.

"So, what are you doing here? What's the work?"

Gerb frowns. "We're… trying to develop something to fight off the Greks."

Logan shifts on his feet and stares at the floor. "I know we're not PhDs or anything, but…"

I nod. This actually works for me. "I'm in. The two of you know a lot more than I do about any of this stuff. I've just been trying to come up with anything I can do to get the people back, all the while running for my life. The best I've come up with so far is to sneak onto their ship and try to disable whatever they're using to control the *humans*, but that's a terrible idea."

"You've seen their ship?" Gerb asks, taking a step forward.

A quick look at Logan, and he looks ready to grab hold of me. "What's going on?"

Logan shakes his head. "We don't really know much about anything. I mean, we knew about the meteorite, but we wondered if a ship landed or what. We both suspected there were ships, and somehow they slipped in while everyone was watching the giant rock fall from the sky. We've had all sorts of theories about it, but no way to prove anything."

"Aside from going out there," Gerb says, "but we'd never do that."

"And what made you invite me into your little club?"

Logan clears his throat and gives me an embarrassed look. "Uh, you seem to be okay going outside. We thought maybe you could help us."

I just wait. They must know I'll need more information than that.

"We need water. We have plenty of food, but we need more water. The recyclers can't keep up. Something's wrong with them. And we need something else," Gerb says slowly, his baby face making him look almost comical with the serious gleam in his eye. "We think if we have a sample of one of the Greks, we can develop something to keep them away."

"Only one problem…" I begin to say.

"We know," Logan interjects. "They disintegrate if they die. We don't know how to fix that problem, yet."

I smile. In the past, I'd always get angry at the soldiers under me if they couldn't come up with a solution to the problem they saw, but these two… they're at least trying. "I can work with that," I say, and both boys smile back at me.

5

A NEW HOME

I wake with a start and scrabble back up against the wall. A noise, something… I heard something.

I don't recognize the room. Not the barracks. Not home. Not one of my many hiding spots. Do the Greks have me? Am I lost?

I close my eyes and calm my heart. I've lived on edge for so long, even my training hasn't helped to keep me focused. The noise comes again. It's a knock on the door.

Just a knock.

Standing up, I stretch and make my way through the dark to the pad beside the door. When I press it, the door unlocks, and I swing it open, revealing a man I haven't met yet.

He's far older than Logan or Gerb. Far older than me. I'd say around seventy. Maybe older than that. Thin, shorter than me, with sparse white hair combed straight back on his head, and wrinkly skin stretched across a gaunt face. He doesn't look like much, aside from that piercing gaze. His eyes, though… he looks like he can see into my soul.

His face slowly breaks into a smile, and he nods. "You must be Xavier. I'm Fred. I thought I'd let ya sleep well before I came to meet ya." His voice is gravelly, but not unkind.

"Thanks," I say slowly, nodding back. "Haven't slept like that for a while, not since before my wife and kids…" I catch myself. No use going down that road.

He nods again. In a compassionate voice, he says, "I understand. Why don't you come with me?"

Throwing on my shoes, I follow him out into the hallway. There's something about this guy, something likeable… but even so, I won't put up with that!

"What do you understand?" I growl at him. He doesn't deserve this, but I haven't been around anyone for a while, and he has no right to act like he gets what I'm going through.

"I get it. The pain. The anger. The everything."

I frown, and he stops and turns to me. "Don't misunderstand me, Xavier. I don't understand *everything* you're going through—how could I?—but I get it."

He turns and walks on, leaving me standing there in the hallway. After a moment, I rush after him. I did little after arriving and meeting the boys, other than eat and head to bed. I don't want to get lost in this place.

Catching up to him just as he rounds a corner, I ask, "Where are we going?"

"Breakfast!" he says with a laugh. "At least for you. It's lunch for the rest of us."

He turns into a room on the right-hand side of the hallway and leads me into a large dining hall. On the far side of the room, Logan and Gerb sit, shoveling food into their mouths. When they see me, they both wave.

I take a seat across from them, and Fred tells me he'll get me some food. I watch the boys eat, surprised at how thin Logan can remain if he eats like that all the time. Then again, I think I ate like that at his age. Of course, I also trained every single day.

"How'd you sleep?" Gerb asks through a mouthful of food.

I nod in reply, and a moment later, a plateful of beans and mac and cheese plops down in front of me. At first, I can hardly wrap my mind around it. Hot food... even what I had last night was cold. But this...

I dive in and, before long, find I'm eating not much different than the boys. Fred sits down next to me and is the only one who eats with any form of control. I forgot how much I missed eating in peace without having to worry that a Grek might spot me.

My fork stops halfway to my mouth, and my face turns into a sneer. Dropping the fork, I push the plate away. "I've had enough."

Logan and Gerb stare at me, and Gerb, his mouth full of everything on his plate, spits out, "What's wrong? Don't like beans?"

I'm about to stand up, but Fred puts his hand on my shoulder. He's not strong, he can't hold me down, but I don't move. Somehow, he makes me want to listen to him. "Just try, Xavier. Try to push through. I felt the same way when I got here."

I grip the table, my knuckles turning white. I'm about to snap at him, tell him he has no idea, but he says to the boys, "You guys remember what I was like when I first came, don't you? Couldn't eat. Felt guilty. All I could think of was those I'd lost."

They nod.

Grinding my teeth, I decide to try to shift the focus a bit. "You guys have anyone?" I ask Logan and Gerb.

"Just a mom," Gerb says. "Back home in Florida. I hope she's okay. I'm... hoping she found somewhere safe."

"Not much else you can do, Gerb," Logan says. Turning to me, he says, "Me, I have no one. No one at all. They all died well before the Greks came."

"Who'd you lose?" I ask Fred.

He smiles at me as his eyes drop to his plate. He slowly scoops up some mac and cheese on his fork and raises it partway up to his mouth. "A lot, Xavier. I lost everyone. Seen my wife out there. Two of my kids. And some of my grandkids, at times. They're all there, as far as I know. Just me left." He smiles again, and adds, "But we'll be okay. We know what we're about." He takes the bite and starts to slowly chew.

"What are we about?" I ask, forcing myself to let go of the table. "None of you have told me anything."

Gerb's eyes flash with pleasure, and his small mouth stretches into a big smile across his round face. A moment later, I think he's almost bouncing. "You wanna tell him, Loge, or should I?"

"You go ahead. I got to tell Fred about it when he got here."

"Okay!" Gerb says, sliding his plate to the side. "We..." Looking back at his plate mournfully, he grabs it, shovels some more beans in his mouth, then turns back to me. "Wumble..."

"Chew first!" I growl. "I'm not in so much a rush that I want to wear your supper!" I'm not in the mood for this kind of thing. All I can think of is seeing Aaron walking next to a Grek. I haven't seen Alliah for a few days, but Aaron's been around.

He nods and quickly chews through his food, swallowing the entire mouthful at once. I watch as his eyes drift to his plate, but I reach across and slide it farther away before frowning at him.

"Oh, yeah, right. I get it. Uh... well, here's the thing." He glances at his plate one more time before folding his pudgy, baby-like hands together on the table in front of him and taking a deep breath. "So, you know we're trying to beat the Greks, right?"

I just stare at him.

"Okay, dumb question. How about I just tell you? No more questions. Yes, that'll be..."

"Gerb!" Logan says with a laugh.

"Sorry. I... uh... not used to this kind of thing anymore. I used to teach kids a bit of chemistry on Fridays at..." Glancing at Logan, he says, "Oh, not important. Okay, we're trying to take down the Greks, but at the moment, we're running into a few problems. One, we're running short on water. We told you that. We also need that sample, but we're wondering if we can create something, like a chemical, or something, to drive them away, if we can figure out one that won't hurt the environment, you know, 'cause that would create new problems, right, you get it? Uh, well, um… if we can do that, well, maybe eventually we can find a way to, um, you know, get it all over the place. Like, right through the atmosphere, and maybe the Greks will leave."

"So, that's what you want the sample for?"

Logan smiles again. "Yup. That's it! But, we don't do well out there. And Fred's really, really, really old and frail and all…"

"Hey!" Fred says with a laugh. "I may be old, but I can still throw my teeth at you!"

The boys laugh, and that one brings a smile to my face. "Okay, so, how do we get the sample? Any ideas?"

Logan and Gerb glance at each other, then Logan says, "We were hoping you'd have an idea. We have some ideas about how to test it once we have it, but we…" Logan laughs and then adds, "Neither of us is the outdoors type, and I just can't imagine how to get the thing. We have tranquilizers here, like, the chemicals, but no way to give it to them—no weapons and certainly no tranq guns. You have any ideas?"

I shake my head. "No, but I can work on it. What do you have for me to work with?"

Logan tries to convince Gerb to leave his lunch behind, but the boy won't move, and in the end, Fred just waves me on. "I'll show 'im. You two just finish your meal."

I follow the old guy out the door, and he leads me down a corridor to a set of stairs. As we go, he explains a bit to me. "So, I'm doing my best to keep this place running. I'm a mechanic, by trade, and did a lot of home renos on the side, so I can figure out a lot of the stuff, but some of it's beyond me or beyond the time I have to give it. The boys don't seem to worry about the elevator much. They'll use it rather than climb the stairs, but the thing needs to be serviced, and I'm not sure how to take care of that, so… I'd recommend you use the stairs. As for the rest, the basement has some kind of sewage seeping through the walls. Not sure what it is or why it's down so low. That seems to be the priority, to me anyway. The boys just want the lights to remain on, but if they're going to be here for a while, years, maybe, that issue has to be fixed."

I listen as he walks me through all the things he's taking care of. It's a lot. He doesn't seem to mind, though. I've worked with guys like Fred before. They're not good guys to have on the front lines—too focused on fixing stuff—but they're the guys to have watching your back, the guys keeping the artillery running smoothly, servicing all the vehicles, and keeping the birds in the sky.

We exit the stairs two floors down, and he takes me to a solid steel door. Swiping his card, he pushes the door open once it clicks, and I step in after him. What I see causes me to gasp.

I stand in an armory filled with enough equipment to arm a dozen soldiers, at least. Everything from vests to XM7s. There's even a few hundred grenades and a fair amount of Semtex.

The distrust bubbles its way to the surface again. In a quiet voice, I growl, "Logan said they didn't have weapons. Why'd he lie to me?"

Fred laughs. "He didn't lie. They were probably going to show you the chemical supplies they have for experiments. They don't know about this, because I just haven't told them about it, and they don't come down this far. If they do, it's just to find me to tell me they're having a problem."

"Why don't you tell them?"

He scowls and shakes his head. "I found chloroform a few weeks back, Xavier. Happened to mention it to them, and they told me right away that they needed it. I came for supper that evening to find they had spent the afternoon trying to chloroform each other—just for the fun of it. If they hear about this, they'll be setting up a shooting range, and the dart guns in the back will probably get used on each other." He turns to me and rolls his eyes. "Likely under the guise of testing them, but chances are they'd treat 'em like paintball guns. Just there'd be no question who got hit."

I nod. That's good to know. Helps me understand a bit more of the kind of people I'm working with.

FIRST SAMPLE

I check my gear and tighten the straps on my vest while Logan and Gerb natter on about something. They're talking about some movie and how it's similar to a video game which is similar to what's going on here. I stopped paying attention about four minutes ago. Gotta focus.

"Xavier?"

I look up, and both Logan and Gerb have their eyes on me.

"Yeah?"

"Were you listening to anything we said?"

I shake my head. "Was there anything important?"

Logan's mouth drops open, and Gerb starts to sputter. Fred chuckles beside me and shakes his head. "Most of it wasn't important, Xavier, but the part about getting the sample here was. They want you to come straight back with it. Something about not passing GO, just come right here."

"Of course, but why? Why's that important?"

Gerb steps forward, and his small eyes seem to bulge out of his head. He does that when something's causing him stress, be it video games or saving the planet. "Well, you never know how fast it can degrade. We need to get it here quick!"

"Where'd you get all that gear?" Logan asks, looking me up an down. "And the weapons. You carry all that in your pack, the one you wore in here?"

I had wondered how I would get past that little issue, but they've made it easy for me. "Maybe," I say, squinting my eyes a bit. I've noticed they seem to think soldiers do that when something's classified. These guys are nothing if not predictable.

Logan squints his eyes like mine and slowly nods. "Gotcha! Okay, won't ask that question again."

I almost shake my head but catch myself. Fred just chuckles again.

"What's the plan?" Gerb asks.

"Gonna try to get you a sample," I say with a frown, and turn toward the door. "How do I get back in?"

"Punch in the code," Logan says. "It's 688-904. The keycard we gave you won't work. If it fell into the *People Greks*—Oh, I like your name for them, by the way, *HGs*—that would be bad. They could just walk in here and take us."

I nod. I'm not one for conversation when I have a mission before me. Gotta get a sample. They don't care what it is, I just have to get it without the *HGs* or the Grek disintegrating. The *HGs* should be simple. Just not sure about the Greks themselves.

I reach for the handle, but Gerb tells me to wait while he checks his tablet, flipping through the various camera angles outside. I feel the weight of Fred's hand on my shoulder and turn to him. "You got this," he says with a smile. I can't help but smile back. This guy's got a good heart.

"You're clear, but it looks like there's a Grek about half a mile or so to the north."

I nod again and swing open the door, repeating the code in my head to get back in. When I step out into the mid-morning light, I take in my surroundings. I've gotten used to identifying where I am by the size of the piles of rubble all around. A few trees off in one direction, a single tree off in another, I think I've got it down. The challenge will be if I have to find the hole in a rush. I make sure the board is back in place and examine it, trying to burn the image in my mind. Hopefully, I'll be back through here shortly.

I set off to the north, careful with each step. My gear is mostly a darker tan color, which makes hiding among the rubble a lot easier than even the camo, but I don't have my suit that hides my body heat. I have a blanket in my pack that'll do that for me, but it also reflects the sunlight, which will turn me into a large mirror. I think that'll likely get a lot of attention… fast.

Usually, the *HGs* aren't too far from the Greks themselves. They seem to work together. Some kind of connection between the two, so if I head north, I should come across a target soon.

Ten minutes later, I come around a larger pile of rubble and see one. Its back faces me. A woman, I think. For a moment, I think it's Connie, but I shake my head. Connie's a little taller and not as heavy set.

The woman's back is still toward me. She's searching the rubble for hiding spots. There's likely another *HG* within a short distance. They're rarely alone. At least this one's not Alliah or Aaron. I don't think I could do this if it was one of them.

I circle the area first to make sure no one else is close. I see another *HG* off in the distance, maybe five hundred feet to the west, but there should be plenty of time before that one can reach me.

Coming around again, I settle behind a few broken boards and a soggy bundle of fabric, the smell of mildew strong in the air. I pull out my dart gun, careful to stay down and out of sight. Once the gun's loaded with the tranq, I pull out a sample jar and syringe. The jar's tiny. Gerb and Logan tell me they only need a small sample. Just some skin and blood. It's probably best not to take more. If we ever free everyone, this woman won't be pleased to wake up without a finger.

Taking aim, I get myself into position. I've used this model of dart gun countless times, but never on a civilian. Never on someone like this. But, I am familiar with the requirement for speed.

I pull the trigger, and the dart zips through the air, landing in the woman's neck. She jolts around, reaching back for it, but staggers for a moment before dropping to her knees. She's fighting it, but I wait until she drops. Once her face hits the ground, I rush to her side, pulling the dart out right away and tossing it into a hole in the rubble near our position. Can't leave any evidence.

Flipping her over, I set to work, blood sample first. Won't take long for that, but need to clean the area. The man I saw in the distance can likely run the five hundred feet in about a minute, maybe less, if it's a straight, clear run, but the rubble will slow him down. Despite how quiet I've been, they always seem to know.

Always.

I get the blood sample, then scrape some skin off the arm. I have maybe fifteen seconds before the man arrives, twenty if I'm lucky.

Thud… thud… thud… thud…

By the sounds of things, the Grek will be here in about thirty seconds. Coming from the north. Syringe and sample jar put away. I take my first look at the woman's face.

My knife's in my hand before I even think about it, my heart filled with rage, hatred, murder. I want this woman dead. She's the one who tried to pull Alliah away from me. She tried to pull my little girl into danger!

For some reason, as much as I can't stand Geoff… this woman… I have nothing but hatred for her.

Ten seconds until the man arrives…

I could kill her. No one would know. I'm outside the range of the cameras. The only risk would be the Greks would know someone was here. I'd get away with it. It's not like I haven't taken a life before.

Five seconds till the man gets here… maybe I have more time. Maybe the terrain will slow them down.

Thud… thud… thud… thud…

The Grek will be here in ten, maybe eleven seconds.

I'd probably be doing the woman a favor. She'd never want to live like this. I'd be helping her by killing her… It'll be quick, merciful, and I'd get what I want!

Thud… thud… thud… thud…

I slide her sleeve back down to her wrist and rush off to the east, slipping behind a pile of rubble as quickly as possible. When I'm safely hidden, I peek around. A man, Geoff, of all people, comes around the corner and rushes to the woman's side. He checks her, then spins around, scanning the area. The Grek arrives, and I nearly slip away, but someone else comes around a pile from the north. Alliah. It's my little girl. She checks the woman as well, then spins around, eyes searching the surrounding rubble.

I take off as quietly as I can. I expect they'll start their search. Hopefully, they'll assume the woman just passed out. Perhaps thinking it's some kind of dizzy spell. The Greks have to know humans are fragile.

Making my way back through the rubble, I reach the area of the lab. There can be no risk-taking with our location, so I circle around. The Grek, the woman, Geoff, and… and Alliah… they're all far to the north. The Grek stands out, but I can't see the rest. I circle around one more time just to be sure. No one nearby.

I move the board off to the side, then slide through, pulling the board back into place. A moment later, I'm punching in the code, 688-904.

The lock clicks, and I turn the handle, then lock it behind me and find myself face to face with Logan and Gerb. Their mouths hang open, and the color has drained from their faces. Logan looks pitiful, while Gerb, with his round face, small eyes and tiny mouth, looks a little creepy. Fred's obviously gone back downstairs.

"What? Did I miss something?"

Gerb shakes his head, his mouth opening and closing like he has something to say. Logan just stutters for a moment before he manages to say, "You survived!"

I frown, and it seems to pull him back. "You sent me out there. You didn't think I'd make it back?"

"Well… no… you survived out there before… but…" Logan begins.

"But, well," Gerb continues, "we just didn't think anyone could survive out there for long. We were afraid they'd get you."

I shake my head and pull out the jar and the syringe. Handing them over, I turn toward the door.

"Wait… where are you going?"

Turning back to Gerb, I laugh. "You wanted a sample of a Grek too, right? The *human's* the easy one. I still have to get you a piece of the Greks. Any reason not to go now?"

Logan shakes his head while Gerb just stares at me. I slip back through the door. Poor boys are just terrified. It's a wonder Logan came outside to find me the other day.

Once out in the open, I head off to the east. I'm not going back to the north today. The Grek might still be on alert. Besides, I don't want to run into Alliah. I want to see my kids, but I can't do that twice a day. Not when she's like this.

I move cautiously along the streets and in between torn down buildings. Now and then, half a building remains, but those structures often contain one, if not five or six, *HGs*. Good way to get caught. An old post office, from the looks of it, stands relatively untouched—by *relatively* I mean only half of it's torn down—and I take the long way around.

On the far side, I catch sight of the top of a Grek body ahead, just past another pile of rubble. Coming around behind it, I check out the area. I have to not only look carefully, but search, watch, and examine everything.

Once I'm satisfied, I move back into position behind the Grek. The closest *HG*, at least from what I can see, is around eight hundred feet away.

Loading the dart gun with a tranq, I use one that I prepared with about ten times the dose I'd use on a human. It's impossible to know what effect it might have, but hopefully it keeps it from disintegrating long enough to get a piece. The boys say they'll need me to cut off a chunk. They don't know what they're dealing with, so the bigger the piece, the better. I plan on either taking a claw from the end of its leg, or one of the tentacle-like-things on its head. Just the tip, maybe. The whole thing is something like twenty feet long. I have no interest in lugging that back.

The Grek hasn't moved. That's not unusual. I think they have some connection with other Greks and with the *HGs*. They'll often just sit in a spot while the *HGs* search around. Which might mean if this goes badly, I could have *HGs* coming at me from every direction.

I aim for the back. The body of this thing, like all the other Greks, is covered in hair. I'd aim for a neck if I had any way to determine what that looks like.

Squeezing the trigger, I watch as the dart slams into the back of the Grek. I'm hoping for some kind of reaction, but aside from a little shift in its position, nothing changes. Perhaps that's a pretty small needle for a creature that large.

I count to ten, then to twenty, and am about to just walk away, looking for another plan, when one of its legs gives out—just a little. It's just enough for the Grek's body to shift to the right before standing straight again. A moment later, it does it again, but stumbles back a bit, then forward.

A smile creeps up on my face. Maybe we've got it.

The Grek stumbles forward this time, then stops, stands straight, and lets out a roar, something I haven't heard from these creatures before! Spinning around, the Grek searches every direction.

Time to get out of here.

I scramble down the pile of debris and take off at a run between two buildings, careful to avoid any *HGs*. Need to head back and…

Thud… thud… thud… thud…

I spin around and see the Grek come up over the ruins of the building I just passed. It's unsteady on its feet, but it still moves fast, and those legs could crush me in an instant if it catches me.

GRRREHHHHK!

I run with all I've got. There's no real way to outrun one of these things when they're right behind you, but maybe the tranq will slow it down.

Off to the left, two *HGs* come out. One's a little boy, and I force myself not to look to see if it's Aaron. Ahead, another two *HGs* pull out in front of me. I don't recognize the man, but the little girl with him is Chloe, Aaron's best friend from school. I'd recognize that wild hair any day.

Veering off to the right, I take off down a small alleyway. Before long, yet another *HG* appears. This one's Geoff. I push on toward him, and at the last minute, I slip around him as best I can, but I feel his fingers grab at my pack. I yank hard, and he goes flying, losing his grip on me, but the jolt from his weight sends me crashing to the ground. It's all I can do to keep my head up as I twist around, doing my best to ensure my pack takes most of the impact.

Scrambling to my feet again, I dive out of the way as one of the Grek's tentacles comes down at me. My knife is in my hand in a second, and I slash at it. A moment later a piece hits the ground.

The Grek lets out another loud roar. I snatch the piece of its flesh and rush out into the street. Within ten feet, the squirming piece of the tentacle goes stiff, then turns to ash, disintegrating and slipping through my fingers. I snarl and drive my elbow into the jaw of a large *HG* as he tries to wrap his arms around me. The man goes down, and I turn sharply to the left, ducking under a fallen tree laying across two piles of rubble and turn again, this time into one of the few remaining structures. A small office building, I think.

The hallway's dark, and I splash through puddles collected from the recent rains as I search the area. With any luck, the *HGs* who usually hide in a place like this were called out to look for me. I shove another tranq into the dart gun and glance back. One's right behind me, and I turn and a moment later, he drops as the tranq works its way through his system.

Circling around through the offices and crouching low behind the desks, I make my way back to the main door until I sit in a small office right near the entrance. I'm hoping the *HGs* will think I'm on the far end of the building, where I tranqed that guy, and I wait. Four… no five… eight *HGs* rush into the building, spreading out, but mostly heading to the back.

One, however, remains here, looking back and forth. There's no need to see his face for me to know who he is. It takes everything I have not to tranq my own son and take him back to the lab. Maybe we could find a way to sever whatever hold they have on him… but that's a foolish move. There's some way they know, some way the Greks know where the *HGs* are, and I'll just lead them right to Fred and the boys.

It takes all my discipline to lower the gun, to throw away my chance to have my boy back again.

Someone steps up next to him. Of all people, it's Alliah. They look at each other, and from my hiding spot, I can see their faces from the side before they move on. Tired faces. Gaunt, hungry faces. But alive. There's always hope if they're still alive.

Slipping out from behind the desk where I've hidden myself, I exit the small office and make my way carefully to the door. Once there, I scan the area. No movement. The *HGs* hide themselves well, for the most part, but when they're on the hunt, they tend to run, not stay in one spot for long. I should be okay.

A few steps outside the building sits a smashed car. I move over to it at crouch, careful not to step on any of the broken glass strewn throughout this area. The Grek's hearing isn't that great, but the *HGs* will pick up the noise with little trouble.

Making my way around the car, I freeze when I come to the far side. Not more than a step away sits Geoff, facing away from me. He's watching the area. If I try to get out of here, the others will be on me in no time.

Pulling out the dart gun, I take aim and shoot him in the back of the neck. Seconds later, he's down, and I run with all I've got.

GRRREHHHHK!

Thud… thud… thud… thud…

Across the street and down an old alley, zigzagging my way through, I run with every bit of energy I have left. The *HGs* should all be behind me, so I head north for a few hundred feet, then swerve to the left and make my way west— not directly, in case they can track me, but in that general direction.

Thud… thud… thud… thud…

The base is farther behind and to the north a bit at the moment. The Greks and *HGs* are having trouble finding me, but still I double back just a little, then head south for a bit, then west again. I have to cross a wide street which is common enough, but always risky, and I'm hoping they're all far enough behind. Even so, I head south for fifty feet along the pavement, hoping if they follow my tracks through the rubble, they'll have a tough time finding my trail again. When I turn west again, I zigzag through alleys, and slow myself down. The slower I go, the more careful I can be.

By the time I reach the lab, the sun's nearly set. I punch in the code and let myself in. Down the stairs, I move to the elevator, but it opens to reveal Gerb, standing there with a look of terror on his face.

"You okay?" He comes up to me, looking intently into my eyes. He moves back and forth as if that'll help him spot some glow or sign that I'm compromised.

After a moment, I ask, "Satisfied?"

He nods slowly. "You've just been gone a long time. Did you get a piece?"

I hold up my hand to show him the ash, and a frown fills his face. "We've tested some of that. Fred went out and got some a few months back. There's nothing to it. We can't get anything from it."

"There's always tomorrow."

He nods. "But you're okay?"

"Just hungry."

Gerb smiles. "We can solve that problem. Fred made a casserole tonight. Not sure what it is, but it's good."

7

PERSONAL

I pick at my "Casserole Surprise," as Fred calls it. Looks like macaroni, tuna, and crackers to me, but the boys seem bewildered about what it could be made of. I'm hoping it's just that their smarts lie in a different area.

"What's the word on the sample from the woman?"

Logan frowns, and Gerb shrugs. Neither boy looks at me for a moment, until Logan raises his eyes. "Nothing. We can't find anything unusual about it. It looks like… uh… she's just a normal woman."

"What does that tell us?" I ask.

"It tells us," Logan begins slowly, "that the control the Greks have on them is deeper. It doesn't change anything in their skin and blood."

"But I've seen one die."

That causes both boys and even Fred to perk up. "What did you see?" Gerb asks. "It didn't turn ash, did it?"

"Not *it*." Fred says. "Not *it*, Gerb. They're people. Gotta remember that."

"I call 'em *HGs*," I say with a smile.

Fred shakes his head. "Too easy to forget what they are, if you call them that."

That makes me frown. "What do you mean?"

"Remember who they are. They're our children, our spouses, our brothers, sisters, parents. That's who they are."

I nod. Having just seen my kids, I get that. "I saw a *human* Grek die once. It turned to ash, but much slower. Much, much slower. The guy got caught in the crossfire when a few people came out with guns to take down a Grek."

"And what happens to the people when a Grek dies?"

I look at Logan a little strangely and shake my head as I say, "Nothin'. Why?" but then I hesitate. "Wait. I'd never really put this together before, but I've seen this happen a few times. When a Grek dies, some *humans*, not always all of them, but some, they just freeze where they are for a few moments and stare at nothing. Most times I just got out of there, but one time… one time I stayed around long enough to see what happened. They just stood there for about three or four minutes before they resumed their search."

Logan stares at his plate. It's empty. The boy eats a fair amount, considering his size, but it's nothing compared to Gerb. That boy's eyeing my plate right now, so I dive in to finish before I lose what I have left.

"So," Logan says slowly, "they're not physically changed in terms of their blood or their skin, but there's something in them that releases whatever chemical or process that turns their bodies to ash. And the pausing…" He stares at his plate for another moment.

"Could that be…" Gerb says, still eyeing my plate.

I've got my appetite back, so I pull my plate closer and frown at him.

Gerb doesn't seem to notice my reaction, but his brain's still spinning. "…maybe there's some control that each Grek has over a group of the *humans* they take. Not just general control, but each Grek has its own people. Maybe that's the pause. After the Grek dies, it takes a few minutes—three or four—to re-sync up with a new Grek." As he finishes, his hand moves in my direction.

I pull my plate even closer. "That would explain it. So each Grek maybe has its own group of *humans*—likely ten or twelve, judging from the groups around each Grek. The *humans* receive their orders from the Greks, and there's something inserted in each person to dissolve them if they're killed or injured too severely."

"So, before we can free any *humans*," Fred says, drawing it all together, "the control needs to be ended. No use trying to get a *human* away when a Grek can just dissolve the poor guy."

I take the last bite off my plate and chew slowly. When I'm finished, I say, "So, we're back to needing a sample of a Grek. I assume we've gotta start there. I cut off a piece, and it dissolved within seconds, while the *human* sample didn't. So, whatever dissolves the Greks is likely all throughout their body."

"So, how do we do that?" Gerb asks. "How do we get a sample?"

I laugh. "I was hoping you two could come up with something."

They shake their heads, but Fred leans forward. "I might have an idea…"

"You can see why I haven't told the boys about this, right?"

I nod.

"I've had to treat the boys three times, each, for frostbite in the last few months. Don't really even know what I'm doin', but there's some good books in the nurse's station that gave a bit of direction. If they knew this was here, they'd freeze everything they could get their hands on, just to see what happens."

I nod again.

Before me is a room with about forty canisters of liquid nitrogen. Fred tells me the labs are all set up for the canisters and there are even some cabinets specifically designed to keep things frozen by a constant source of the stuff.

The boys seem to be smart, that's for sure, but what they have in intellect seems to have crowded out all hope of common sense.

"I've been working with them, trying to help them think a little further ahead, but it's slow going. They've gotten this far in life on brains alone. You know they were both more or less in their second year of university?"

"They told me third year."

He laughs. "That too. Sort of. They both managed to convince the university to let them take a full double load of courses. They completed years one and two, all in one year—and aced the courses. As soon as the summer started, they jumped into third year. I think they both wanted to finish all four years in about sixteen months—at least, that's my guess."

"How do you know all this?"

Fred laughs again. "Read their files. It's all in the office. They might not look like much, but they're smart guys. Just need a little time to grow up, that's all."

"So, you think we can use the liquid nitrogen to freeze the Greks?"

"That's my guess," Fred says. "I don't know how to do that; I just know this stuff comes out cold. Real cold. Cold enough to freeze flesh instantly. But I don't know how to make it all happen."

I frown while I stare at the cannisters. "So that's what we gotta figure out."

I spend the next four days watching the Greks and the *HGs*… no, the *humans*. I gotta see them as people. All of them, not just my kids. "*HG*" is too easy… easy to forget who they truly are.

The *humans* don't follow much of a pattern. They tend to move in a seemingly random manner. I can't figure it out, anyway. The Greks, on the other hand, they move through an area, stop, remain there for upwards of an hour, then move, stop, remain in place, move, stop, remain…

It feels like some kind of search pattern, with the *humans* covering all the details, searching all the cracks and crevices. I've nearly been caught by the *humans* once or twice every day, but I always manage to get out and away before they see me. My luck will run out eventually, but maybe if this plan works, we can force them back.

I see Alliah and Aaron quite a few times every day. They're always part of the search. Alliah's fast and Aaron's so small, I can see why the Greks make such good use of them.

At the end of the fourth day, after selecting the location to take down a Grek, I carefully make my way back to the lab, circling around the entrance twice before I slip inside. A moment later, I'm through the door, and the lock clicks behind me.

"What'd you find this time, Xavier?"

"Same thing as the other days," I tell Fred. "They're consistent. I think we can count on the pattern they've set."

"Your plan taking shape?"

I nod. "Yep. I have a spot that should work. It's to the north. I think I can do it without hurting any of the *humans* and, hopefully, without losing the Grek sample."

"Good news!" Fred says with a smile.

I pat him on the shoulder as I pass by and head to my room to clean up, then move on to the dining hall to get some food and fend off Gerb's attempt at stealing my meal. There's enough food he doesn't need mine, but I think he wants everyone else's food. His own is boring. My meal is a challenge.

"Whoa!" Logan says with a laugh as I walk in. "You don't normally come to supper armed! What's with the gun?"

I place my hand on my 9mm and frown at Gerb. "This is to discourage that one from trying to take my food."

Gerb steps back, but then his eyes fill with excitement. It's almost like he craves the extra challenge.

"Can I hold your gun?" Logan asks.

"Touch my weapon, and I beat you silly!"

Logan slowly nods as he backs away. Gerb, on the other hand, looks like that threat hasn't even registered, other than to up the stakes.

I drop into my seat and wait while Fred brings the food over. I don't really know why I came to supper armed. I think… I think these guys are growing on me. Fred is very fond of them, despite their… weirdness. Maybe I'm growing fond of them as well. I actually enjoy the banter. I left the bullets in my room, anyway. It's just strapped to my side for show. No use taking the risk.

"You see 'em again today?" Fred asks as he puts my plate down.

That catches me off guard, and I'm no longer in a joking mood. "What do you know of it?"

"They know what they're doing," Fred explains.

I just wait. He's got something to say, and I'm not going to drag it out of him.

"It's targeted, Xavier. It's all been strategic, right? You told me it was from the start. It's not become some random thing now that they rule the planet. If it was strategic at the beginning, it's still strategic."

Staring down at my plate, I force myself to remain calm. "It doesn't seem like it, Fred. It's just patrols. They're not up to anything other than catching whoever they can find."

"And yet it's personal."

I take a deep breath and force down the rising anger. "It's not personal! They don't know where I am or if I'm even still around. They just want to catch anyone they can. If they catch me, they might just catch us all."

Fred takes a bite and slowly chews. I hate it when he does that. He's in no rush. Ever.

When he finishes, he asks, "Are you sure?"

I don't have any reply to that. There's no way I can be sure. It just doesn't look like some grand strategy is at work. They're just hunting down strays right now.

"Xavier, they're not after just anyone. They're after you."

I force myself to loosen the grip on my fork and take another deep breath.

"Not trying to upset you, Xavier," Fred says.

The boys slide down the table as if to get away from us. They're strange boys, but at least they can pick up on the tension in the room. This time, anyway.

"What are you trying to do?"

"Trying to give you some focus. They're after you, Xavier."

"You said that already. If you have some proof, Fred, let's hear it!"

"Did you live around here, Xavier?"

I shake my head. "No, my home was about ten miles to the west."

"Were your kids taken around here?"

"Nope. That was more like twenty miles to the south. Maybe a bit more. Near the Grek ship."

Fred nods slowly and raises his fork to take another bite.

I grab his hand and snarl, "Out with it, old man!"

He smiles at me and sets his fork down. "You see anyone else you know?"

"Yeah, a few. A kid who was close with my son, a few people my wife worked with, a couple people I don't like."

"Ahh… yeah, that makes sense."

"Why?" I'm feeling the tension in my chest. Fred takes his time getting anywhere.

"Doesn't it seem strange that your kids are here, not back where they were caught? What about your son's friend? Why would that kid be in this area? Ten miles is far enough that I'd say it's quite the coincidence. And the people you don't like… doesn't that seem strange that they're here too? And… even some of your wife's coworkers." He shakes his head slowly before adding, "Strange."

"Out with it, Fred!"

"The ones you don't like, that's a draw to attack. You could attack them, even kill them, and you might get away with it, as long as the Greks don't catch you. And… the ones you love, that's a draw to rescue. Xavier, anytime anyone goes out there, they see people they know, and not so many they don't. It's how the Greks draw you in." Fred takes a deep breath and sits back from his plate. "Never told the boys this, but you might as well all hear. I lost a lot of people I love. When I was out there, it wasn't Xavier's kids coming after me, searching for me. It was my grandkids. My two daughters. My sons-in-law. Even my best friend, and the two guys I worked with for over thirty years. I couldn't stand either of those guys, but they're out there. They're all out there when I go outside."

I drop my fork as I stare at him, trying to accept what he's saying. "They know… They know who's going out. It's targeted. They're preying on our weakness, trying to use everything they can to pull us in. And they're using our loved ones. And Geoff."

"Who's Geoff?" Gerb asks.

I shake my head. "Just someone."

"I saw… Amber…" Logan says. "She came after me. On my way here, months ago. She was the one who chased me here."

"Who's Amber?" Fred asks.

Logan doesn't answer, so Gerb speaks up. "Just the love of his life. He had a mad crush on her. Couldn't stop talking about her all the time. She's cute, has really wild hair. Even when we both got here, he talked non-stop about her for a week. I…” He looks over at his friend and adds in a quiet voice, “I didn't know she'd chased him like that.”

“So even a girlfriend…”

“No!” Gerb says. “That's the strange part. Amber didn't even know Logan existed. He tried to talk to her a couple times but chickened out.”

Logan nods vigorously at that. “Yeah, man. I tried like eight times. Each time I couldn't get within like fifty feet of her.”

I frown at that. “So, if she didn't even know Logan existed, why's she out there? Does that mean they can read our thoughts?”

That gets both boys' attention, and I have to look away. Now's not the time to laugh, but Gerb's shocked face with that round head, tiny eyes, and small mouth is about the funniest thing I've ever seen. I push it out of my mind. Focus, Xavier! “That must be it. Obviously, they can't do it to the point where they can find us, otherwise we'd be overrun by now, but they can read enough to know that I'm here, and I'm the one going out every day.” To Fred, I ask, “You went out again a few weeks ago. See anyone you know?”

He nods slowly and a mischievous smile creeps up on his face. “Yes. Despite my advanced years, I went out. In fact, that's why I went out. Curious if I was just wrong about it all… but I went out and within ten minutes, came across my daughter and my twelve-year-old grandson. They were searching for me, pretty intently.”

I take a deep breath and let it out slowly. “So, it is personal.”

“Yes, it definitely is,” Fred explains. “But that changes nothing.”

Gerb twists his head in one of his awkward reactions. “What do you mean?”

“I mean,” Fred says with a look of deep compassion on his face, “it doesn't mean we hate them. It means we just have to be more careful about our hearts. It's easier to be fooled when those you love are pulling you in. Or those you hate are offering themselves up to you."

"But it still means we need that sample," I growl. I'm struggling with this whole thing. It all makes sense now. I kept wondering what would bring Alliah and Aaron here, along with all those others. I just assumed maybe they were all dropped in this area, but Chloe was an odd one.

I finish my meal in silence, then get up and walk out. I can't help but remember Aaron and Chloe playing together in our backyard, digging in the sandbox, or imagining they were dinosaurs, or any number of games. Her parents, just getting to know them, they…

I shake my head as I move down the hall. Too much pain. The Greks have taken too much.

SECOND SAMPLE

I have my plan all set, I've gone over my strategy with Fred countless times, and I'm ready to put everything together. Fred's an interesting guy. He's done nothing in his life that would make me think he could speak into my mission parameters at all, but when I go over the plan with him, he asks all the right questions, pushes me in all the right areas, and finds all the weak points in my strategy. We could have used him on some of my ops, to be honest. He has a brilliant mind.

The problem now is that I'm only the only one who can do this. The others aren't soldiers, so it's going to take a lot of work putting everything into action. I set out early in the morning with the first two tanks of liquid nitrogen. I have about a mile to go, which means I'm risking exposure that entire time. It also means I have to take a route that allows me to push the cart, and instead of running the mile in little time, it'll take me close to an hour to cover that distance and another hour back. At least.

By the time I have eight bottles at my chosen location, and still nothing set up, it's getting dark. Most of my trips back and forth were fairly uneventful, but on one of them, I had to hide out for most of the afternoon while two Greks and over thirty *humans* combed the area. After what Fred told me, I paid close attention to all the *humans*. I think I knew every one of them, from both my kids to a guy who changed the oil on my truck a few months back.

Still no sign of Connie, though. I'd think they'd bring her out at some point, if they're after me. But either way, if I doubted Fred's take on the situation before, I no longer do.

I figure I need about twenty tanks, so I head back to the base to settle in for the night, stopping at a small creek to get some water on the way. The boys will complain if I don't.

———•——•——●——•——•——

Early in the morning on the fourth day, I'm ready. The liquid nitrogen is all in place, I have my diversions set, and far more sedative than I think is necessary. The Greks can sometimes react quickly, so everything needs to happen with precision. Typically, I would have trained with this specific strategy over and over and have a team of about six or more SEALs to implement the plan, but nothing is typical anymore.

Those days are long gone. Even if I get my family back, nothing will ever be the same again.

But today is where my focus must remain.

If the pattern holds, the Grek should arrive in somewhere around ten minutes, and the patrols should start immediately after.

When I see the Grek, I breathe a sigh of relief. It's right on schedule. Despite all my effort, there's still a lot of guesswork involved. Most is based on what I've observed. With some of it, I'm just shootin' in the dark.

As hoped for, the Grek moves along the open street, pausing every few moments, and then climbs down into a lower area. My initial assumption about the creatures was that they would seek high ground if they were communicating with people, but this Grek appears to control all the *humans* in the area while it stands in this low area. The area appears to be a construction site where I expect they were laying the foundation for some skyscraper.

I watch as the Grek settles in on a slab of concrete held up by four solid pillars. I'm assuming this was to be part of the subbasement, but I know little of construction, other than to see that it's perfect for my needs.

Part of the challenge, what took me so long to set up, was to get everything in place without changing the landscape in any significant manner. On top of that, there are so many aspects of the plan, all of which must fall into place just perfectly.

Moving down into the construction site, I stay hidden by advancing from object to object, careful to keep myself out of sight. The sun's barely up, which helps, and I've wrapped myself in my heat reflective outfit with camo.

When I reach the bottom, I settle in and wait. The Grek, if it follows the same pattern, should sit here for approximately two hours. The *humans* then move out from here, searching through this area, and I've been careful to make sure I time everything so the *humans* survive.

When the sun sits high enough that I think all the *humans* can see well in their search and therefore will move out far from the Grek, I pull out both dart guns. Each one carries a single dart filled with twice the dose I used on the Grek the last time, the maximum amount the dart can handle.

A quick peek at my watch… five minutes. I pull a suit out of my pack, one designed specifically to handle extreme cold. A coat isn't enough. I need something to keep all the cold out.

Another quick look at my watch. Two minutes. That should place the *humans* where I want them.

Counting down the time, I go over my plan, once, then twice, then a third time. At the precise moment, I let a dart fly. It hits the Grek, and this time, as expected, the Grek stumbles within seconds. Perfect.

I flip the safety and press the button on the first of several transmitters, and the Semtex I've set about five hundred feet to the west detonates. Immediately after, I grab the other dart gun and fire the second tranq into the back of the Grek. I can't see any *humans*, but I'm hoping the Grek will have ordered them to search out the source of the noise. As low down as we are, there's no chance for me to see what's going on up top.

The Grek doesn't roar this time. Instead, it stumbles forward, then backward, while its legs wobble. Flipping open the safety, then hitting the button on the next transmitter, I hear the second Semtex charge detonate about six hundred feet to the west, then I grab a large pole off to the side where I'd left it.

This will be the trickiest part of the entire plan as I'm hoping the Grek will be unstable enough to push it off the edge. It sure looks like it is. Running up behind the Grek, I slam the pole into the back of the creature, pushing it forward until it reaches the edge. Giving it one more shove, the creature's front two legs slip off, and down it goes, over the side and out of sight.

Below, a cloud shoots up as the liquid nitrogen releases, and I turn on the small oxygen tank I have in my suit. I should be okay, but nitrogen can force breathable air out of the entire area as it expands, and I don't want to pass out.

I scramble around the concrete pad and down into the area below. The liquid nitrogen has stopped spraying, and the Grek isn't moving. Not even a twitch.

I grab the sample jar I stored down here, protected from the Grek by another slab of concrete, and rush up to the large creature. The jar itself is now frozen, the nitrogen should have dropped it and the Grek to around -300 or more, and I snap off a chunk of the tentacle and drop it in the jar. I also grab a crowbar I'd left down here and smash one of the creature's claws, dropping it in the jar, then sealing it up.

On my way up the hill, I stuff the jar into my pack as I shed the suit. It's cold throughout this area now, but we're in direct sunlight and there's enough of a warm breeze that I'll be okay. Once I've stored the jar away, I throw on the pack.

I'm not too concerned about the jar itself. Not only can it handle the cold, but it's tough. It can take quite a beating before it's damaged.

I already laid out my escape route. I'm hoping all the *humans* are far to the west right now, which means I can swing east just a little, then head south, hopefully without even a sign of anyone. If all goes well, I'll be back in the lab in half an hour.

I get to the top of the hill and come to a halt, my heart racing. I can't move. My feet feel like they're rooted to the spot. Standing just a few steps in front of me... is Aaron. It's... Aaron. My boy... just... staring right at me. He's still wearing the clothes he had on when I lost him—just a lot dirtier and with a few extra rips. He might be a little thinner than before, but he looks just like he always did.

Aside from his glowing, yellow eyes.

He opens his mouth, and I hear the first words I've heard from my son in far too long. "Daddy? I need you, daddy."

My hands shake, and my mouth goes dry.

I try to think through it all, try to understand, try to figure out how to react, but all I want to do is grab him and run. Take him back to the lab, barricade the door, and do everything I can to free him while the Greks beat down the door.

"Can I go home with you, daddy?"

My feet move beyond my control, and I take a step forward before I can stop myself. I can't... I can't fall for it. I didn't know the Greks could do this, get him to speak to me, but I know this isn't my boy. He's in there somewhere, but he's...

This isn't him.

Footsteps, quick, light footsteps.

I spin around. On the far side of the construction site, Alliah runs full out, circling the pit, coming for us. Coming for me. Her voice rings out across the distance, "Daddy! I need you, daddy!"

I turn back to Aaron and nearly fall back as he slams into me. At first, I wrap my arms around him, but he scrambles, grabbing, pulling, climbing. He's up on my chest, around my neck, swinging his body around. Before I quite figure out what's happening, Aaron's secured himself to my back, piggyback style, holding on with all he's got.

I grab his arm around my neck, then spin back to see Alliah has made it nearly half-way to me. She's still fast. I'll never outrun her, especially with Aaron holding onto me.

I take off to the east, zigzagging through the buildings and around the construction machinery. A large crane takes up a huge amount of the area around here, and I race around the back of it. There's something I can make use of back there. As I run, I grab hold of Aaron's arms again.

I can't stop, but I can't hurt my son either. I see what I'm looking for and run toward it. When I get there, I wrench his arms apart, and his small body comes loose. I twist, and my boy goes sailing through the air, hitting the pile of sand. I look back to see him rolling over to keep his eye on me.

He's safe, so I run. Hard.

Aaron won't catch me, but Alliah… If I slow even a little, she'll catch up.

I follow my escape route. I created it with this in mind, knowing it could be Alliah on my tail. A lot of the ground I cover is asphalt, so my boots leave no tracks. Heading east for another block, I come around a corner and turn south quickly, doubling back a bit and slowing my pace, both to catch my breath and hoping to lay eyes on my daughter. I need to know she can't follow this turn.

I come to a halt at a corner of a torn down building, hiding well behind a few pallets leaning up against a post. From there, I watch and wait. A few seconds later she comes tearing out from an alleyway, eyes fixed forward, chasing me with a look of intense focus on her face. In another few seconds, she's out of sight, and I head south. I still zigzag a little and do all I can to maintain my pace and remain out of sight.

There's a spot I'm aiming for, not far away. It's a taller pile of rubble, but the way it's laid out, I can actually get up there and sit on top without being seen. I push on until I reach it, run around to the southern side, and scramble up under the cover of broken beams and piles of stone and brick.

When I reach the top, I can see out over a long distance. The broken crane marks where I got the sample, and I can see the torn down building where I came around and caught sight of Alliah as she hunted me. I even see the pile of sand where I dumped my son. But none of that's what worries me. What worries me is I also see a dozen, maybe more… no… more appear, coming up and over piles of rubble… maybe fifty or even a hundred *humans*. They're all searching. I see Alliah among them, but she's not running anymore. They all move back and forth, searching, hunting, almost like they're trying to smell their way along. But what scares me is every last one of them, regardless of how much they move back and forth, they're all consistently moving in the same direction.

South.

And not just south, but specifically towards me. Somehow, they know where I am.

I scramble down the hill. Not sure what to do. I can't lead them back to the lab, but then I need to get the sample to the boys. If I don't get it back to them, this is all a waste, and I don't think Fred or the boys could pull off what I just did.

I run again, heading in a southwesterly direction. After about ten minutes, I climb another pile. This one isn't as safe— easier to be seen on top—but I climb carefully and keep myself low. When I reach the peak, I scan the area. Sure enough, all the *humans* are heading toward me again. I must be leaving a trail…

Somehow, they can track me.

I scramble down again and run west, maintaining my speed for another ten minutes. When I stop, I crawl into a small hole and pull off my pack. I assume it must be the Grek sample, so I take the jar out of the pack, along with a bottle of rubbing alcohol, and douse it. Throwing off my gloves, I douse my hands as well. I think that's all that's touched the sample, aside from the pack itself, which I leave in the hole.

With the sample jars under my arm, I run off to the south, this time for another ten minutes. If I'm right, I think I'm somewhere directly east of the lab. Sometimes, it's hard to know exactly where I am when all the landmarks are broken buildings.

I climb up onto an enormous pile of rubble once more and look back. I can't see all that many, maybe two or three *humans*. No Greks. It's like they're staying back right now. I can't tell for sure if the *humans* are heading this direction or just searching generally.

But… no Greks.

That's strange. Do they think I'll hurt them? They must know by now that I won't hurt a *human*. Is that what they're up to? Trying to protect themselves?

I turn to slide down the rubble, and my heart jumps into my throat as I see what's really going on. Directly ahead, maybe a quarter of a mile away, a line of Greks—possibly sixty, maybe seventy of them—are all heading this way.

I now have two choices. Either east towards the lab, or west away from it all.

I can't lead the Greks to the boys and Fred… but maybe I can do something else. They're obviously tracking me somehow, but it's hard to know if the alcohol fixed the problem. Just no way to test it anymore.

I race off to the east, heading directly towards where I think the lab is. After fifteen minutes, I see some familiar piles of rubble. I adjust my direction accordingly and head straight for one of the main cameras. I told the boys to watch the cameras today for when I came back. Let's see if they can listen.

I reach a tall maple tree. The Greks didn't tear down all the trees like they did the buildings, and this one's likely eighty or ninety years old. I jump up and down, hollering, "One of you, come outside, quick!"

I jump up and down a few more times and repeat the message. I'm taking quite a risk here. Not risking myself, but them.

I run around to the lab door but stay back a good twenty feet.

After a few minutes, I hear from behind the board covering the hole, "Xavier? What's going on?"

"I can't come in, Logan!" I holler. "They're tracking me. I don't know how. I've doused the canister in the rubbing alcohol you gave me. Hopefully it's clean and the samples are good."

He pokes his head out, his eyes filled with terror as he tries to look in every direction at once. "What do we do?"

"I'm going to set the sample down here. I won't come any closer. After I leave, you come get the sample then seal yourself in. Change the code in case they get me. I'm gonna lead them east. Do you understand?"

There's a pause, and I shake my head. "No time, Logan. There are both *humans* and Greks chasing me. DO YOU UNDERSTAND?"

"I do… but…"

I set the sample jar down. "I'm going now, Logan. Be safe. If I can lose them, I'll come back, but otherwise, do what you can."

"No, Xavier… wait."

I hesitate. "I know it's hard to lose a member of the team, Logan. Tell the others…"

"NO! Xavier, wait a sec…" The board shifts to the side, and Gerb is here. He's breathing heavy. I think he just ran up from below. He hands something to Logan who steps out and tosses it to me. "Follow that. Gerb rigged it up. If it lights up, follow the lights."

I don't get it, but I was a soldier. Sometimes, orders don't make sense. I nod to both boys and, without another word, take off to the east, not sure if I'll ever see either of them again.

HOPE LOST

As I run, I shove Gerb's gadget into my pocket. For now, I need to get away. I make sure that I don't change my direction at all. That means, of course, if they're tracking me, they'll walk right by the lab entrance, but if I shift directions at that point, it might draw attention to the fact that I stopped there.

That's the last thing I want.

Once I've run about a quarter of a mile, I shift slightly to the north until I find a taller pile of rubble that looks stable enough to climb. Scrambling up the side, I crouch down at the top and look back.

My breathing catches in my throat, and I grab my binoculars to confirm what I think I'm seeing. A moment later, I'm grinding my teeth and trying to figure out what I can do.

The Greks have all stopped and are standing in a large circle. At the center of that circle, hundreds of *humans* search through the rubble. Some are even up in the maple tree as if they think they'll find me up there.

I close my eyes and drop my head down onto my arm. A groan escapes my lips. They weren't tracking me. Not at all. Somehow, they can track the sample! Now I'm safe, and Logan, Gerb, and Fred are surrounded. It's only a matter of time before the Greks find the lab entrance.

I scramble back down the side of the pile and reach for my pack, only to remember that I'd left it in that hole. I had some more Semtex in there, along with another two detonators. So much for a simple distraction.

I run back towards the lab, and when I'm within a few hundred feet of the nearest Grek, I climb a small pile of rubble, stand on top, and yell, "Hey! Hey Greks! And all the rest of you! I'm here! Come get me if you want me!"

Two of the Greks spin around, but I can't see any of the *humans*. The large creatures stare at me for a moment before turning back. They don't want me… at least not as much as they want the samples!

That tells me two things: first, there's something in the sample they don't want us to see; second, and this is the worst part, I can't save Logan, Gerb, and Fred.

I'm just about to climb down as I mentally add them to the list of people I want to rescue when movement catches my eye. Three shapes, moving fast, coming through the rubble and debris.

The one's definitely Alliah. The second is definitely Chloe, Aaron's friend. She was a fast one. Small and fast are two strong qualities in a world of shattered buildings. The Greks must also know I'd never hurt a child, least of all those two. And the third… a taller, thin man I don't recognize. He has the build of a runner, and he's coming fast.

Scrambling down the rubble, I take off to the east again, and then veer to the south, zigzagging for a bit, then running all out to the south. I have to get away from them if I'm to rescue the boys and Fred.

I turn back to the west again, not to head back to the Greks, but I doubt Alliah and the two others will expect me to backtrack. When I've moved far enough, I see the remains of a building—just a wall, basically, but enough of a floor sticks out of the second level to give me what I need.

I climb up the side and use the extra height to look out over the ruined city. It takes a bit, but eventually I lay eyes on my three pursuers. They couldn't track me—at all. All of them, though they've spread out, are to the north and east of me. When I look back toward the lab, more to the north and a little west now, the circle of Greks has closed in, and the people, they're all congregated at the entrance.

All hope is shattered as I come to grips with the fact that my friends are lost. I couldn't save them anymore than I could save my family.

———•——•——●——•——•———

I move south, wandering aimlessly for the rest of the day and well into the night. Obviously, the Greks can sense my presence to a certain extent. Fred was right. The searches to pull me in are very personal, and as I learned today, very direct. The words of Aaron, his voice, his pleading, still ring in my ears. And Alliah… the same words. *"Daddy! I need you, daddy!"*

How could I have left them? How could I… No! That's not them. I know it's their body, and their voice, but if either of them could understand what was going on, neither of them would try to pull me over to the Greks.

In a way, I want to give up. I'm all alone, again. What's the point of fighting? Perhaps it would be easier to just hand myself over.

But then again, if I truly am the only free human left, the only one not taken by the Greks… then I think this would all go down differently.

I've seen how they try to pull me in. If they want me that badly, and I'm the only one left on the entire planet, they would certainly devote more attention to capturing me. I would think I'd always have hundreds, if not thousands, of *humans* after me. And the Greks… they'd come in force like they did when I took the sample. They'd tear what's left of this planet apart to get me.

But… they don't.

That means one thing. There are more free humans. Many more. I'm not alone. I just have to find the others.

And I have to remain strong for my kids and my wife. I made a promise. The kids first. If it takes me twenty years to get them back, to free them… Alliah will be in her early thirties, and Aaron his mid-twenties. If it takes that long, I'll get them back.

I just can't do it alone, so I have to find the other free humans.

A memory tugs at me, and I stop. Logan gave me something… Gerb's little gadget thing. I pull it out, and I'm surprised to see a light flashing. *"If it lights up, follow the lights."*

That's about as cryptic as it gets, which is definitely the way the boys like to do it. *Follow the lights.* There's only one light. *Not helpful, Logan.* I smile and shake my head.

The boys are weird, and they like mystery, but they're also brilliant. They won't give me something that doesn't work.

It's dark, but by the light of the moon, I try to look all over the little box to see if there are any other buttons or anything to give me a clue about what's going on. The light isn't that bright, but with no other lights around, it's almost blinding, forcing me to cover the bulb with my hand as I examine the gadget. Nothing. I uncover it again and turn it over in my hands, and when I do, the flashing lights speed up.

I turn it back, and it slows down. Smiling to myself, I hold it steady, but turn slowly around. As I turn, the more the little gadget faces north, the faster the light blinks until it's almost a steady light, but when I turn back around to the south, the speed of the blinks slow down.

That's a good enough sign for me.

I set off to the north, careful to keep my eyes out for Greks and *humans*. The Greks aren't very active at night, but they stand out with their height. The *humans*, though… aside from their glowing eyes, they're hard to spot. And some of them seem to close their eyes almost to slits.

Pushing on with my reclaimed enthusiasm and energy, I creep along. For the most part, I keep the gadget in my pocket. The flashing light is bright enough that it makes it hard to see in the dark, and it can function not only as a beacon to light my way, but also as a beacon to draw attention to my location.

I walk for hours through the darkness, careful to keep my footing when any step could mean a hole and a broken ankle. Whenever I pull out the beacon, I try to find some area to shelter myself from view and use my hand to cover the light, but so far, north is the direction. It's not exactly where the old lab was, but it's close.

When I finally reach a point where the lab is directly to the west of me, the sun is just lighting up the eastern horizon. The gadget continues to lead me north, so I push on. Greks swarmed through this area as of just a few hours ago, but it now feels deserted. They're so quick when they set to work, when they destroy. So aggressive to zero in on what they want to tear down, and so effective in doing it.

I stop at a small stream running through the area just as the sun begins to peak above the horizon. The water is far from clean, but I need it. While sitting on the bank, I pull out a bit of food, all that I have left. The rest was in my pack. At some point, I might go back to find my hidden pack, but for now, I need to see where Gerb's gadget leads me.

When I've had a bit of a rest, not much, just enough to ensure I can run if needed, I set out again. Still north. When the old lab is about six miles behind me, I check the gadget again and come to a halt. The light, it's still flashing, but slow. I turn to the west, then south, then when I turn southeast, it speeds up again. I must have passed whatever I'm looking for.

Setting off in the new direction, I travel this time with the gadget in hand. The sun's far enough above the horizon that the lights won't give me away, and within ten minutes, I pass a point where the speed of the flashing slows. The spot I'm looking for is right around here.

I spend the next hour circling through this area, getting the lay of the land. It's not much different from any other area I've been in. The odd tree here or there, piles of rubble, some small, some massive. Few hiding spots.

Hiding spots… what if…

Labs were big money… discoveries could make people rich. And the lab the boys worked in was definitely military. The first one was underground…

I search the area, looking for anything that might have gone unnoticed in the Grek's destruction. How would they miss it? It would have to be under a building. The other one was covered in a lot of debris. This one could be the same.

I search and search until I find what I'm looking for. I doubt the boys will be overly creative with this kind of thing, so I figure a board over the entrance will be the sign that I've found the right place.

When I find a large broken sheet of wood, I shove it aside and slip through into the dark crevice. I don't pull the board back over the entrance right away but instead wait until my eyes adjust. In the dark, cramped area, I push a few beams out of the way, and a moment later, I'm grinning like a fool as I stare at a steel reinforced security door.

I slip back to the entrance and pull the board over the opening and then return to the door. Not sure what else to do, I punch in the old code.

688-904.

Nothing. No unlocked door, nothing. The lights on the keypad just go out.

Obviously, the wrong code.

There could be a similarity between the two. Perhaps it could be 688-903 or 688-905. I try each of those, but nothing happens. My hand on the palm scanner doesn't work either. There's no reason it should, but I try anyway.

Think, Xavier, think! If Gerb led me here… what could the code be?

I shake my head. I don't think there's any chance I could just guess it. It's not an overly secure system if someone like me can figure it out. I also can't break through. I saw the door at the other lab. It was solid. I'd need to blow it open, but then we'd have a new problem.

I pound on the door, but that does nothing. The door's thick enough that I can't really hear much of a thud myself, let alone could the boys or Fred if they're in there and on a lower level.

I need to find another entrance. Maybe my code will work on a different door. Perhaps this keypad is shorted out.

I'm just about back at the entrance when I hear the door unlock behind me. When I turn around, it opens to reveal Logan and Gerb with a smiling Fred behind them.

I nearly shout for joy but keep my cool. Can't give away our location.

Moving inside, I swing the door shut behind me, and when I turn around, I nearly stumble back as Gerb slams into me, wrapping his thick arms around me. While Gerb holds on, Logan stands there awkwardly, grinning like a fool, unsure how to act or react. When Gerb finally lets go, he's sniffling and wiping his eyes while I pull Logan into a hug. He seems to need it. I think I do too.

When I'm done with Logan, Fred stretches out his hand, and I shake it. "Thought you might find your way through."

"What is this place? Why didn't you guys tell me about it?"

Gerb wipes a tear. "I'm sooorrrrry…" he wails.

Logan shakes his head. "We didn't think we'd ever need it. There are a few of these labs around. I think four or five of them, although we've only been to these two. It's a good thing we came here. Otherwise, we'd never have met up with Beth."

"She goes by Elizabeth," Gerb corrects.

"But everyone always called her Beth," he says, a seriously distressed look filling his eyes.

I'm not entirely sure what to make of Logan's reaction, but I'm pretty sure I don't care. I'm just happy to be back with these guys. "How did you get here?"

Both boys start talking at once, but Fred cuts them off. "You eaten?"

I shake my head. "Just a snack a few hours ago."

He waves for me to follow, and I do right away. Food sounds good. Maybe they can tell me while I eat.

This lab seems to follow the same layout as the previous one, which helps me feel right at home. When we reach the dining hall, however, there's no tv set up for the boys, but there is a young woman here.

When we enter, she frowns at the three of them. "You sure he's safe? Not a spy or anything for the creatures?"

"Nope, no spy," Gerb says. "We know him."

She eyes me warily. I don't blame her.

I'd say she's mid to late twenties. She wears glasses, and her light brown hair is curly and held back in a ponytail. The hair looks like it's trying to break out and free itself. Not sure how to put my figure on it exactly, but she has a smart look to her.

"This is Elizabeth," Gerb explains. "She's Amber's older sister."

At that, Logan seems to choke a little, but Gerb doesn't notice.

"You knew Amber?" she asks me.

I shake my head. "Nope. Never met her."

"Then…" she points at me and Gerb, "why'd you introduce me as Amber's sister?"

I raise my eyebrows at Gerb, hoping he'll get the hint that he's made it all awkward, but he just seems to understand that things are always awkward and charges forward with total abandon. "Because we were talking about Amber since Logan had a mad crush on her and we told Xavier this and so Xavier knows about her because we told him and Logan really misses her but he never talked to her so she never even knew that Logan had a crush on her and…"

I put my hand on Gerb's shoulder. "You really gotta stop, Gerb. This is one of those moments when you shut your mouth and refuse to make things worse." Fred just chuckles to himself as he heads into the kitchen, probably to grab some food, and I turn to Logan. "Just go with it, man. Crushes are pretty normal."

Elizabeth sits down across from me and opens her mouth, I think to ask a question, but then stops. Turning to Logan, she says, "She actually had a crush on you, too, but you never spoke to her. She said she tried to start up a conversation with you once, asked you how your biology class was going, and you just walked away."

Logan frowns and sticks out his bottom lip. "I thought she was talking to someone else, then after I walked away, I looked back and saw her standing there by herself. I… wanted to go back but thought I couldn't… 'cause she'd be mad… and I didn't know what to say."

I can't take any more of this, so I ask, "Bring me up to speed. What happened?"

No one speaks this time as they all seem unsure who should explain it, so we sit in silence until Fred comes back. When he does, he drops a plate in front of me and takes a seat.

"Well, since no one else seems to want to spell it out, I will," Fred says as he turns his chair around to face me and leans back. "So, it turns out the boys aren't all that bad in a crisis." He pauses at that and gives me a look that lets me know he's as surprised by that as I am. "They brought the sample in and ran some tests on it, startin' right away. They were all set up to go when you got back. Didn't want to waste a second. In fact, once they had all their equipment ready to go, they sat there, watchin' the video feed—I even made them some popcorn—while they waited for you to return. Once they had the sample, they went at it, but then about an hour later, the Greks started pounding on the door."

He laughs and shakes his head. "I figured it was over, but the boys split the samples up and grabbed me. They had packs all ready to go—even one for you, but, of course, you weren't around, so we only needed the three. I didn't think to mention this before, but there was a back way out of the lab. It's a tunnel that leads out to a shipping entrance. The Greks destroyed it like everything else months ago, but we picked our way through the rubble."

"And then they came straight here," Elizabeth says, her face bunched up in a sneer. "No regard for whether or not they'd lead the Greks to this location."

"Did the Greks follow you?" I ask.

Logan shakes his head. I notice he hasn't made eye contact with Elizabeth since Gerb started babbling about his friend's crush. "They were just after the sample."

"What's this about splitting up the samples?"

At that question, the corner of Gerb's mouth curls up. "Loge guessed that maybe they couldn't track it all. Maybe they could only track the blood or the soft tissue. So, we split it up into three sections: the piece of the tentacle, the shell, and the goo inside the shell."

"Do you know what they tracked?"

Logan shakes his head. "Nope. No way to tell without going back there."

They both look at me expectantly, but Elizabeth just frowns. "What's going on? Is this new guy your leader or something?"

Logan shakes his head. "No, he's the guy who gets stuff done."

"So you want me to go back there and try to retrieve the samples, or at least find out what they left?"

"Wait, why this guy?" Elizabeth asks.

"I used to do this kind of thing?"

"Collect alien samples?"

I smile and shake my head.

"So, the army look isn't just for show?"

I shake my head again. "Navy."

"What'd you do?"

"SEAL."

"I don't know what that means," she says with a frown.

"It means I did stuff that no one else wanted to do."

Gerb speaks up, his voice all defensive. "He got us the samples, didn't he?"

She shrugs and asks, "What if you lead them back here, too?"

"I'll take precautions," I explain. "The last time, they hunted me with it. If they've left something behind, they likely don't know it's there, but I'll keep an eye out to see if I'm followed, just in case."

She nods slowly. I see she's not convinced, but that's okay. I have to be careful, and I will. Leaning forward, I look her in the eye and ask, "So, what do you do?"

A frown fills her face, and she asks, "What do you mean?"

"These two guys are third-year biology and chemistry students. Fred here fixes stuff and throws out wisdom at unexpected intervals. And I go get chunks of alien body parts. What do you do?"

"I… I'm a PhD Candidate. Molecular Genetics. I worked out of this lab under Dr. Terrance. She oversaw all five labs, but mainly worked out of the one you guys were at. This was one she rarely came to."

I glance at Gerb and Logan. "Well, this is perfect. I can't help but think the three of you can figure this out."

"You'll go see if they left anything behind?" Logan asks.

"Of course. But first, I want a nap."

10

NO GOOD CHOICE

I set out early the next morning.

A calm breeze is already blowing, and the air has the feel of a storm coming on. The clouds in the sky roll along smoothly, and I can't help but think of Connie. This was exactly the kind of weather she loved. Warm, cool breeze, storm blowing in. The only thing that could make it better in her view was lightning.

But for right now, I'd rather the storm hold off for a few hours. Or better yet, longer.

I move cautiously today, unlike yesterday on my way to the new lab. Yesterday, all I could think of was reaching my friends, hoping to find some comfort with them. I didn't bring up with Fred or the boys what happened to me. My kids' pleading voices, Aaron's arms around my neck… The boys wouldn't understand, Fred doesn't need any extra grief, and Elizabeth… I really can't read her. She's stern, focused, and suspicious. But then again, she's been alone in that lab for months. She's perhaps more sane than most people would be after all that time.

Although… I'm no longer convinced that I'm a good judge of proper levels of sanity.

Every ten minutes, I climb a pile of rubble to scout out the area ahead. I'm not going straight toward the old lab, as much as I'd like to salvage what I can find quickly so I can get back. I'd rather anyone who tracks me think I'm moving aimlessly.

When I get to the area I want to find first, I take a few minutes to locate the hole where I left my pack. Once I retrieve it, I check through everything, just in case it's been tampered with. I can't find anything that looks out of place, so I throw it on my back and climb out.

Now, for the old lab. It's good to know they aren't tracking everything that's come in contact with the alien samples. My pack touched nothing of the sample itself, but it touched the sample case. So, whatever is traceable by the Greks is not transferred from object to object.

By the time I reach the area where Gerb, Logan, and Fred described as being near the shipping doors for the lab, I've had to skirt around three *humans*, all of whom I recognize, and one fast-moving Grek. I gather it was on a mission of sorts, and I'm happy not to get in its way.

The shipping entrance looks like everything else here—just a pile of rubble—but when I look a little closer, I find some decent sized holes and slip inside. Once I get in there, I find the doors, which were forced open from the inside, and slip through.

My flashlight comes out, and in my other hand, I hold my dart gun. I have four tranqs with me. Hopefully, that's enough.

Moving along the corridor, I pass unpacked pallets filled with boxes. None of it looks helpful to us, so I move on. Truthfully, I wouldn't know if I passed something they need for their studies and research, but I have no intention of learning that anytime soon.

When I enter the main lab, I see why I didn't notice the shipping area. The inside door leading to it looks like a door to a closet.

Inside, the lights are mostly out. Some flash on and off again, and I hear some doors lock, then unlock. Something's messed with the system controlling everything here. The heat is up as well, which is strange, because the air feels cool.

I've entered on the top floor, and I need to get down to the third floor. So far, everything's clear, although any rooms I pass have been trashed. Little remains that's not smashed and broken. The Greks can't get in here, but the *humans* have done a good enough job of it.

I reach the stairwell and move down two levels. I keep hearing noises. I wish I had someone to watch my back.

When I reach the right level, I quickly turn off my light. I'm sure I saw a flash through the window in the door. The lights flicker on and off, so that could be it, but this looked more direct—like someone else is here.

I reach the door and peer through the window. I can't make out much in the hallway. At least there's no sign of anyone.

But then I hear it. A crash. Nothing huge, more like something falling. Like if someone were to move a large metal object or throw it onto the floor.

Someone's here, and the chance of whoever it is being a friend is pretty slim. The good news is, I don't think the sound was in the direction I'm going.

The door opens easily, some of the few in this place that don't need a keycard to access them, but the lab where the boys left the samples will certainly need one. Which means I might have a problem.

Stepping into the hallway, I carefully make my way in the opposite direction of the noise I heard earlier. I hear a few grunts from back that way, and some more crashing. Whatever is going on, I think they're still destroying something down there. The Greks or the ones they control leave nothing intact.

When I get to the lab, I breathe a sigh of relief at the sight of the doors sitting wide open. Enough lights flicker in this area and in the lab, so I don't need to worry about my flashlight. I set to work immediately, searching the room. The boys told me they left the samples in three different areas of this lab. It's a large room, maybe twenty feet one way and nearly fifty the other way, so there's plenty of room to hide things. Down the center of the room, running from left to right, the workspaces run the length of the room. There are two rows of them, so to get to the back of the room, I have to move to the far right before I can move to the back wall.

I head for the tentacle first. It's in the far right corner. I have to be more careful in this area. So much has been smashed and destroyed in this room that it's hard to move about without making a lot of noise.

When I get to the corner where the tentacle was, I quickly locate what I'm looking for. The canister is here, but its contents are incinerated.

Now, that's interesting. The other samples turn to ash quickly and on their own, but this one, it had to be incinerated from something outside. The burn marks are both on the outside and the inside of the canister.

I turn to find the second jar when I freeze. No more noise. I could hear it a moment ago, even in this room. But now, nothing.

I make my way carefully back to the door and slowly slide it shut. With everything destroyed, it's easy to find a few broken pieces of steel shelving supports lying around, and I quietly slide them through the loops of the door handles to secure the door shut.

That'll at least keep whoever it is out while I search for the other canisters. I turn around and head to the far left corner. That's where they left the inner "goo," as Gerb calls it. When I reach that corner, I find the cabinet where they'd left the canister. It's still closed, but scorch marks cover the outside. A moment later, I have the cabinet open, and I see this canister is just as burned as the last one. Nothing left inside other than ash.

The third one… hopefully it's intact. That's the hard shell of the Grek's claw. Gerb suspected the Greks were tracking one thing, not all of it. Separating it had been an attempt to determine what they could track.

I head to the left-hand corner of the lab on the same wall as the door, and search for the canister. Nothing looks burned in this area. Hopefully that's a good sign.

The noise from down the hallway hasn't resumed. Maybe whoever was doing it just finished. Maybe they left.

I quietly slide boards and chunks of construction material out of the way, along with shelves and broken glass. I'm doing my best to be quiet, but I cringe every time my boots crunch on a piece of glass or plaster.

In the flickering light, I catch sight of a canister. My heart jumps as I see it's not burned and not broken. It's intact and might be just what we need!

As I reach out for it, I hear a crash behind me. Spinning around, I catch sight of the door as it heaves inward, creaking under the weight of someone trying to push it open. A moment later, a flashlight beam shines through the window, searching for anything… anyone.

The canister is in my hand, and I'm shoving it into my pack in seconds. No way out of this lab, other than the way I came in. That seems like a bit of a safety hazard… but then again, I didn't know there was a back door to this lab until after it got overrun.

I keep low as I skirt the back of the lab, looking for anything that I might have overlooked. Some of the taller cabinets could always be a door, so I pull them open, but I just find shelves full of instruments and supplies.

The banging on the door has grown far more intense. Whoever's out there is either in a panic, or worse, there's a lot of them.

A moment later, I have a tranq in my dart gun. I just don't know how many are out there. They might think this is just something wrong with the door right now, but the moment they realize I'm in here, there could be a dozen *humans* coming after me.

I don't want to kill any of them, but maybe I can fight my way through. They might not know how I got in. Just have to get to the exit.

The pounding on the door has turned from incessant banging to a steady, single crash every few seconds. Someone's running their shoulder into the door. In between, the light flashes briefly through the windows. So, at least two out there.

A large steel sheet, a broken section of a shelf, sits off to the side, and I carefully move it to the doorway, far enough in that the doors won't hit it. On the floor, it sits low enough that it'll function just the way I want. Counting… counting… the person crashing into the door hits every four seconds, maybe a little longer between crashes, but not much.

I slide up next to the door, careful to stay out of sight of the beam that shines through every ten or twelve seconds. It's mostly just the guy slamming into the door right now.

My pack stays on for this. It'll slow me down a bit, but I can't afford to leave the pack behind. Once I get a clear path to run, I have to take it. When I'm ready, I put my hand on the steel shelving supports, the ones I slid into the loops of the door handles. I wait for a slam, count to four, and then as soon as the next slam finishes, I slide the support back enough, then yank open the door on the count of three and a half.

A large man comes barreling through the open doorway, trips on the shelf I've laid on the floor, and crashes into the cabinet doors under the first row of workstations set out in the room. His huge frame collapses to the ground and doesn't move.

One down.

Another man runs into the room, flashlight on. I briefly hope to slip around the open door and into the hallway, but he turns in my direction first, the beam of the flashlight blinding me for a second. Before I can react, he kicks the dart gun out of my hand.

The *human* lowers the light, and I see his eyes. Yellow… attack.

He lunges at me and wraps his arms around my neck. I know he doesn't want to hurt me. He just wants to hold me, slow me down. That means others are on their way. They might even be just down the hall.

I drop low and twist my body, shifting his grip on me and forcing my head out from his grasp. Once out, I slam my fist into his stomach. He grunts, but other than that, it doesn't slow him at all. That's when I get my first good look at his face.

Geoff!

I briefly wonder who the big guy is, was… no… is, but I push that out of my mind. Geoff lunges for me again, and I throw him back against the wall behind me. Spinning around, I take off for the exit, but the open door slams shut as Geoff runs his shoulder into it, and I crash into the steel door. Before I can recover, Geoff has me by my legs.

We twist and fight as the seconds tick by. Any moment, another one, two, ten, a hundred *humans* could pour into the room. I have to get away. I'm a soldier! This guy is built like he doesn't know the meaning of exercise, but I can't shake him! Pain doesn't slow him. Injury goes without notice. Something in the control keeps them focused on their objective, no matter the cost.

I slam my fist into his side yet again, and he pushes back on me. Something under my feet shifts, and I go down, Geoff on top.

I can't get away. Only two options: fight him until I get an opening and can make a break for it… or kill him.

I grab his arm and twist it to a point where any normal *human* would cry out, but Geoff just knees me in the side, and I lose my grip. I can't even get him in a chokehold. Every time I try, he worms his way out!

My mind spins through my two options, back and forth, as I wrestle against my stubborn opponent. I can't kill him. It's not his fault. He's controlled by the Greks. I can't take his life… but then again, if I don't get the sample to the boys and Elizabeth… their lives might be forfeit. Is it Geoff or them? Are their lives worth more? Or his?

I know I'm just rationalizing murder, but in the brief seconds between grunts and hits and more, I hear more footsteps. Someone else is coming.

I whip out my knife in my desperation, and a moment later, Geoff drops to the floor.

He stops moving just as someone else steps into the entranceway.

Her eyes… glowing yellow at first, change to white.

Caution.

My little girl's face fills with fear as she looks back and forth from my knife to Geoff's lifeless body. All I feel is guilt… remorse… shame.

"Daddy, what did you do?"

Can't remember at first even how to breathe and can't hear anything other than my heart pounding in my ears. Her accusing voice, even controlled by the Greks as it is, haunts me.

But… I can't stay.

Focus, Soldier! I quickly wipe off the knife on Geoff's shirt, put it away, and grab a short piece of rope, one I've secured to the side of my pack.

I've prepared for this.

I lunge for Alliah, grabbing her with my left arm and pulling her back into the room. She struggles and twists, but she's far weaker than Geoff. A moment later, I have one loop of the rope around her ankle, and another around a support post near a workstation.

While she twists and tries to free herself, I tie her tight and roll away from her.

"I'm sorry, Alliah," I whisper as I turn and race out of the room, grabbing the dart gun on the way. The rope won't hold her long. Even if it does, I expect the *humans* will release her. And the big guy, the one unconscious on the floor, he's stirring. He'll be up in a moment.

I hear footsteps behind me. A glance back shows four humans coming my way, while others file into the room I just left. They'll want Alliah after me. If they want me, they know what it'll take.

I make a few turns and enter the stairway. I'm hoping they're far enough behind not to see I went for the stairs, but a moment later, I hear the door below swing open and footsteps echo up the stairwell. When I reach the main floor, I get back into the hallway and come face to face with one of my old neighbors, Ms. Gillingham.

I feel sick to my stomach for doing it, but I plow into her and send her tumbling back. At the corner, I look back and see she's already on her feet and moving after me. I race around another corner and see the doorway to the exit is still open a hair. I slide through, trying to leave it exactly as it was a moment ago, then I race down the hallway past the pallets.

When I get to the end, I come to a halt. Through the small opening, I see at least three Greks patrolling the area. I don't think they know I'm here, but I won't get away if I just run out there. Those tentacles are quick. I might get past one, but not three. No… wait… that's four Greks.

I slip back into the shipping area. So far, none of the *humans* have come down the corridor. They must not have noticed my exit yet. The pallets are close together. I could hide behind one, but it's not a decent hiding spot.

Slipping into an office on the side of the loading ramp, I jump onto the desk and push back a ceiling tile. Not much room, but perhaps enough for me. I have to take off my pack for this one, and it goes up ahead of me, propped up in a spot where it shouldn't shift. I pull myself up and squeeze in next to it, then slide the tile back in place.

Just in time.

Footsteps echo through the area as *humans* run through. Can't see anything, but I'd guess there's a dozen or more. All I have to do now is hold out until they leave.

11

CHASE

The minutes tick by, then the hours. My left ankle hurts where it's wedged up against a beam, and my right side feels like it's on fire, but I've pushed through worse pain than this. Now and then, someone comes into the office below me, and I slow my breathing to keep from making any noise, but so far, no one's thought to look above the ceiling tiles.

The last half hour or more has been quiet. Very quiet. I haven't heard so much as a footstep. That could be good or bad. It might mean they've left, or someone could be sitting right below me, watching, waiting for me to move my hiding spot.

I do my best to wiggle my ankle, making no noise, hoping I can loosen it up just a little. One tile, not the one I came up through, but the one right by my head, sits loose, and I pry it up as carefully as I can.

The lights in the room below are off, but there's enough light coming through the windows to show me that at least the office is empty. Now it's just the shipping area that I have to worry about.

I pry up the tile some more, but at this angle, I can't see my way out. If I'd thought ahead, I would have positioned my feet at this end so that I'd have a better angle from which to see.

I briefly consider trying to turn myself around, but where I'm lying is the only solid spot up here. Wires support the ceiling in this area. If I want to see anything below, I have to drop down onto the desk.

Since the room is empty, I might get down there without being seen, even if there are a dozen *humans* out on the receiving dock. The tile in the center where I came up slides out easily, and I push it off to the side. My legs are first, and I bring them over, doing my best to ignore the stiffness. Once my legs are hanging down, I give it a moment or so for the blood to rush back into that area, and then I lower myself down onto the desk, careful not to disturb anything.

Crouching down, I peer through the window. The lights in this area, just like throughout the rest of the lab, flicker on and off, giving me enough of a view of the receiving dock to see it looks clear—at least from this angle.

My pack comes down next, and I slip it on, securing it tightly to my waist. Down on the main floor, I see a bit more of the room through the window, and when I reach the door, I scan the area and listen carefully. No sound… not at first… but then I hear it. Quiet steps. Careful steps.

Someone's here.

I slip out of the office and move in behind a pallet stacked with crates. I suspect the Greks themselves have moved on. But they've left a *human* behind.

If they know it's me—and they likely do—the person patrolling will be Alliah or Aaron. I force the thought of Geoff out of my mind because the more I think of him, I'm left torn between guilt for what I've done and rage toward the Greks for what they've done to all of us.

Neither emotion gives me a clear head.

The footsteps begin to slowly retreat toward the lab, and I wait, hoping whoever it is will just go back inside. Instead, I hear the footsteps come to a stop and turn back this way.

A sentry. On patrol.

Forced to wait again, I sit tight until the sentry has moved past my position again, but just as the person goes by, I hear a sniff… like the sentry is crying. They should be past me now, so I peer around the edge. I can only see her from the back, but it's a woman, brown hair, about the height and build of Connie.

My heart races. I haven't seen her since I lost the kids, but she's still wearing the same outfit. Her leg must have healed. She walks fine, but… she's crying. I haven't seen anyone taken by the Greks cry before.

I'm hidden well enough that I risk watching until she turns around. Her eyes glow green—searching. Yellow is attack, and that's when they move fast. White is caution. But green seems to be just regular searching. As she walks, she wipes her eyes, and I see her shoulders shake.

She's weeping.

My heart goes out to her, but I pull back and remain hidden. Closing my eyes, I force myself to think rationally. They're getting more aggressive, playing more to my emotions. No longer content to just try to capture me, they're now getting my kids to call out to me, to play to my emotions. And today, they're using my wife. The first time I've seen her in months, and she's weeping. Everything in me wants to go to her and comfort her. But I know it's a trap.

I wait while she comes up again and passes me, heading back toward the receiving doors. The floor in this area is clear, and my boots make little noise on the concrete. The problem will be the exit. I don't know how I'll manage that without shifting a lot of the rubble under my feet.

When I get to the hole through which I can reach the outside, I hear her, and my heart grows cold. "Xavier? Is that you? Xavier?"

I don't look back. If I do… No! I can never look back. But even so, I can't bring myself to slip away.

"They told me you killed a man. Murdered someone! But… I don't believe it. You wouldn't do that, would you?"

Squeezing my eyes shut for a second, I force myself to push down my emotions before I scramble out the hole and run out into the open.

Thud... thud... thud... thud...

GRRREHHHHK!

Thud... thud... thud... thud...

The Greks are on the way. By the sounds of it, I have about half a minute before they come into view. I race off toward the east. Connie might see me go, but she can't know what direction I'm ultimately heading.

I pass between two ruined piles, all that's left of whatever stood in this area of the city, and circle around to the south, then zigzag in that direction.

GRRREHHHHK!

Thud... thud... thud... thud...

They're moving fast. I'd say there's at least two on me, if not three.

I zigzag more to the east again, then turn north. By this point, if they can follow me, they might think I'm just running wildly all over the place. I feel about a thousand different emotions all at once, from grief to guilt to exhilaration to determination. But I won't let them get me! I blew it. I killed a man, but they won't get me. I'll take them down before they *ever* get me!

Thud... thud... thud... thud...

GRRREHHHHK!

Thud... thud... thud... thud...

My feet take me east again, and I focus all the emotion into running, pushing myself harder and harder. Somehow, the Greks still follow me. I can't seem to lose them. I haven't seen them yet, but they're always back there!

Thud... thud... thud... thud...

GRRREHHHHK!

Thud... thud... thud... thud...

Something catches my eye, up on an enormous pile of rubble, off to my left. Just for a second. Not even sure I actually saw anything, but… as I run, I look again, and I see it. A face. Yellow, glowing eyes. To my right, I catch sight of another face. Ahead, a destroyed building with only one wall standing rises before me. Perched in the window of the second floor, balancing precariously up there sits Aaron.

They're not searching for me. They have eyes on me! All the time.

I pick up speed, thinking maybe I can get out of this area and lose them if I can get past all the *humans* watching. But… it could go on for miles! They'll know where I am no matter where I go!

I grind to a halt. Time to see how my XM7 holds up against a Grek. The first one comes over a pile of rubble just to the right of where I thought it would be, and I put two rounds through it almost immediately, right through what I think is the mouth.

The Grek stumbles but then recovers itself and comes at me again. I put another two rounds in it, careful not to waste ammo, and it crashes to the ground. The creatures are somewhat fragile in terms of our weapons… but their strength is in numbers. I saw them swarm a few months back. Glad there's only a few right now.

A moment later, the next Grek comes over, and I put another two rounds in while the first one disintegrates. Another couple shots finish the second one off, and I throw my weapon back over my shoulder and take off again. At first, I hear nothing, but then I catch it. From off to my left and a little ahead of me, I hear it again.

Thud… thud… thud… thud…

One more, at least, if not two.

I run as hard as I can, still heading east. Eventually, I have to get past all the *humans*. Certainly, they can't be everywhere now. Heading one direction seems to be the wisest move.

The next Grek comes within sight. I skid to a halt before punching three holes through it, then throw my weapon back over my shoulder to free my arms and run. The wind blows the ash directly at me, and I just hold my breath for the few seconds while I get through.

Thud… thud… thud… thud…

I can't keep this up forever. Despite being on the run for so long, I'm not in as good of shape as I was when I'd constantly trained for missions. I'll run out of steam in a few more minutes.

The next Grek comes at me from down a street, but this one has a shield of *humans* in front of it. It's tall enough, though, that I can shoot over their heads. Four rounds, and that one's gone.

They're changing up tactics on the fly. All it will take will be a Grek that can truly hide behind a group of *humans*.

It should know by now that I won't kill *humans* and…

Wait… that's the difference. The Greks aren't sending *humans* after me because they suspect I'll kill them. Or at least most of them. Aaron can't catch me. I tied Alliah up, and besides, she's far behind. Connie's way back there and was never really a runner. Those are the ones they likely know for sure I won't harm.

The rest of the *humans*, however… the Greks might think I'll kill them.

If they think I'll kill either *humans* or Greks, they may no longer be trying to catch me. I might no longer be a target. Now I'm a threat!

But if so, what will they do differently?

I look for more *humans*, and I feel relief flood through me when I don't see any. Maybe I'm past them all.

Bricks and mortar and beams explode out of a pile beside me as a Grek comes barreling out of the debris right on top of me. I drop to the ground, letting the pack take the brunt of the fall. The canister is strong, hopefully it'll survive. As I slide under the body of the creature, I pull out my 9mm and put a few bullets in the underside of the creature. It's not enough to kill it, but it reacts and pulls away. By the time I stop sliding, it's recovered enough to attack, but I get my XM7 out before it can reach me.

I take off running before the Grek turns to ash and veer to the north. I still don't see any *humans*, which means I might escape.

Thud… thud… thud… thud…

I hear the Grek… off to the south. Then another, just ahead of me to the northeast.

Thud… thud… thud… thud…

I scramble behind the remains of a wall. The Grek passes right by me, heading in the direction I would have gone if I'd not switched directions.

I scramble out and head directly northwest, hiding every few minutes when I see or hear a Grek, all heading towards where I used to be. They really want to get me, that's for sure.

I push on, hiding, traveling, hiding… until I get within a few minutes of the new lab. Come to think of it, they still haven't given me the code to get in the door. I gather Elizabeth doesn't trust me.

I settle in a small little hole for a bite to eat. There's no way I'm heading straight to the others. The Greks have changed up their strategy enough in the last while, they might even now be following me, hoping I'll lead them to everyone else.

Once I've taken a few minutes to refresh myself, I stare out the opening of my hiding spot for about five minutes, examining everything I see for any signs of a *human* or anything out of the ordinary. When I'm finally content, I climb out and still take a few minutes to circle around until I'm certain they haven't followed me.

The trip back to the lab takes me another five minutes from that spot, and when I arrive, it's only a few minutes of banging on the door before Logan lets me in.

Anxiety fills his face, but when I pull out the canister, his shoulders relax, and a huge grin takes over. Without another word, he runs off into the elevator, leaving me to close the door and take the stairs.

I gladly lock up as I feel the weight of today's chase slide away, and the weight of what I've done and faced take root.

I stir the hash browns on my plate. Out of the corner of my eye, I catch sight of Gerb hungrily eyeing my food. I think if he took my plate from me, I'd either just walk away or attack the guy. Not sure which, I just know I'm a wreck.

"You see them?" Logan asks. "You see your family again?"

I nod. "Yup. Even my wife this time. Haven't seen her since they took her."

"Why'd they bring her out now, do you think?"

"They changed up a lot of stuff." I take a deep breath and let it out slowly. "This time and last time."

"Like what?" Logan asks, obviously not picking up on my mood in any way.

I take a mouthful of my breakfast, chew it up, swallow, then shovel in another mouthful. When I finish chewing this time, I stand up. "Don't want to talk about it."

As I leave the room, no one speaks. Probably for the best. I think I realize now if Gerb had taken my food, I would have… well… it wouldn't have been good for him.

I move down a floor and enter the small gym. This place, like the last lab, was built as a self-contained living base of operations. Weapons, living quarters, food stocks, powered by geo-thermal energy… even a gym. Not huge, but the equipment's good. And there's a punching bag. I never used to take out my anger on something like this, but then again, I was never stuck living in a world where the only people I could talk to were three young academics and a retired mechanic. Fred's okay, but the boys and the PhD… they get under my skin at times.

"What is it, Xavier?" I spin around and see Fred sitting on a weight bench. He's got his plate on his lap and a fork in his hand. "You don't mind if I eat in here, do you? You might be fine with only a bite or two of your hash browns, but I'm a growing boy."

Despite everything, I smile. "If you continue to eat like Gerb, you'll definitely be a growing boy."

Looking around slowly at all the equipment, Fred says, "This place, in some ways, is a lot better than the last one. It's slightly larger, fewer problems on the mechanical and structural side of things, at least as far as I can tell, and it's better stocked than our last home."

I nod. Not much else I can do. Not sure why he's here.

"But then again, as long as we have a roof over our heads and food in our belly, I'm not sure it matters that much. Not when those we love are out there." He takes a bite, slowly chewing as he looks around the room again. When he finishes, he points his fork at me and asks, "What happened?"

"Don't want to talk about it."

A small smile creeps up on his lips as he takes a moment to poke at his food. "I think you do, Xavier. Or, at least, I think you know you should."

"What do you think you can do about it?" I ask with a growl.

"Probably not much. I mean, I can't change whatever happened, but I might be able to help you make sense of it. That's really what's going on, isn't it? You can't make sense of somethin'."

Dropping to the floor, I lean back against the wall and slowly pull off my gloves. "I did see Connie. And Alliah. Aaron too."

"What made that so rough? I mean… more so than other times you've seen your kids."

"Connie… and Alliah, they both spoke to me."

Fred's eyebrows shoot up. "They spoke… now… none of my family spoke to me. That's… that's quite a change!"

I nod slowly, staring at the floor.

"But… that's not what's got you all worked up." Fred takes a deep breath and sets his plate aside. "You gotta forgive the Greks, Xavier."

I look at Fred like he's crazy, and all I can do is laugh. "What?"

"You gotta forgive them."

"What are you talking about?"

"I see the hatred in you. That kind of thing is not right to hold on to. It's like a poison inside."

I toss my gloves to the floor and shake my head. "They don't deserve it. Besides, you telling me you forgave them for everything? You're okay that they took your family?"

He smiles. "Those are two different things, Xavier. Forgiving is one thing. Thinking the bad stuff is okay is totally different. I can forgive them for what they've done without ever saying what they did was good. What they've done is wicked! It's pure evil. That's all there is to it! There's no justification that I can see for any of it. None! But that doesn't mean I can't forgive."

He shakes his head slowly and pokes at his food. "No, Xavier, it means I'm no longer bound to a life driven by revenge. And it means I have the capacity now to show compassion to them."

"You'd stand by while they took more of us?"

Fred laughs. "I wouldn't. But, once again, forgiving those things doesn't mean you agree with the bad stuff. Forgiveness means you give up the anger. You pay *that* price." When I frown at him, he says, "You pay a price either way. Either you pay the price of the anger and the hate eating away at your soul, or you pay the price of accepting the hurt and loving them back."

"That seems dumb."

"Depends on whether or not you can see what's eatin' your soul. And dependin' on if you see that as a problem."

"I hate what they've done."

"That's good. I'd hate to see the day when someone like you is okay with it. There are really only two options. Holdin' a grudge or givin' it up. You know if you killed every last one of them and got your family back, it still wouldn't make up for it. You know that, Xavier. The grudge option just allows you to wallow in anger. Givin' it up…"

"You're saying if I give it up, then I prove to them that they have no hold on me!"

"You're still trying to get them back, Xavier," Fred says with a laugh. "No, to forgive means you no longer need to get them back. And it means you can be driven by doing what's right. Not by revenge."

I sit there, seething in my anger. I love my anger. And I hate it. It eats at me, but it also satisfies me.

"About ten years back," Fred says as he sets his plate down on the bench beside him, "a guy I worked with, nice guy, good sense of humor, everybody liked him… he came into work one day actin' a little funny. I don't mean really weird or anything, just… different. I thought maybe he was frustrated with the job he was workin' on. Some rich guy had brought in an old Datsun and wanted the engine rebuilt but didn't want to pay all that much… anyway, shouldn't have taken the job… but that's beside the point. I thought he was just frustrated. He started snappin' at everyone, even the boss. About halfway through the day, the cops came in and arrested him. Turned out he'd… well… doesn't really matter what he did, now does it. Not anymore."

"Why you telling me this, Fred?"

"Because, Xavier…" and with this, Fred leans forward, his eyes boring into mine. "…that look he had in his eyes? When he came into the shop that morning? You got the same look. The look that man carried with him all morning long." He paused for a moment and asked, "What'd you do, Xavier?"

"Back off, Fred!"

He nods slowly, his eyes dropping to the floor. "Hey, I know when I'm steppin' somewhere I shouldn't, but Xavier?"

"What?"

"You gotta deal with this. I mean..." He stops and frowns at me. "It's not just you here. There's five of us. This is all we've got. We can't afford to have one of our number goin' down like you're goin' down right now. We need to stand together. If you have somethin' ripping you apart inside, it affects us all."

"I'll keep it under control."

"Yeah, perhaps," Fred says, "but we still need you. Not as a soldier. We need a friend. Part of our team. You can't be a team all alone. And we can't be a team with a fifth of our number standin' on the outside. Whatever you did, you gotta find peace with it."

With that, he grabs his plate, stands up, and walks out.

When the door closes behind him, I whisper, "That's easy to say, Fred," but all I can hear over and over in my head is my little girl's voice. *What did you do, daddy?*

SAMPLES

"Any progress?"

Gerb's giddy. I mean, he's almost bouncing off the walls. Elizabeth looks irritated, but pleased, and Logan looks awkwardly out of place. Something good has happened, that's for sure. I haven't left the lab for a week and a half. I know these things take time, but I'm hoping for a quick breakthrough.

Gerb opens his mouth to answer, but then stops, looking at Elizabeth. It appears a hierarchy has developed. The PhD at the top, and Gerb and Logan at the bottom. Probably best. Elizabeth knows her stuff, and hopefully she can focus the other two on what's important.

She sets down a clipboard she'd been writing on and takes a deep breath. "We were trying to develop some kind of gas or liquid that would kill the Greks. We tried all sorts of things, but nothing really seemed to work—at least using what we have here. But then Gerb had an idea. Rather than kill them, what if we kept them away?"

I nod. That's not an answer, but sometimes I think these three need the buildup, or they won't be happy.

"You have something to keep them away?"

"Yeah, we do," she says, and I see one of the first smiles I've seen on her face. "We found a compound that softens the exoskeleton on their legs. In fact, it almost turns it to liquid."

I frown. "So, if we can dump this on a Grek, its leg shells will wash away, and it'll be standing there with naked legs? We're going to embarrass them to death?" Somehow, I'd hoped for more.

Elizabeth's smile fades quickly. "No, well, I guess that's possible with a little more work. Maybe we could figure out how to do that… I mean… if you want to…"

I shake my head. "No, I don't want that!" I take a deep breath and ask, "What have you got? What did you develop?"

Her smile comes back, and she puts both hands down on the workspace in front of her. "We can put it into a spray. Here's the thing. It only works for a few seconds." In response to my frown, she adds, "But that's plenty of time. You see, the exoskeleton turns soft and starts to run together, liquifies, then the spray loses its effectiveness, and the exoskeleton hardens."

"I'm missing something."

"What it does," she says, "is it softens the exoskeleton enough that it actually flows together at the joints and then hardens again. You spray this on a Grek, and in a few seconds, it won't be able to move its legs!"

"And people? The *humans*?"

"It shouldn't hurt us or them. The boys call it Grek Spray."

"It definitely doesn't hurt humans!" Gerb says with an enormous grin.

Elizabeth scowls. "Gerb, you didn't!"

He smiles back at her, and I see Logan snickering in the corner with his head down. "I did!" Gerb says, the elation filling his face and leaving him nearly shaking with glee as he speaks. "I sprayed all over me! Didn't hurt me at all!"

"You…" Elizabeth looks horrified. "But it… you… it could have killed you! We don't know anything about it! It might affect you in ways you don't expect over the coming months or years!"

"Nah, it loses its effectiveness after about three point four seconds. It didn't hurt me at all in that time." As if to add to the absurdity of it all, he looks at me and says, "I still haven't showered it off, and that was two days ago!"

"Two days ago!" Elizabeth hollers. "We didn't even know what it did back then! It could have killed you!"

"I know!" Gerb says and high fives Logan. "And I'm still here! I even tasted some of it."

"You what?"

"Yeah! I mean… it didn't taste good. In fact, it kind of tastes like shoelaces, but it didn't make me sick."

Her hands are balled tightly into fists, and her shoulders are scrunched up against her neck. "How do you know what shoelaces…?" She closes her eyes, and her lips move wordlessly for a second. When she speaks again, it's in a whisper. "Never mind. From now on, don't test anything on yourself without checking with me first." She pauses and then quickly adds, "Or anyone else! No one! You don't test anything on anyone, even yourself, at any time, for any reason, without getting permission from me first. Got it?"

"Supper last night tasted a little funny," I say, but Gerb shakes his head at me quickly, glancing over at Elizabeth as if she can't figure it out.

Elizabeth puts her face in her hands, and I think she's on the verge of either tears or throwing both boys out to face the Greks. She's definitely the most normal of the three.

"So, when will it be ready?"

"It's ready now!" Gerb hollers.

"No, it's not," Logan says. "We have to figure out a way to put it in a spray. There's a lot to work with in all the storerooms in the lab, but we just haven't tracked down what we need yet. We can put it in a small aerosol, but then you kind of have to be standing right next to a Grek to spray it."

"That's not ideal," I say.

Logan shakes his head quickly, still not making eye contact with Elizabeth.

"How long?"

Elizabeth shrugs. "We're going through the inventory. The problem with the computer system is the inventory's organized in a way that someone who doesn't know the technical names can't find anything. We know, for instance, that we have eighteen units of P977-46."

"What's that?"

She shrugs again. "That's our problem. Everything's labeled like that, and we can't find the list that explains what it is. So, we're just exploring rooms, one by one."

"Fred and I will take the third floor down," I say. That's where the armory is, and I still don't want the boys knowing about it. I've kept them away from that floor as much as I'm able, and Fred's rigged a padlock for the door to add to the security.

"Thanks," she says. "We were going to hit that floor next."

"Oh," I say with a smile, "what am I looking for?"

"Anything that looks like it can dispense the Grek spray. We'll take anything… anything at this point."

"So, they really called you old?" Fred asks with a laugh.

"Yep. On my way out, I overheard Logan say, 'If the old guys take the third floor, we might finish exploring all the storage rooms by the end of tomorrow.' I don't know how I feel about being one of the old guys."

"Age catches up to all the lucky ones," Fred says, again with a laugh.

We've been through about half of the third floor. This floor's actually easy. Few rooms on this level are storage. The armory is here, the gym is here, the offices are here… nothing to draw the boys to this area, unless they learn about the armory, of course.

"You're sure none of that in the armory can be converted to use in this way?"

I shake my head. "The dart guns are probably the best option, but they send a single dart. We need something that can spread the chemical."

"None of the explosives will work?"

"Not without risking blowing my head off, and besides, once it explodes, it'll incinerate the chemical. Oh, and we can't just release it into the atmosphere because it's only effective for a few seconds. After that, I guess it goes inert. It has to be delivered directly."

"Like… with maybe a leaf blower?" Fred asks.

I laugh. "That might work. Got any of those floating around in your workshop?"

I stop when I notice Fred staring at me. "Well, there was one in the storeroom off the receivin' dock in the last lab. There might be one here. I gather they used it in the fall when leaves blew into the loadin' dock."

We both turn and make for the stairs. Once we reach the top level, we head to the shipping and receiving area. These doors, like the ones leading out to the receiving docks in the last lab, are not only solid, but are easy to miss. They almost look like part of the wall.

Fred swipes his keycard, and I hear the click of the door unlocking, so I give a shove. It opens just a little before grinding to a halt. I put my shoulder into it, and the door opens a bit more, then a bit more until I can finally squeeze myself through. A moment later, Fred easily slides in.

"Well, look at that!" Fred says with disappointment in his voice. "Not sure what to make of this."

The floor, what I can see of it as I squeeze through the opening, is covered in stone, concrete, wiring, plaster and rebar. One lightbulb, off to the far left, is still on, but it sits on an angle with exposed wire above it. Fortunately, there's nothing flammable in this room in case it shorts out. I can't even see any light from the opening at the far end.

"Where was the storage room in the other lab?"

"Back there, not too far from the light hanging down," Fred says, pointing to the left.

I crawl carefully in that direction, but before I even get there, I know it's a lost cause.

"You mess with that too much, it's likely to come down on you," Fred warns. "I don't think we can confirm if there's a leaf blower here, let alone get it out."

I shake my head and back away. He's right. I hate it, but he's right.

But what I hate more is the thought of going back to the old lab. They might still be guarding it. There could be hundreds of *humans* in that area and far more Greks than I can handle.

But… the leaf blower may be the answer to our problem.

I wave for Fred to follow me, and he does. We seal the door back up again and then head downstairs. Neither of us says the obvious, but we have another problem. If we don't finish searching the third level, the boys might decide to finish searching it. Then, they might kill themselves playing with the guns in the armory.

It's like raising toddlers! If we want to keep them alive, we have to Gerb-proof and Logan-proof our actions and choices.

When we finish the floor, it's nearly time for supper, and I give Fred a hand. He enjoys being the maintenance guy and the cook. He's not bad at either.

"Any luck?" Gerb calls out as he and Logan come into the room.

"Not really," I reply. "We finished level three, though. You guys?"

"No, we've finished this level. Level two and four are left. Two's going to be easy because it's mainly living quarters and meeting rooms. Level four's gonna take a while, though. It's mostly storage."

Elizabeth comes in next. She's frazzled. I'm not surprised. She's been working with the boys all day. Fred and I enjoy them, most of the time, but they get under her skin.

Half-way through our meal, I bring up the topic on my mind. It's ripping me apart. Not the risk, but going back there. Back to the place where Connie and Alliah… no, it's not just that. Back to the place where I killed Geoff…

"Listen, if we don't find anything on the fourth level, there's another option."

"It's not a good option," Fred says. "There's a lot of risk."

"What is it?" Gerb asks without bothering to swallow his food first.

"Xavier would have to go back to the old lab," Fred says. "Again."

They all look at me like I'm crazy. I haven't talked much about the last trip there, but I've shared enough that they know the Greks were aggressive. "Fred remembers seeing a leaf blower in the receiving area of the lab. I didn't go into the room, but I remember it when I was there last time. The doors looked fine, unbroken. I expect I can get in there and find the leaf blower, if it's not wrecked."

"What do we need the leaf blower for?" Logan asks.

Elizabeth flashes him a look of death and shakes her head. "Do you always miss the obvious, Logan? It's to clean up that mess you left in the boardroom on level two!"

I glance at Fred, and he's just picking at his food and laughing. I decide to just carry on. "The leaf blower might be exactly what we need to disperse the Grek Spray. And… just so everyone knows, I wouldn't risk my neck to get cleaning supplies. I just want to be clear on that."

I see the wheels turning as they all consider the possibility. "So," Elizabeth begins, "we'd need something to slowly drizzle it into the leaf blower, so it doesn't just pour out. If we can get something like that, it might work."

Gerb's face twists in a way that makes me think he just figured something out. His eyes fill with concern as he says, "But…"

"But… we're taking a risk," I say, interrupting him. "The Greks might still patrol that area heavily, and last time I was through there, they were very aggressive. Very personal and very aggressive. I'd venture a guess that they're still monitoring things there. Even if they're not, they seem to have a general idea of where I am when I'm out, so I expect they'll figure out I'm in the lab pretty quickly."

"Which means you have to get in and out within minutes," Logan says.

"Maybe seconds," Fred adds. "Hey, so, this was my idea at first, but the more I think of it, the worse an idea I think it is. That entire lab might be trashed by now. There might be nothing there you can bring back. It's quite a risk."

I nod. My plate's empty. I don't remember eating it all, and Gerb looks full. I must be distracted. "We don't need to decide until we finish searching level four, but if we do and we're left with no means to disperse the Grek Spray, then I think it forces us to take this route. Otherwise, we just sit here in this lab for the rest of our lives."

"Well, maybe it's not worth the risk," Elizabeth says slowly. "I mean, what's out there now? It's just a destroyed world, and all the Greks and the *humans* they've pulled in. What's the point? We could just be fine here."

"You really think staring at my ugly mug for the rest of your life is what you want?" Fred asks with a laugh.

Elizabeth's eyes drop to the table, but Gerb leans forward. "She won't have to do that, Fred. You're really old. Like, really, really old. Whatchu got left in you? Six months? A year at the outside? I doubt she'll have to put up with looking at you for much longer at all."

Fred laughs as he picks up his plate and mine. "The rest of you can clean up after yourselves."

"I think this might work," Fred says, handing me a small contraption. "The leaf blower is electric, which is probably good 'cause it means you won't have to start a gas motor that's been sitting for a while. You'll have to unplug it, though. I think it was charging when I was there. I'd recommend you bring the cord as well, just in case it's a different connector. Could probably rig something up in a pinch, but I'd rather focus on being old and decrepit. Apparently, that's my thing now… for the rest of my short, miserable, arthritically dominated life."

Gerb snickers as I shove Fred's contraption in my pack. We found nothing of use on Level Four, and I wanted to make sure I had a way to use the Grek Spray if I went out. Elizabeth and the boys came up with a jar that would slowly drain when turned upside down, and Fred made the contraption that he thought would hook onto the hose. I'll have to cut a hole for it to work properly, but it seems like I'm good to go. Just have to hold it upright. No turning it sideways.

"I'll walk you up to the exit," Fred says while the others head back to one of the labs. They're always working on something or playing some game. Turns out Elizabeth is quite a gamer, so those three spend their evenings racing or shooting each other.

When we reach the door leading out into the open, I turn to him. Somehow, I gotta get this off my chest. "You asked what I did, Fred. I killed a man. His name was Geoff. He knocked the dart gun out of my hand, and I thought I had to kill him before anyone else came. I couldn't get away from him."

Fred nods slowly. "I see."

"I didn't want to kill him. I… I just didn't have time. Others were on their way."

He nods again.

"It's eating me up inside. I keep thinking I could have found another way. There's nothing he could do. I mean, Geoff. He couldn't do anything to stop this. I knew him briefly before. He was a total jerk—arrogant, obnoxious, full of himself—but he didn't deserve this."

"Would you say what you did was evil?"

I grind my teeth for a moment, but then close my eyes. "Yes. I know it was. Geoff couldn't help what he was doing. I should have found another way. It wasn't an accident. I knew what I was doing…"

Fred holds his piercing gaze on me for what feels like an eternity. When he appears satisfied, he says, "You know… I don't know what motivates the Greks. Not at all. I don't think they're gaining anything from our planet. They just destroy and take."

I laugh. "And you want me to forgive them?"

"We're all given something. And often with what we're given, we do horrible things."

He stops and looks at me as if I should get it.

"I didn't conquer a planet and brainwash an entire population!" I say, nearly spitting the words out of my mouth.

"No, they did. They took what lay before them and did something evil with it. They have longer arms than you do, in a manner of speaking. A longer reach. They're able to do a lot more. They took what they could, an entire planet, and did evil with it. But you took what you could… and you know what you did was evil. The whole, 'It was him or me' doesn't hold up very well in reality. Their evil might have been worse, but now you know what it's like to do something really wicked."

"How's that help me?" I growl at him. "I want them all dead. Not the *humans*, the Greks! ALL OF THEM!"

"Sometimes, Xavier, when we see the stuff we've done, it helps us forgive others. And… when you see your old, decrepit friend standing in front of you, and he's forgiven you, as best he can, and he holds nothin' against you. When you see all that, it helps you see that you can forgive as well."

I open my mouth to argue, but he puts up his hands. "Xavier, what I'm sayin' is this: when you forgive, you aren't sayin' the thing they did was okay; you're sayin' that you choose love instead of anger. If someone does somethin' truly wicked, you can't say what they did is good without makin' yourself wicked as well. But you can love the person. What you do is accept the pain they caused you and love them. Nothin' more, nothin' less. I don't know what's drivin' these Greks, but they're clearly intelligent. I think you can actually forgive them and find some freedom in your heart. If you don't, it'll eat you from the inside."

I take a deep breath and nearly argue back. I don't know what to say to him, but I want to tell him it's all garbage. Before I can, he just points at the door. "But… you have something you need to do. Go do it, but on the way, try this… try to think of not only the *humans* but also the Greks as controlled. Maybe none of them want it. Who knows? I don't. But, one thing's for sure, your anger will eat you alive. Sure, you may be free of the Grek's control in a way, but you're just stuck in a very different prison."

Facing away from Fred, my hand grips the handle of the door, but I stop. Without turning around, I say, "I get it, Fred. I really do. I just…" I take a deep breath and turn back to him. "It's just hard. They took my family."

"I know, Xavier. I know."

A moment later, I'm through the door and alone in the wide-open world.

GREK SPRAY

The early morning sun shines brightly through a light haze, all that's left of the fog that drifted in sometime during the night. I love the feel of a morning like this. The quiet, the still air, the coolness on my face and neck. It almost makes me forget how much I've lost, and how badly I want them back.

I head south through the streets and alleyways. At first, I don't see any Greks or *humans*. They're certainly out at night and in the early morning hours, but never as active as they are in the full sunlight. After about an hour, I catch sight of a *human* and hide in a pile of rubble to wait while she approaches.

I haven't seen this woman for a while, but it was the one who tried to get Alliah to go with her. That familiar rage builds in my heart again as I watch her walk along, passing right by my hiding spot, eyes shining an eerie green glow as they do when they aren't pursuing anyone. I can't believe someone would try to get an eleven-year-old girl to go with her and abandon her family.

A smile creeps up on my lips, and the same thought hits me again. I could get away with this one. I got away with killing Geoff. I bet I could…

I gasp hard and scramble out of my hiding spot, out of sight of the woman, and down a small alley. Pulling myself behind a half-crushed trash bin, I slam my back up against a crumbling cinderblock wall as my heart races. All I can think of is how disgusted I am at what I just thought... what I just considered.

Not just thoughts. Not just ideas. I seriously considered...

Scrambling to my feet again, I run wildly down a street, stumbling past old cars and destroyed buildings until I find a small river going under a road and crawl into the dark, mud-caked culvert underneath. I sit back, the trickle of a stream washing over my boots and feel like throwing up.

Daddy, what did you do?

My breathing quickens, and I can't hear anything other than the pounding of my own heart. I want to block it out, but my entire body convulses.

Daddy, what did you do?

Sweat pours from my hair, my back, my arms, my legs. My breathing speeds up, and my hands shake as I cover my head, then curl up in a little ball.

Daddy, what did you do?

I try to escape... get my thoughts back... back under control... remember where I am... who I am... what I have to do... but I can't think of anything else...

Daddy, what did you do?

Daddy, what did you do?

DADDY, WHAT DID YOU DO!

I gag and then cough the water that's flowed into my mouth back into the small stream flowing by. I'm... laying in water. In a culvert.

Noise!

I scramble out. Not sure what happened. Have to get out of the culvert. Away from here. My cough in there... works like a megaphone, alerting everyone around to my presence. I stumble forward, trying to look in every direction at once and find myself in a field of tall grass. My arms, shoulders, legs, everything... so weak.

Can't keep going, so I do the only thing I can.

I collapse.

<hr>

Daddy, what did you do?

When I come to, I'm on my side and crickets chirp in my ear.

I roll onto my back and try to remember. The woman. I wanted to kill her. Actually considered it. Then I ran and hid in the culvert... I...

I'd seen panic attacks in others many times. Never had it happen to me. Not even close. Always been focused, thought I was too strong to panic, too strong for anxiety to knock me down.

Too strong.

I'm no longer strong.

I'm no longer the SEAL everyone looked up to. No longer the guy in charge. No longer... *strong.*

I feel weak.

And I *am* weak. Weaker than I've been my entire life.

But strangely, I'm glad. Relief floods my heart. I needed this. I've been arrogant. I've been angry. Filled with hate.

I will forgive that woman. Don't know her name, but I forgive. And Geoff. Him too. And the Greks. All of them. I forgive them all. I won't let them take me, nor will I let them have Fred, or Elizabeth, or Logan, or Gerb... well... maybe Gerb...

I smile.

That might be the first genuine smile I've had since the day I lost Connie, then Aaron, then Alliah. Since I lost them all.

I lay there for a long time, soaking wet, weeping and smiling as the sun sets. The others will be worried, but I can't be what I was anymore. It's not all duty and power and winning. For the first time in my life, I think I understand what I see in Fred's eyes.

Peace.

Daddy, what did you do?

I find my smile turns sad. In a whisper, I say, "I did something evil, Alliah. I wasn't the man I wanted to be. I wasn't the man I should have been for you, or your brother, or your mom. But, I will be. And I'll start by forgiving the Greks for taking you from me. I'll continue by protecting the others from the Greks. And one day, I'll get you back. I'll never give up hope for you, my dear, but today, I forgive."

I close my eyes and take a slow, deep breath. It's time.

Sitting up, careful to keep my head low until I know it's safe, I freeze where I am. It's dark out, but from where I sit, I can see at least a dozen *humans*, all of whom I think I know. Alliah, Aaron, and Connie are out there, so is that woman who tried to pull Alliah away, so is the guy who used to work at the store where I bought milk. My commanding officer is out there, too… all areas of life.

They know I'm here, somewhere. They just haven't found me yet.

I pull out my suit, the one that hides my body heat. The silhouette of two Greks rise above the piles of shattered buildings, about four hundred feet to the north, so I can't be careless. The suit will hide me from them, but it's also made of dark material which will help me travel at night. In a pinch, I can crouch in it, and at night, I should look like not much more than a pile of dirt.

I wait a little longer for the darkness to settle before I slip carefully through the grass. I'm maybe a good hour from the old lab, if I can walk at a steady pace. At the speed I'll need to move, however, I expect I'll be most of the night.

I slip past a few *humans* and settle in next to an old car, then move along to the broken remains of a building. When I get my chance with no one looking in my direction, I slip around a corner and make my way down a wide street.

Ideally, I would move along alleyways, but they're darker at night, and with the sun set, I'm just as likely to bump into a *human* as avoid everyone. The best I can do is creep along the streets as the night wears on.

Hour after hour, I slink through the shadows. By the time I reach the area of the old lab, the sun's up, and I'm eager to get that leaf blower and get out of here. Perhaps I've been more careful than I needed to be. I've seen no one, not even heard the thuds of a Grek, for a couple hours now.

At first, I can't find the entrance to the shipping area. It was small and difficult to find before, but now the entire area has changed. The Greks obviously did a lot more tearing down.

But the problem now is I need to get inside that receiving area. Unfortunately, where I think the entrance used to be is now an immense pile of broken chunks of concrete.

Moving slowly in the early morning light so as not to attract attention from anyone in the area, I work my way along, trying to find a hole or crevice or anything that might provide a way inside. When I finish circling the entire area, I'm left with nothing.

A sound catches my attention, and I remain still, trusting my camo suit to do its job. Carefully turning my neck to look behind me, I see a man walk by. I don't recognize him at first, but then I remember him. He was a neighbor of mine, a man I barely knew. I think we went to their house once for something or other.

So, they know I'm in the area. I have little time before they zero in and figure out what I'm up to.

As the man walks by, I sit there, covered in my suit, which against the rubble likely looks like just more of the mess, and consider how to proceed. I could try to get in through the front entrance. There's always a possibility it's still accessible.

But… they might have tried to collapse the entire area. If so, they'd likely do that from above. Which might have created an opening…

I glance back to confirm the man's gone before I slowly move up, climbing the rubble, careful to keep my footing and not disturb any of the loose gravel and rocks. I don't want to draw attention, but I also don't want to create a landslide and bury myself.

When I get to the top of the pile, I move not only slowly, but more cautiously than I had before. If there's an opening, and I slip in, well… the shipping area has a high ceiling.

I nearly shout for joy when I find something. It's small—only big enough for me to squeeze through—but it'll work. Carefully searching for a larger chunk of rock or concrete, I move back down the side of the rubble pile. When I find one, I tie a rope from my pack around it, making sure it's secure, then move back up the pile. At the hole, I drop the rope down into the darkness. I think I'm around thirty feet from the floor, so the rope should reach the bottom. Unfortunately, I can't see anything down there right now. I'd drop a flare, but the flash and smoke might give me away.

I take the risk and whip off my camo. It'll do nothing but catch on stuff on the way down. A moment later, I'm sliding carefully down the rope into the darkness.

Halfway down, I wait for a moment for my eyes to adjust. It's dark in here, but after a few seconds, I can see enough to find I was wrong about the height. I'm still about eight feet above the floor. That's not a problem going down, but it'll be a big issue on the way up again.

I drop to the floor and whip out my flashlight. I need to get this leaf blower, if it's still accessible. Heading to the door of the storage area, I'm careful to walk around any broken glass or anything that might crunch loudly under my feet. The main entrance to this section is caved in, and the floor is far more covered in debris than it had been before.

The storage room Fred told me about is easy to find, but the door's been ripped off its hinges. I'm assuming that means they got a Grek inside here. The *humans* couldn't do that on their own. Inside, everything's turned upside down, but with a little searching, I find the leaf blower.

I close my eyes and let out a sigh. The damage isn't terrible, but a cabinet fell on it. I hope Fred knows a bit about fixing battery powered tools.

The plug is still in the outlet, and a shower of sparks makes me jump back when I pull it out. The cord goes in my pack, and I take the time right away to hook Fred's contraption to it. There's no benefit to doing this later. When I have it, I hit the switch on the leaf blower, but it only clicks. Giving it a shake, I press it again, and the leaf blower turns on! It runs just fine for a few seconds as I reach for the lever on the bottle to turn on the drizzle, but sure enough, it cuts out before I can get the drizzle on.

Maybe it's a simple fix. The damaged side has a crack with exposed wires, and I shine my flashlight in that area. One wire barely hangs on with most of the braided wire torn from the solder. I don't know for sure that this is the problem, but it's all I have to work with, so I pull out my multi-tool and lighter. A moment later, the small blade is under the flame. This isn't likely going to be a permanent fix, but it'll hopefully do for now.

When I think the blade is hot enough, I use it to push the braided loose wire into the solder and then wait for it to cool for a few seconds. Once I think we're good, I press the *on* button for the leaf blower, and it kicks right in!

I head into the main area, moving close to the light shining down through the hole, and turn the knob on Fred's contraption, opening the nozzle for the chemical to flow. A smile breaks out on my face as I stare at the mist moving through the light. We've got it.

One more thing to take care of. I head back into the lab through the broken doors, taking the leaf blower with me. It's a mess in here. The lights are all out now. Most appear to be smashed. I don't need the light, though. My flashlight provides all I need as I move down to level three. This lab's laid out a little different from our new home. Most of the laboratories here are on level three. When I get down there, I make my way to the room where I killed Geoff. There are two things I need.

When I get to the room, I smell the ash in the air. I had wondered if they would clean up the mess since it was one of theirs, but I guess not. Geoff outlived his usefulness to them.

But what I look for first is to make sure Alliah's not still here. I knew the rope wouldn't hold her long, but I had to be sure. The tiny piece of rope sits there without her in it. I have a half dozen lengths of rope like that to use in situations where I can get away from the person by tying them up, but I add this one back into my supply.

I look forward to the day when I won't have to use any of them.

But the second thing I need to do has to do with Geoff.

I kneel next to the pile of ash, all that remains of the man I killed. The smell and tiny particles float through the air, but I ignore it. Instead, I take my time to say what I need to say. "I'm sorry, Geoff. You didn't deserve this. If I could, I'd give you a proper burial, but there's no way I can get you out of here. At least all of you. You'll have to rest here."

I sit there for a moment, wishing I could do more. "I really am sorry. But I forgive you for working with the Greks—I know it wasn't your fault—and I forgive the Greks. I won't let them continue doing this to others, as much as I'm able, but I won't hate the Greks anymore."

I don't have anything else to say. I thought I'd have more, but that's it, so I just nod to what's left of his body. Before I leave, I take a small amount of the ash in a little bag I keep for samples, then take a lab coat from the floor, pick it up, shake it out, and use it to cover what I can of what's left of Geoff. I'm not sure if it's the right thing to do, but it's all I can think of.

Once I reach the receiving area again, I carefully slide a large crate over and check the rope. I need to make sure no one has come along and untied it by chance, but I also can't just grab it and yank on it. Anyone up there within sight of the rope will notice that.

Once I'm confident I won't fall—at least right away—I start up the rope. The leaf blower with Fred's contraption hangs just under my pack. I'd say it weighs about ten pounds, which doesn't add much to a walk, but to a climb, every ounce makes a difference.

Halfway up, I feel the exhaustion kick in. I'd like to say it's the weight of the blower, but I know that's not true. I do my fair share of running, but I need to train a lot more intensely in the gym if this is going to be my life from here on out.

At the top, I use the rafters to push myself up until I can peek out. No sign of anyone. I still take a few minutes, however, to scan the area. I want to be sure.

It looks clear. I cautiously pull myself up a little more, then fully out until I sit crouched on top of the pile of rubble as I pull on my camo suit. Again, I look around. Nothing.

I finally relax and climb down to the large rock. The leaf blower unclips easily, and I set it carefully on the ground while I retrieve the rope.

GRRREHHHHK!

Thud… thud… thud… thud…

I spin around as a large Grek comes barreling over the pile of rubble behind me, heading straight at me. At the last second, I dive off to the side and roll, grateful that my pack is taking a lot of the abuse from the rocks, bricks and more. The Grek comes at me again, and my knife comes out. I've found if I'm fast enough, I can slice the tentacle off when it shoots down to grab me. With the camo suit on, I can't quite get the XM7 out, so my knife will have to do.

The Grek reaches me, and I'm shocked to find the tentacle doesn't come down at all. Instead, one of its legs swings around, and the Grek drives it right at my chest. I dodge and then dodge again as leg after leg comes for me, then roll out of the way as the Grek drops its entire body right down where I had stood a moment before.

"You're not trying to catch me anymore!" I gasp in my shock as I catch sight of a second Grek coming up the street from the south. At the speed they move, I have about twenty seconds, maybe less, before I'm facing both.

I dive again, but this time position myself where the leaf blower sits, grateful that the Grek's stomping hasn't crushed it. Pressing the button, I growl as it doesn't start. "Not now!" I leap to the side and press the button again, and this time, it kicks in. Twisting the knob to release the chemical, I swing around and point the mist at the Grek. I can feel some of it coming back on my face. I hope Gerb's right about this stuff being safe for us.

I scramble to the side again as it lunges forward, but once it's past me, it doesn't turn. Instead, it struggles, one leg bent as though lunging forward, the other three straight as can be. Turning to the next one, I see it's halted its approach about thirty feet away, eyeing me warily.

I take a few quick steps toward the new arrival, and it backs away. When I glance back at the first Grek, its legs still haven't moved, but its body struggles as if it's tied down in place.

The leaf blower cuts out at that moment, and I quickly switch off the drizzle. I only have so much of it, and I'm unwilling to waste even a drop. At first, I fear the new Grek will approach when the blower cuts out, but it doesn't. It's either that it can't hear it, or it can't figure out how it works.

"Back!" I holler. "Back!" The creature doesn't move, but its eyes have gone white. Fear… caution… at least that's what I think. I've only seen the eyes glow white a few times. "Back!" I holler again, but only when I walk toward it does it back away.

I try backing up myself, but it just follows me, always maintaining that same distance, approximately thirty feet away. "So, you understand at least a little of what's going on, eh?"

Scanning the area, I try to take stock of the situation. Aside from these two Greks, I see nothing else. No… wait… I see a *human*, peering over the rubble to my right. Off to my left, I see a bald head poke up, not even enough to recognize the face. They're out there. Just staying back, like the Grek.

I take a moment and examine the wiring. Sure enough, my little solution wiggled its way out. Maybe while they're holding back, I have time to fix it. I pull out my lighter and multi-tool again, keeping my eye on the Greks and the *humans*. This time, before I heat the blade, I strip off a bit more of the wire, which means pulling the wire right out of the solder.

I can't take the chance that they'll charge, so I strip off my camo suit and pull out my weapon. If they come at me now, I'm not defenseless.

Taking a deep breath, I hesitate as I consider what's changed, not in the Greks, but in me. After all that's happened, I don't think I want to shoot a Grek if I don't have to.

The knife goes into the flame, and I wait as patiently as possible. I don't think it'll help to let them see me afraid right now. Can't help but think they can sense that. Once the blade is hot enough, I put the wire onto the solder, then try to melt the solder around the wire.

For good measure, I start it up again and keep my hand on the knob of the contraption. I'm ready to move on, but this standoff won't do. I don't want to hurt anyone, so I take a chance. Charging toward the Grek, I holler and yell, hoping it can hear me and that the sound will scare it away.

The Grek backs up a few steps, eyes glowing a bright white, then scrambles back more before turning and running in the opposite direction. I can't help but laugh. After all these months, to finally see a Grek flee! I laugh again and again.

Looking around for the *humans*, I can't see them either. I wonder if they're afraid too, now.

I take another chance and walk down the open street. Generally, the streets are clear of debris—just have to navigate around the empty cars—but this road has no cars on it at all.

But also no Greks and no *humans.*

At this rate, I'll be back at the lab in half an hour, maybe forty-five minutes. I...

I come to a halt. The danger's not gone simply because I have a weapon against them. Eventually, they'll figure out it doesn't affect *humans,* and when that happens, I don't want them knowing where we live.

I turn and run between what's left of two buildings, and when I come out behind them, I see a half dozen *humans* scatter in every direction. They're staying out of sight, but they're watching me. Following me. And I'm leading them right back to the others!

Going back to my old style of travel, I slip off down another alley, then zigzag, heading southwest for the time being. When I come to where the lab sits just to the east of me, I continue going for another ten minutes, then circle around. At first, I see no one else, but then as I come out from behind a dump truck, I catch a quick glimpse of a man skirting around behind an old row of cedars.

This is almost worse than when the Greks chased me down! *Humans* are hiding, but extremely well. At least the Greks I can fight, but knowing someone could be just out of sight at any moment... how do I avoid that?

Perhaps another distraction...

I don't want to hurt anyone, but I need to get away. Maybe I can distract them. Pausing where I am, I set some Semtex with a detonator on the side of a car. It won't be big, but it'll be loud and get their attention. At the next car, I set another small explosive.

Ahead of me is an alley leading between two large piles of rubble. I take it, then slip in behind what used to be a few smaller buildings, then into another alley. It takes a bit to find what I'm looking for, but when I find it, I quickly slide back into my newly found hiding spot and put on my heat resistant suit. The *humans* don't see the heat, as far as I know, but it's better camouflage than my fatigues.

The alley I sit in is perfect. I wanted one I could enter and hide. I know they can communicate, but I suspect that once I'm out of sight, they lose track of me. If I don't exit the alley, the *humans* watching each side, if there are *humans* there, will hopefully think I slipped past them.

I remain as still as I can while I wait. Ten minutes… twenty minutes… after about thirty, I see a *human* enter the alley. I think I recognize her, but I can't quite place her. She walks along, stops not far from me, spins around slowly, looks every which way with her glowing green eyes, then moves on. Before she's out of the alley, however, I press the button to detonate the first explosion.

As hoped for, she turns immediately and runs back through the alley toward the sound. I then detonate the second, and two more *humans* come around the corner, also racing down the alley toward the sound. Once they're out of sight, I wait another minute. This is the tricky part of the plan. I have to move while they're distracted, but I can't move too soon, or another *human* might see me flee the area.

I give it to a count of thirty again, and then move along the alley, away from the explosions. When I get to the end, I carefully look around. No one, as far as I can see, so I move on, zigzagging through the area, and eventually swing around until I get to within a hundred feet of the lab's entrance.

I think I've lost everyone, but just to be sure, I circle the area three times. When I'm satisfied that I'm alone, I find a spot in a small, grassy area and use my knife to dig a tiny hole. "This isn't much," I whisper as I pour the ashes into the dirt, "but it's the closest I can get you to freedom." I open my mouth to say more, but no words come out.

With my hand, I scoop the dirt back in place and try to push the grass I dug up back into the hole. Somehow, this seems like the right thing to do for Geoff.

Truthfully, it's the only thing I can do.

Wiping the dirt off my hands, I slip into the entranceway to the lab, and punch in the code, grateful that

Elizabeth has finally decided I'm worthy of it rather than banging on the door, waiting for someone to come.

Inside, no one is here to greet me. That's no surprise. They wouldn't know I'm back until I approach the door, and they'd never have enough time to get up here. Besides, I've been gone for over a day. I head to the dining hall and am pleased to find them all there.

Before they can get too worked up over what took me so long, I hold up the leaf blower. "Good news, everyone. It works!"

14

NOT ALONE

"So… it just stopped. I mean, it struggled and more, but it didn't keep running after you?"

I frown at Gerb. "That's what I just said, isn't it?"

"But… yeah… so… it really just…"

"Gerb! I'm not saying it again. I've spelled it out for you six times. You know what happened."

"Yeah, I mean… it's just so hard to believe!" Gerb says. Everyone's either smiling or staring at each other in shock.

"Well, believe it! If you have new questions, I'll answer them. But I'm not telling you the same things again!"

"I'd like to hear it all from the start."

I spin around to face the owner of the unfamiliar voice, my 9mm in my hand, the safety off, ready to fire. "Who are you, and how'd you get in here?"

The woman is in her mid-fifties, I'd say. Fair amount of gray hair, tied back in a ponytail. Glasses. Army fatigues. Somehow, the fatigues are out of place on her. She doesn't look like a soldier, but her eyes are clear. No green, yellow, or white light.

She smiles and holds her hands up. "It's my lab. I think I should be the one asking you who you are and how you got in here."

"Dr. Terrance?" Elizabeth asks in disbelief.

Gerb and Logan come around from behind the table, and Gerb says, "Dr. T! How's it going?"

She frowns at Gerb and shakes her head. "You realize I've told you repeatedly that you can't call me that."

"Gerb's not great at listening," I growl. "How do we know you're not with them? With the Greks."

She shrugs. "I'm not. The eyes should be a dead giveaway, but if that's not enough…" She shakes her head again. "I don't really have anything else, other than to say that I've been fighting the Greks from the beginning." She smiles again and then says, "Why don't you put down the gun? I have eight soldiers with me out in the hall. If bullets start flying, your 9mm isn't going to protect you or anyone else. I think it'd be better just to talk."

"Who's out in the hall?" I ask.

"Marines. I'm told we could use you. That Marines are so willing to work with a SEAL tells me they're quite impressed with your record. You just have to lower your gun."

Without taking my eyes off the woman, I call out, "Elizabeth!"

"Yeah, Xavier?"

"Anything about her seem off? She seem like the Dr. Terrance you remember?"

"Mostly, but… to be honest, I didn't know her all that well. I met her a few times."

"Gerb? Logan? How well did you guys know her?"

"Oh, really well," Gerb says. "We were like besties with Dr. T." Dr. Terrance rolls her eyes and shakes her head, but Gerb remains undeterred. "I mean, you always talk about the *humans* taken by the Greks, you know… that their movements are a little off, like, what they focus their eyes on is different or something. I mean, Dr. T seems exactly the same as always. She's got that piercing gaze, that smile for me or… frown… but I know she likes me a lot, even though she frowns a lot at me."

"Logan?"

"Uh, yeah, I'd say that's her. The only difference is I've never seen her in camo, but aside from that, I think we're good to go."

I nod and holster my 9mm. "Okay, but I keep my weapon."

She nods. "That's not up to me." Turning around, she hollers, "Major Gordon? Come on in."

A moment later, eight men, armed to the teeth, come into the room. A few seconds later, I'm disarmed, and they search everyone. Aside from an impressive pile of snacks hidden on Gerb's person, they find nothing of interest to them.

"I think he can probably have his gun back," Dr. Terrance says.

The Major shakes his head. "Sorry ma'am. Not until he's cleared back at L-O."

Not sure what this "L-O" stands for, but I get that about taking my gun away. I hate to be defenseless, but I'd do the same thing in his shoes.

She looks at me and asks, "Are we good, Commander?"

I nod, not much else I can do, and Dr. Terrance motions to the table. "I'll bring you up to speed."

We all have a seat, and the Doctor lays it out. "My labs were all working under military contracts. Most of what we worked on was highly classified, but the second we got word that the Greks were here, that became the primary focus. Unfortunately, most of my staff cleared out and went home to their families." She pauses and holds up her hands, "Not that I blame them, of course, it just meant that the work boiled down to nothing in short order, so the military moved me and my staff—what was left of them—off to a base a little less than twenty miles southeast of here. We've been trying to come up with a way to fight back against the creatures everyone calls 'Greks' ever since it all started." She smiles at us. "But it looks like you beat us to it. Aside from bullets, we don't really have any decent way to push them back, and bullets only work if they don't overwhelm us."

"Hey Dr. T, in the movies," Gerb pipes up unhelpfully, "the army always wants to nuke 'em. Are they wanting to do that?"

"Doesn't matter what the army wants," she says, rolling her eyes just a little. "The Greks took out nearly all our defenses before we knew it, and that includes all our nuclear arsenal. We have limited weapons. Very limited. That's why we're clearing out your armory as we speak."

"We have an armory?" Gerb asks.

"So, you're leaving us here defenseless," I growl.

She shakes her head. "Not at all. You're coming with us. We want your help. We need to band together."

"And if we don't want to come," Fred says slowly, "we're left here defenseless."

"We can't leave the weapons here. They're not yours, anyway. They belong to the Marines. You can either come with us or stay here. We need your help, though. We've observed what you did to the Grek to the north of here. I assume whatever you did had to do with that leaf blower by the door. We needed a way to fight back, and you may have provided one." She leans forward and speaks in a lower voice. "There aren't many of us left. We really could use your help, even aside from the leaf blower. We need each other. We need you."

"The others…" Elizabeth says in a quiet voice, "how many are there? Like… left in the world?"

"There are a few," Dr. Terrance says with compassion. "Not many, but some. It's hard to know how many pockets of free humans exist around the globe, actually. We have some access to a few of the satellites the Grek's ships didn't destroy, and we search continually. When we find those still not taken in our general area, we try to track them down, but most are hard to find. They don't trust us because they think we're part of the Greks. They're usually scared of us."

"How come you took so long to find us?" Logan asks.

She laughs. "We can answer a lot of this back at the base if you're coming, but I'll say this: you were all really hard to find. We saw the Commander a few times on the satellites," she explains, pointing at me, "but we couldn't track where he was hiding or who he was with. A few weeks ago, we identified him but then lost him again." Glancing at me out of the corner of her eye, she smiles and says, "You're certainly good at what you do! So, when we saw what he did with that one Grek, we took a closer look and tracked him to this area. Since he used to return to the area of the previous lab and then started coming back to this area, we took a guess that you'd found yourself in the company of someone connected with this place. We didn't know anyone was in either location. If we had, we would have come sooner."

Turning to the Major, I ask, "You all seem to know a lot about me. How'd you identify me?"

"One of our men spied you out in the city a week ago. He lost sight of you after a few minutes, but he got a photo of you. We looked you up."

"Can we have a few minutes to discuss it?" I ask.

Dr. Terrance turns to the Major and raises her eyebrows.

He nods and says, "We're gonna wanna move within the hour. They have that much time to decide and pack up."

"You have that long, Commander," she says, turning back to me.

Once she's back with the Major, I ask everyone, "Thoughts?"

"I want to go!" Elizabeth says. "Dr. Terrance knows what she's doing. We're just guessing here."

Gerb and Logan look unconvinced. Logan speaks up first. "What if they don't give us any free time? I still wanna game."

"That's a biggie," Gerb adds.

I shake my head and turn to Fred. He nods slowly, and says, "I'm open to going. Might be nice to see we're not the only ones left."

I turn back to the boys and lay it out for them. "Look. We gotta do this. You might lose some of your game time, or all of it, but I think it'll be worth it. We might keep the Greks back on our own, keep 'em away from us, but we can't free anyone. We're kind of isolated here."

"But… games," Gerb says.

I shake my head. "Dr. Terrance?"

"Yes, Commander."

"We'll join you, but the boys want to take their gaming equipment."

"We don't take kindly to slackers, Commander," the Major barks.

"Yes, but the boys and Elizabeth were the ones who developed the Grek spray that has the Greks running scared. That's the condition. They need some downtime to…" I glance at Fred, and he shrugs. I can't believe I'm pushing for this. "They need their game time."

"Agreed," Dr. Terrance says with a smile.

The Major steps forward and barks, "We leave in fifty minutes. Be at the main entrance by then or we leave you behind."

"So, what does your rank mean with these guys?" Gerb asks. "Are you like one of the big ones or small ones?"

I smile and check the straps on my pack. I don't have much to carry. Most of what I owned I got at the first lab, minus what the Marines confiscated. Which was pretty much everything. "What do you mean, Gerb?"

"I mean, they all have ranks, but they called you Commander. Does that mean you command them?"

"It means, I'm Navy, they're Marines. We don't always mix like this, but my rank would be equal to about a Lt. Colonel. The base commander will work out how I fit in, though. That's not my call."

"Is Major bigger than Commander?" Gerb asks.

I turn to him and shake my head. "Bigger?"

"Yeah," Logan adds. "Like, you know, more powerful."

"They think this is a video game," Fred says. "Everything in video games is about power and bigger and stronger. They think of it like who would win in a fight."

"I would!" the Major barks, coming up. "I'm a Marine! They send us in when the Navy can't make it through."

"Oorah!" the other Marines holler out.

"However," the Major adds, "he'll likely outrank me. The General will want to talk to you first thing, Commander. I don't doubt you'll have a lot to offer us, despite a foolish early decision in your military branch. The General's a forgiving man, though. He even brought a Space Force Captain in under his wing for a time. I think he'll find a spot for you."

"For a time?"

He nods. "It's an unforgiving world, Commander. But, as for you, the General will fit you in somewhere."

"That'll be good, Major," I say with a nod.

I'm tempted to ask for my weapon back, but the Major doesn't strike me as a flexible man. I just hope the Marines can get us through. Turning back to the boys, I ask, "Where's Elizabeth?"

"She's with Dr. Terrance. Fred walked her through how to work the leaf blower with the chemical, and now Elizabeth is talking through the composition of the Grek Spray," Logan explains.

"Why aren't you there with them, Gerb?" I ask. "You're the chemist, right?"

"Yeah," he says, his eyes drifting off to the side, then down, then up. He's not making eye contact with me.

Logan smiles and looks like he's made a decision. "This is for embarrassing me in front of Elizabeth the other day, Gerb." To me, he adds, "Gerb figured out most of it, but then nothing was working, then it suddenly did."

"What made the difference?"

"I don't think we need to bother the Commander with this, Loge," Gerb says, his eyes on the floor.

Logan just laughs. "Gerb was eating a chocolate chip cookie, and a crumb fell in one of the test samples. He was too embarrassed to say anything, so he just let it go through, and that one worked. Turns out, a chemical used in the chocolate chips made all the difference. Once we isolated the right substance, we could reproduce it. He'd be there with them now, but he's just too embarrassed."

"I like cookies," Gerb whispers.

"We'll finish up at the base lab," Dr. Terrance says as she enters the room with Elizabeth trailing behind. To Gerb, she says, "I take everything back I said about your eating. Your snack attacks might have saved all our lives."

"All set?" the Major asks.

Dr. Terrance nods. "Lead the way, Major."

The Major leads us up to the top level and signals to his men to head out. A moment later, they're through the door.

"Clear!"

The Major signals for us to go out, and I lead the way. I don't enjoy being out here without a gun, although I spent months among the ruins with my family and on my own unarmed.

Outside, the sun sits right above us, the hot rays beating down on my head and shoulders and the sweat breaking out down my back almost immediately. The heat doesn't bother me—I don't mind sweating—and Fred seems fine, but the boys and Elizabeth all shy away from the sun as if they're afraid it'll come down and attack them. But comfortable with the sun or not, all four of my friends stand close to me. I guess I'm the only one used to the outside anymore.

My mouth drops open as two of the soldiers pull back a large sheet of camo to reveal a jeep and then another truck. I want to tell them it's impossible, even though both vehicles sit right before my eyes! "How do you drive that without attracting attention?" I ask, but the Major doesn't respond.

"Hit it!" he orders one of his men.

The soldier, a tall, thin man with a shaved head, pulls out a detonator, flips off the safety, then presses the button. A moment later, I hear a loud sound—more of a vibration than anything else—off to the north and another one off to the south.

"Load up!" the Major hollers at all of us, and we pile into the open back of the truck. When the vehicles start, they're quiet.

"Corporal!" I bark, speaking to the woman who activated the detonator. The Major's up in the truck's cab, and it's us and four soldiers in the open back. "How're the vehicles so quiet? And what was that noise?"

"We've taken great care to quiet the vehicles down, Sir. If we're quiet, we can move without notice. It's throttled down the power significantly, but we have few battles when we're out. As for the noise, we've found a specific frequency, a vibration of sorts, that attracts the big Greks. We can generally get them all out of the way. We pulled them off to the north and south, which gives us a clear run east. After about a mile, we'll head south."

"What about the *humans*?"

"What about them?" the soldier says with a laugh. "They don't bother trucks or Jeeps. They tend to just go after people on foot."

I didn't know that. Then again, I didn't know how to pull the Greks away aside from a bit of Semtex, but even if I had known all this, I still never had a Jeep.

"It's a strange feeling, being out here in the open, eh?" Fred calls above the wind.

I smile and nod. "Thought for a while we'd always have to slink in the shadows."

I glance at the boys and Elizabeth and barely hold back my laughter. Gerb is pale. Not just a little. It's like his skin has never seen the sun. With Logan's darker skin, he doesn't have that problem, but he looks terrified, as if he suspects we're going to die at any moment. And Elizabeth, she looks like she's about to lose her lunch. She actually looks a little green.

"Elizabeth," I say with a laugh. "I gather you're not used to…

GRRREHHHHK!

I grab the railing for support as a Grek, one of the biggest I've seen, comes barreling over one of the countless piles of rubble on the right-hand side of the road, straight at the Jeep in front of us. The Jeep swerves to the left and barely recovers as a second Grek follows the first, then another.

From the left, a fourth, smaller one leaps out in front of our truck, and I slam into the soldier in front of me as the driver hits the brakes. We don't stop in time, and the truck runs right into the legs of the Grek, its body crashing down on top of the cab.

The truck's still moving somewhat as I jump to my feet and throw my shoulder into the body of the beast before it slides back off the cab onto those riding in the back. Two other soldiers join me, then another one comes from behind and puts his hands on it. "Everyone out of the truck!" I order.

The soldiers move immediately, and Fred goes to follow, but the other three, the boys and Elizabeth, just sit there shaking. Fred grabs Elizabeth first and pushes her to the back, while another soldier grabs the boys, one in each hand. Logan goes easily, but Gerb moves with an urgency not entirely unlike a sack of potatoes.

"MOVE!" I holler, and Gerb shakes his head before running off the end of the truck and hitting the ground with a thud.

I'm about to order the three soldiers by my side to move as well, not sure if they'll follow my lead or not, but the weight shifts, and a moment later, my hands fall through a cloud of ash. The Major's out of the truck by now, taking charge, and gunfire rips through what little quiet we had left. The Greks are here in force. Another six have arrived, and new ones show up as quickly as the old ones turn to ash.

I pull a scarf up to cover my mouth as the air fills with the fine black powder left from the attacking Greks and find my way to the boys. Elizabeth comes running out from behind the truck, and Fred joins us a moment later. "Cover your mouths!" I holler, trying to get above the noise of the gunfire.

A soldier whips out the leaf blower, and the moment he turns it on, everything changes. The Greks run from it every which way but won't leave the area. They move back and forth and attack from any angle away from the man with the leaf blower, forcing the soldier to run in circles, never fast enough to catch them.

"Everyone, gather at the truck!" the Major hollers.

The soldiers herd us together, and the soldier with the leaf blower gets in the back of the large truck while the rest of us stand around the outside. It feels like a solid strategy, only the leaf blower isn't fast enough for this approach.

The Greks circle our truck, eyeing us warily.

GRRREHHHHK!

GRRREHHHHK!

GRRREHHHHK!

"They ain't happy, Major," a soldier hollers out unhelpfully.

I know the Major won't leave anyone or anything behind. All the supplies he collected at our lab sit securely, tied down in the bed of the truck. But… we have to get out of this area.

"Commander?" the Major calls out. "How did you drive them away last time?"

"There was only one of me and two of them that time," I holler back from the other side of the truck. "Besides, their strategy changes often. Once I got one of the Greks with the spray last time, the others stayed back."

"That one!" the Major hollers, pointing out a Grek at random. "Marines! Pick your targets, but we leave that one standing." Then he yells, "Millar!"

"Yes, Sir!" replies the man in the back of the truck.

"When the others go down, you go right for that one."

"You got it, Sir!" he calls as he starts up the leaf blower.

A moment later, the soldiers open fire and a half-dozen Greks turn to ash. Millar leaps out of the back of the truck and charges toward the Grek still standing. By the time he reaches it, the creature's backing away, but Millar still manages to get one leg of the Grek. The creature pivots on that leg and lashes out with a tentacle, but Millar dives to the side. By the time he gets to his feet, the Grek is lumbering away, doing its best to run with only three working legs.

Gunfire erupts again, and I spin around. A half dozen Greks race over the mounds of rubble and debris behind us, one after another, turning to ash.

I've heard of this strategy… they did this at the beginning.

"They're swarming!" Major Gordon calls out. "Civilians in the center!"

I take a moment to wrap my mind around the idea that I fit into that category right now, but I move to join the others. When I'm just about there, a strong hand grips my arm, and Major Gordon shoves my XM7 into my hands. "Get the civilians out of here, Commander!"

I grab Elizabeth and Logan and pull them away from the truck. Fred follows immediately, but Gerb stays rooted to the spot with a look on his face of equal parts terror and fascination.

"Gerb! Move!"

He shakes his head as if coming out of a trance and follows, along with Dr. Terrance and Millar, the Sergeant with the leaf blower. A moment later, we're running in the direction the injured Grek had fled.

"Sir," Millar hollers out. "My orders are to get you and the civilians back to base. The Major put you in charge."

I nod, slipping back into the role I'd lived for so many years. "Lead the way, Sergeant. Is the base's location a secret from the Greks?"

"No, Sir!"

"Then, as we run, you tell me the way we're heading loud enough for the civilians to hear."

"Yes, Sir!"

As we run along an alley with Millar taking point and with me watching our six, he shouts the directions back to us. The sound of gunfire echoes along through the streets, giving me hope that the Major still stands.

The Greks aren't letting up. As we travel, we have to move slowly, mainly for Gerb. He's struggling the most, but Elizabeth and Logan aren't doing all that much better. Fred's managing, but with his bad knee and extra few years, I'm concerned for him.

A shift in the debris to my right catches my attention, and I turn and fire, taking out a Grek, and getting back up to speed the moment it starts to fade to ash. Another one comes at us from the other side, but Millar hits this one with the Grek spray. As soon as he does, I realize our mistake. If the Greks were holding back with the Major at all because they thought he had the Grek Spray, they won't anymore. A few moments later, the gunfire stops.

I hope that's a good sign.

We're coming up on a street ahead, an open area. I can't imagine that's what we want right now.

As we run toward the street, a figure steps out in front of us. Just one, but it's enough.

"Who's that?" Gerb asks.

Before anyone else can say anything, I growl ahead, "You shoot that little girl, Millar, and I shoot you!"

"No, Sir! We're not in the habit of shooting civilians, except with tranqs. You okay if I tranq her?"

I'm really not okay with someone shooting anything into my daughter, not at all, but I don't think there's much else we can do. "Do it, soldier, but you better pray she falls onto something soft!"

He pulls out a small dart gun and holds off until he's just about upon her. When he shoots her, it lands right in Alliah's thigh, and he gets to her just as she's falling, catching her and setting her down gently in the grass.

"It's just a small amount, just enough for about ten minutes, maybe fifteen, with her size. She'll be okay, Sir."

As we run past, I pull the tranq out of her leg and toss it aside. I almost lean down and wrap my arms round her… just for a moment… just one more time… but I can't leave the others.

I catch up quickly as we run out into the street. Millar says nothing at first, but once we see the area's clear, he hollers back, "You knew her?"

"I *know* her, Sergeant! That's my daughter."

"I'm sorry, Sir. We're always careful with the ones the Greks have taken. Every one of them is someone's daughter, son, brother, sister, Sir. The General has a zero-tolerance policy for any cruelty to the *Taken*."

"Is that what you call them?"

"Yes, Sir. The *Taken*. The General feels it's a constant reminder that our job is not to fight them, but to get them back."

I like that. Much better than *HG* or even *human*. I force myself not to look over my shoulder to see my little girl again. To see her helpless body, laying there, waiting for me to come get her…

But… I can't leave the others.

From the Sergeant's description of the route ahead, we shouldn't be far from the base. Gerb looks like he's about ready to pass out, and Fred's not far behind. Poor guy's knee… bothers him on good days, let alone when he has to run. I have my doubts he'll be walking tomorrow.

A pile of rubble just to my right explodes outwards as two Greks launch themselves from their hiding spot. I bring my weapon around and fire into the body of the one closest to me, then turn to the other one as the first turns to Ash.

GRRREHHHHK!

A tentacle snakes out from the body of the remaining Grek and knocks Millar to the ground, then whips over and smacks my XM7 off to the side, with only the strap holding it to my shoulder.

Before I can get it back up and around, the tentacle wraps around Gerb's chest and hoists him up onto its back. With a screaming Gerb on its shoulders, it races off to the west.

"Gerb!" Logan shouts and starts after him.

I race up the side of a pile of debris and raise my weapon. Bad idea to take this shot… too easy to miss, and a miss of the Grek could be bullseye for Gerb as he bounces along. I take aim, relax my shoulders, let out my breath… and fire.

The Grek jerks forward, slowing down considerably. I hold my aim steady and put a second through the large, round body of the creature. A moment later, it begins to fade to ash, and Gerb drops.

Millar's back on his feet and climbing toward me, but I shout, "Millar, get the others to the base. I'll get Gerb."

I take off running before I see if he's following orders. If I were the commanding officer, I'd never let a single soldier outside the base walls if he or she couldn't follow every order. Perfectly.

I have to assume the Marine General is the same.

Halfway to Gerb, another Grek climbs up and over a pile of debris. Every one of these creatures is different in size, speed, and to an extent, even shape. The same goes for how much it takes to turn one to ash. This one requires six shots before it stumbles and another two before it begins to fade. A moment later, I've reached the boy, and I check him right away. He's breathing, but in a lot of pain.

"What did I land on?"

"Bricks," I say. "No time for Gerb-ness. Can you walk?"

"I can't… walk…" he says, his face filled with anguish. "…they tied my… shoelaces… together."

A growl escapes my lips, and I punch him in the chest, just enough to knock some sense into him. "Get up and get moving. You stay here, you get glowing eyes."

I turn around and scan every direction. No sign of Greks. No sign of the *Taken*.

"Time to move, Gerb."

He's on his feet. I see he's banged up pretty bad, but he's lucky. A fall like that could have killed him if he'd landed on rebar or something just as sharp. As it is, he's walking, and that's more than anyone could hope for.

As we climb down to the small road, he hobbles, but I can tell he's being uncharacteristically undramatic. I gotta hand it to him. To be hurt like that and still be joking around… even so, I want to punch him one more time to knock some sense into him.

We follow the road to the north for two blocks, then turn east around the corner. The roar of gunfire echoes up from the south of us having just restarted. I expect that's Millar and the others. I jog along slowly to allow Gerb to keep up as he limps along.

"How much farther?"

I shake my head. "Not sure, but I think we should be just about there. Maybe another three or four minutes if we're lucky."

We come to an enormous wall of debris, and I smile. A camera sits on a pole ten feet above the top. Gerb sees it too and starts lumbering up the pile, but I grab him. "We're new to them! Best to use the front door."

I lead us along, following the pile, heading south as the makeshift wall slowly curves around to the east. It looks like they set this wall up as a barrier that runs all around the base. I smile at the thought of standing with others—a large group of others—not just fighting alone anymore.

I glance over at Gerb, his beet-red face filled with a cross between terror and excitement, lumbering along, grunting in pain with every step. No, not alone. I guess I haven't been alone for a while.

Ahead, something stands out a little differently than the debris barrier they've built along our left. A concrete wall leads out twenty feet from the debris, and as we come closer, I see it frames an opening. With a laugh, Gerb cheers and somehow finds a bit more energy to picks up speed. On top of the wall, two enclosures sit with openings large enough for the 50 caliber guns manned by soldiers. I assume they have something a little less deadly in case the *Taken* show up, but that's something we'll learn soon enough.

The one 50 cal is trained on us, and I hold out my XM7 to the side while I jog along with my hands in the air. I try to get Gerb to hold his hands up, but it's all he can do to keep moving. They watch us carefully, but aside from that, there's no reaction at all.

When we reach the gate, it's wide open, and we just walk in, but within a short distance, we're both surrounded by a half dozen soldiers, and I'm disarmed. They search Gerb but only find a bag of crushed cookies in his back pocket. The soldier holds it up with a confused look on his face, but Gerb just shakes his head. "I won't apologize for that!"

Once they've thoroughly searched each of us, they take us through a door large enough for three eighteen wheelers side-by-side to move through comfortably. A large hangar spreads out before us, filled with soldiers, Jeeps, trucks, fork trucks, and more. They lead us to the right wall and push us through a smaller door into a room about ten feet square. "Sit here and don't move!"

"Well, I was expecting a better welcome than this," Gerb says, shaking his head. "I thought they'd celebrate our arrival."

I furrow my brow and ask, "Why?"

"Well, they should be excited about a chemist joining their team."

"You're a third-year undergrad student. I don't think you get the title 'chemist' for a little while yet."

"Hasn't it been long enough? I mean, it's been months since I was a third-year student."

I turn back to stare at the wall. Less frustration there.

In a whisper, he asks, "You think the others made it?"

"Focus on what's going on now," I say as I put my hand on Gerb's shoulder. "Don't worry about them. Just focus on here and now."

"Well, what about…"

The door opens, and Gerb's mouth snaps shut. The woman who enters is about my age, pretty, and pushes a cart in with her. Behind her, three soldiers, armed to the teeth, enter.

Under the watchful gaze of the Corporal and two Privates, the woman smiles at us. "Hello, my name is Doctor Liu. I'll be doing an initial screening on you. I just need to…"

"What…? WHAT???"

I look to my left, and I'm not sure how to respond. Gerb's mouth hangs open, and his hands shake. "What… what is involved in this… SCREENING!" the final word comes out in nothing short of a shriek.

Doctor Liu smiles kindly at Gerb as the soldiers chuckle, and she explains in a soft voice. "It's nothing to worry about. We do a retinal scan, take a sample of your saliva, and draw a little blood."

"Bloo… blo…"

I grab Gerb as he passes out. Shaking my head, I say, "I think you'd better take the blood while he's out cold. I'm guessing needles aren't his thing."

She nods, and, with the help of a soldier, we keep Gerb propped up enough to get the sample. By the time he wakes, the only thing left is his retinal scan.

"Do you really… need… my blood…" he begins, but she shakes her head.

"Don't you worry. We just need to take a quick scan of your eye. It won't hurt at all." She holds a small contraption up to his left eye and asks him to hold still while the machine does its thing. A few moments later, she's taken my scan, a sample of my saliva, and then begins to draw some blood. The soldiers catch Gerb as he passes out again while watching the needle enter my arm.

Before the doctor leaves, I say, "We have some questions."

She smiles sweetly at me but shakes her head. "I'm not the one to answer questions. I'm just here to do the initial screening. An officer will arrive shortly."

She then leaves, pushing the small cart in front of her. The three soldiers file out after the doctor, and the door closes.

I spend a moment trying to revive Gerb, but he fights me every step of the way. Eventually, I just make sure he's breathing okay and leave him to his little nap.

There's not much I can do. I heard the lock on the door click shut after the last soldier left a moment ago. Even if I could get out, I'd likely face more than just the three soldiers, so I just sit there, close my eyes, and try to relax.

I mentally go through everything. If I were in charge, I wouldn't give any new arrivals any information at all. The priority is not for them to understand, but for the base to maintain order and security. Second, the eye scan likely has something to do with the glowing eyes of the Greks, which means, there must be a way for the *Taken* to hide the glowing lights—something I hadn't considered. Third, the blood sample. There's no way you can draw a blood sample and test it immediately—unless you're just checking blood sugar or something that will show up quickly, but that's not likely to need an entire vial of blood. They're looking for something specific, and they'll need some time. However, this would be a priority for me if I were the base commander. I'd want to know right away if someone is a threat. So, the testing will start immediately.

I likely have a good half hour, maybe an hour, before I'll know if they're going to trust me. And Gerb looks like he's in no rush to wake up.

I move my chair up against the wall and lean back. In a few moments, I feel myself drift off to sleep.

PART II
STAND

15

THE LAST OUTPOST

The door unlocks, and I'm on my feet in a second. At first, I don't know where I am—an unfamiliar room, a table, chairs, Gerb snoring—but then it all comes rushing back. I'm still on edge, but I force myself to settle a little.

A man steps into the room. From the shade of green, and the star on his shoulder, this is the Marine Brigadier General I've heard about. I snap to attention and salute.

He smiles and gives me a quick nod before pointing to my chair. Once I've picked it up and set it upright again, I take a seat. Two other Marines stand at the door.

"Lieutenant Commander Ghulam," the General says as he takes a seat opposite me. More of a statement than a question. He has a slight smile on his face, and I get the impression he finds Gerb's situation funny, more than anything else. The boy's still sound asleep.

"Yes, Sir," I reply.

"Pulled your file the other day, once we figured out who it was taking on the Greks, getting samples, and more. Impressed with your work."

"Thank you, Sir."

"You've been up to a lot over the last couple months. You obviously work well alone." He hesitates for a moment, then leans forward a little. "Now, can you work on a team?"

A strange question. I gather he's just testing me. "I'm a SEAL, Sir. SEALs don't survive alone. Even over the last couple of weeks, I didn't operate alone. I had my team."

"And I suppose one of your team members is this young man, Maverick Thompson?"

A smile breaks out on my face. "Yes, Sir. But he goes by Gerb. He's an odd one; I can't deny that. But he's brilliant."

"I get that impression." The General takes a moment and flips through the file, but I can see he's not really reading it. I gather that means he's already gone over it a few times. Finally, he closes it up and looks me right in the eye. "Here's the situation, Commander. Everything's changed. The Navy no longer exists. The Air Force is all but grounded, what little is left. The Army has been demolished, and the lowest ranking General in the Marines might now be the highest-ranking officer on the planet."

I nod. "I see, Sir."

"Do you? Then tell me, Commander. What am I getting at?"

"You're telling me that the division of the military is now entirely unimportant. If we're all that's left standing against the Greks, and if we have the same mission, we're all the same."

"Exactly. As of this moment, you are a Major in the Marines. You should be a Lieutenant Colonel, and honestly, I might have just made you a full Colonel, but I won't promote you above my only other Senior Officer, Major Gordon, until I see how you lead."

I nod, and a smile breaks out on my lips.

"Is something funny, Major?"

"Not funny, Sir. It's just good to be back in the chain of command. I was alone for a long time. Then, when I had the others, it was good, but there were only five of us. I always prefer to work with a full team."

"Good. The others of your little group from the other lab are all here. Major Gordon arrived shortly before you with them in tow." The General pulls out a folder below the one I assume was all about me and drops it in front of me. "There's your reading material. Learn it fast. I want to see you in uniform at 1900 in my office."

He gets up, walks to the door, and is gone before I even have a chance to salute him again.

Taking my seat, I grab the folder.

Gerb's snoring.

I flip through…

No, Gerb's not snoring, it's like he's trying to out-suck a vacuum cleaner through his larynx.

I flip through the folder, doing my best to concentrate. Gerb's snoring is growing in intensity, but I try to block it out. I'm reading things I not only guessed on one level or another but also stuff I'd never have imagined.

"Gerb!" I reach out to shake him awake. His snoring… or gasping… or the power struggle between his breathing tube and sleep apnea has gone from a conflict to an all-out war. I'm not sure he's going to win this one. When my hand touches his shoulder to shake him, his arm jerks up, and he slaps my hand away before diving back into his full-scale battle.

"Okay, have it your way, buddy."

The information before me is fascinating. They've determined that the Greks are communicating with the *Taken* somehow. I had already figured out that much. They haven't yet determined how the Greks do it. Of course, we've come up empty on that one, too. But what I hadn't imagined was…

"Gerb! Seriously! You gotta wake up!" I decide to take another approach. "Soldier!"

A moment later, a soldier enters the room. "Yes, Sir."

Shaking my head, I order, "Wake him up, Private!"

The soldier has the briefest hesitation, understandably, but then grabs Gerb by the shirt and yanks him out of his chair. "Wake up, man!" he hollers.

Gerb spasms in his hands for just a moment before his eyes open, and he panics at the sight of the soldier holding him. He starts swinging his arms like he's trying to attack the man, but rather than land a single blow, his arms just flail more than anything.

"Gerb, have a seat!"

Gerb turns to me, his eyes wild with panic, but then, in an instant, he calms down and smiles. "Oh, hey, Xavier. How's it going?"

"I said sit down!" Turning to the Private, I say, "That'll do."

He gives me a strange look again. I think he's wondering if I have the authority to order him around. Likely hasn't heard the General's orders.

Once he's gone, I slide the folder over for Gerb to see. "Look at this."

"What am I… ahem… why's my throat sore?"

"Just look at this, Gerb."

"Okay, but… wait… what's this little bandage on my arm from?"

"Gerb!"

He leans over the table and looks at the page for just a few seconds before his mouth drops open and he tries to turn to the next page.

"No, read it all, Gerb."

"I did."

"You really read that fast?"

He just looks at me, and I shake my head. Once he turns the page, he goes over the next one just as quickly. It turns out this is the last outpost they know of anywhere that stands against the Greks. The creatures have typically tried to capture, rather than kill any resistance, but that's not always been the case. It looks like entire nations were wiped out for resisting too hard. But, as of now, the Greks have focused their efforts on capturing this last resistance.

It also turns out that the resistance has spoken to the *Taken* frequently, and there have even been times when a member of the *Taken* has come into the base. Welcomed in, even.

Gerb whistles in admiration when we get to the page where it explains that the outpost, referred to as the Last Outpost, or L-O, has procured some tech from the aliens. Apparently, the scientists have been able to work with a lot of it, and even figured out how a fair amount of it works.

Finally, the thing that shocks me the most is the final piece of information. As they worked with the Grek technology, they determined first that it was not the Greks that developed it. Second, they picked up a form of communication going back and forth between the *Taken* and Greks, confirming what they had determined earlier, although they still cannot comprehend what the signals mean. And third, they only recently discovered another signal. This one's not going between *Taken* and Greks but is traveling from their ships out into space, directed toward the center of the Milky Way.

"So, they're in contact with their home planet?" Gerb asks.

"Maybe. There's a lot here we don't know. Hopefully, we can figure it out." I close up the folder and get to my feet.

"Where are we going?"

I shake my head. "I'm going to get cleaned up and changed. Don't know where you're going."

Panic fills his eyes, but I put my hands up. "Logan and the others are here somewhere. We just need to get you to them."

I swing open the door and come face to face with two soldiers, one of whom was the man who woke Gerb. "I need to be taken to my quarters." I'm only guessing that's where I need to go. The General told me I need to get into uniform.

It's gotta be somewhere. "And this guy needs to be taken to the others who were just brought in."

The one signals for Gerb to follow him, and the other leads me through the large, open hangar into the base. Neither soldier salutes me, which means they don't know my rank or position. As we walk, it's not long before I see the base is, like the labs, built underground, but unlike the lab, which was comparatively small, this base… this Last Outpost is massive. And it's set up like a fortress. No wonder the Greks have had a tough time taking it. They'd have to fight for every step.

The Private leads me down a busy hallway. At first, I see mainly soldiers, but the civilians come and go, entering rooms, leaving rooms. We turn down another hallway, then take a set of stairs down a level, then two.

As we move along, the Private explains a little of what I'm seeing. "Sir, the L-O is twelve floors below ground, and then, of course, the ground level. The top level is simply called Ground, and then the descending levels follow their number, so the level below ground is 1, then below that is 2, and so on. Every floor has both military and civilians on it, and you are in with the officers on Level 2. The Command Center is on Level 1, right near the center of the L-O."

We walk through a large group of men and women who part to let us through in a hall where the lights flicker somewhat. None of these people are soldiers. Some have grease stains on their clothes and skin. Some are clean. Everyone appears content as they talk and laugh together.

It feels strange, at first, to be around so many people again, but a familiar suspicion grows in my heart. Hard to give that up after so long with so few. As I pass one woman, my heart goes cold when I see a flash of glowing green eyes, just a flicker as she moves past me. Grabbing the woman's arm, I spin her around. Her eyes widen in shock, but they're not green. She has brown eyes. Just regular… brown… eyes.

"I… I'm sorry…" I say as I let go of her arm. "I thought I saw something."

After a brief hesitation, she pulls back her fear, and a small laugh escapes her lips. "You're new here, right?"

I nod.

"Everyone's jumpy when they first arrive." Her smile grows, and she places her hand gently on my arm. "Don't worry. You're safe now."

I nod again at her and turn back. The Private leads me on, and once we're past that group of men and women, he asks, "Did you see glowing eyes?"

"I did."

"It's something to get used to. In crowds, and especially under certain flickering lights, a lot of us see a flash of glowing eyes here and there. They say we're just jumpy. Nothing to worry about."

"You ever have one of the *Taken* make their way in here?"

"Of course! But if we do our job well when everyone first arrives, we rarely have a problem."

"Rarely?"

"There was a time one got through, Sir, but that was a long time ago. The bigger problem we have is the question of who runs this place. The civilians want a civilian leader, but the General hasn't allowed an election yet as we're under constant threat."

The Private comes to a stop in front of a door and turns back to me. The name of the door says Colonel Carter. "What happened to the Colonel?"

"The Colonel got too close to a Grek, Sir. We lost her two weeks ago." I hear the grief in his voice.

"You lose some people yourself, Private?"

"We've all lost people, Sir." He pauses for a moment, then asks, "Anything else, Sir?"

"No, Private, you're dismissed."

I watch the man walk away and smile. I enjoy the purpose and focus of the military. People know what they're doing and what they're about. Turning back to the door, my

smile grows, although I feel sadness for the Colonel. Perhaps…
perhaps we can get her back along with the others we've lost.
If we can figure out what this signal is…

The door handle turns, and the door opens. No lock.
Interesting. Not sure what to make of that. Perhaps the people
here are trustworthy. Or perhaps no one has anything worth
stealing. Aside from a few treasures I've kept of my kids and
wife, I myself have nothing.

I'm pleased to find I won't be sharing a room with
anyone else. Depending on the situation, even officers lose
their privacy. I'm also pleased to find a latrine complete with a
shower. It's small and cramped, but I'll take it. On my bed sits
a uniform with a gold leaf. Major. Going to have to get used to
that.

The clock on the desk says I have a little less than an
hour until I see the General, so I get myself cleaned up and
showered. Twenty minutes later, I'm doing up the buttons of
my uniform. Before I step out into the hallway, I settle in the
single chair in the room at my desk and take a deep breath. I'm
grateful the others made it. I'm grateful I'm here. I'm grateful
that I have soldiers to work with to get my family and the others
back.

A smile creeps up on my face. After all this time, I once
again have hope!

And it feels good.

I grab the folder with all the information the General
left me off my desk and head out. No one else is in this hallway,
but to my right, the hallway ends at another hallway heading
right and left, and it's the one the Private brought me down. A
steady flow of people move back and forth.

When I get to that hallway, I enter the stream and make
my way back to the stairway the Private and I used. I have to
concentrate hard when I get to the hallway with the flickering
lights because I'm sure I see three, maybe four others with
glowing eyes. Perhaps it's some kind of PTSD.

I focus my thoughts and make my way to where I'm going. When I reach the command center, a Corporal and a Private stand guard. The Corporal is one of the young soldiers who led us back to the L-O. Her uniform says her name is Adesina.

At first, neither move from the doorway. I would have thought my uniform would be enough, but then again, it's a small group here. They don't know me yet.

"Name, Sir?"

"Major Xavier Ghulam."

The Corporal nods and then opens the door. "Sir? There's a Major Ghulam here to see you?"

"Send him in, Corporal!"

The Corporal moves out of the way and holds her hand out to direct me through the door. When I step through, she closes the door behind me.

The room is laid out differently than I would have expected. View screens cover the wall on my left, showing camera angles of outside, mostly, and a few inside, all of which are the hangar bays and entrances to the L-O. Ahead, a large map of the area covered in pins and markings fills most of the wall, with a few smaller maps showing specific locations on either side. On my right, desks line the wall, but only one desk is in use. In the center, a table, large enough for a dozen or more people to comfortably stand around, sits covered in reports and maps and coffee cups.

I stand at attention and salute the General. At first, he doesn't look up from his desk as he finishes what he's doing, but when he stands, he smiles and nods back at me, which I take for his acknowledgement and finish my salute.

"A little early! I don't mind that kind of thing," General Williams says with a laugh.

He waves me over to the desk in the far corner. Up close, I see it's a coffee nook. He makes himself a cup and offers me one, which I decline.

"Do you simply not drink coffee, or is it something else?"

"I'm meeting with my General for the first time, Sir. I'll have a coffee once I know where I stand."

He smiles again. "You stand in the command center, Major. Have a coffee, and we'll sit and chat. You need to understand the situation a little better."

"Yes, Sir."

I make my coffee and have a seat where the General points. He takes a few sips and stares off at a point somewhere behind me while he collects his thoughts. Finally, he says, "I'm going to lay it all out, Major. First, don't call me 'Sir' when we're alone. Call me General. Second, we're short on officers. Very short. By that, I mean we've started training and promoting some of our NCOs. I have three former Sergeants operating as Lieutenants. I no longer have any Captains. As of today, I have two Majors, you and Major Gordon, but Gordon came in pretty banged up after his run-in with the Greks. And then there's me. All this for a military base that houses nearly three thousand soldiers and roughly the same number of civilians." He leans forward in his seat and says with a grin, "Perhaps you understand why I drink a lot of coffee."

"You seem to have maintained a sense of humor."

He chuckles at that. "I didn't have much of one before the Greks came, but I've learned to laugh my way through a lot of troubles and difficulties." His eyes focus on his coffee cup for a moment, then he says, "I need to fill in my command structure. I'm looking at you to be my Colonel. Major Gordon was my first pick, but he's out of his element as it is. I promoted him up from Lieutenant less than a month ago."

"He does seem a little young."

"That he is. He's a good man, good heart, trustworthy, but he just needs a bit of time."

"And what stopped you from making me your Colonel right away?"

"Don't know you, Major!" he says, his voice growing stronger and a little louder. "I need someone I can trust, but you're new to me."

I stare at him for a moment, taking in his movements, where his eyes focus, his hesitations… "There's more going on here than you put in the file."

He nods slowly but says nothing. I take that as a sign that he wants me to say a bit more.

"You're not interested in just taking a stand. You don't want to just sit here and collect people. You want to fight back."

"In a manner of speaking," he says, and then he turns his head just slightly as if he wants more.

"From what I've learned, you're careful to see all the people out there not as completely lost, but as those who can be rescued. You want to drive the Greks from the planet and put a stop to their hold on humanity." I stare at him for another moment before it finally hits me. "But you already have a plan. You have something in mind. It's perhaps even in motion right now. You just need the right people in place to make it happen."

"I think we're going to work well together, Major."

"Good. I'm tired of focusing just on trying to survive and protect ourselves. It's time we get the people we lost back."

The General leans back and flips open a folder. "Tell me, Major. Are…" He takes a moment and reads a few words from the file. "Connie, Alliah, and Aaron… were they all taken?"

I don't really want to talk about them, so I give the Private's response to me. "We've all lost people, General."

He closes the file and nods. "That we have, Major." He stares at me again for an awfully long time before he continues. "So, part of everything we do as officers is to train up others. That means you cannot merely give orders, you also have to help those below you learn how to think like an officer. Right now, officers won't learn through coursework or years in the field. We have to be intentional. We need to create officers."

"Yes, General. That makes sense."

"One more thing before I talk to you about our plans." He takes a deep breath, closes his eyes for a moment, and then says, "I'm going to be blunt. I'm also taking quite a risk in trusting you with this, so you better not disappoint me, Major!" His eyes drift to the floor while he hesitates. Finally, he says, "I believe we've been infiltrated."

My eyebrows shoot up, and my mouth drops open. My first thought, as ridiculous as it is, is that Greks have made it inside, hiding here and there, but that can't be it. "The *Taken?*"

He nods.

"How many?"

The General shakes his head. "No idea, Major. Maybe a dozen. Maybe a hundred. The NCOs and the general population believe it's just a trick of the light in certain hallways. I believe the *Taken* can hide their glowing eyes long enough to fool us, but the flickering lights, perhaps the flashing of it, disrupts their control, and you can get a glimpse of it if you're careful."

"We have to root them out."

"We do, Major, but most people won't see it that way. When they find out, they'll either distrust everyone, or they'll defend those they care about who are clearly hiding what they really are."

"And their purpose here?"

"I've noticed that those we suspect are often the ones who spread division, distrust, and sometimes even try to convince people to set out on their own, leaving the safety of the L-O."

"I saw a few eyes flicker after we spoke earlier. The soldier leading me to my quarters convinced me it was a trick of the lighting in that area."

"That's what most think. We'll have to deal with it, or we'll lose more people." He stands and waves for me to follow. "But for now, come look at this."

We walk to the table in the center of the room, and he stops in front of a map of the area. "Major, you read how there's a signal coming from somewhere out in space, right?"

"Yes, General."

"I want to deal with it. Cut it off at the source."

"How do you propose we do that, General?"

He smiles. "We go to the source!" He gets a mischievous look in his eye and adds, "And cut it off."

I just stare at him. I'm sure he's not insane, but I can't imagine what he's talking about. Rather than make a fool of myself, I wait.

"Wise move there, Major," the General says with a smile. "Here's the situation. We have a lot of the alien tech now, and our people have figured out some of it... not necessarily how it all works, but at least how we can use it. We have enough now that we believe we can actually fly a Grek ship. I'm suggesting that we steal their mothership and fly it to their home world."

"We don't know what will be there... what we'll face, General."

"No, that we don't, but we know what we face here, and it's either annihilation or slowly get overrun by the *Taken* posing as us. We're not at war with the *Taken*, Major. We're at war with whatever holds them."

"I agree wholeheartedly, General. What are my orders?"

He smiles. "Yes, Major. I think we're going to work well together!"

VISITORS

Major Gordon limps up next to me. His injury the day he brought us to the L-O has never quite healed. The x-ray machine is down, and the best Doctor Liu can figure is that he'll need a complete knee replacement. Unfortunately, that's entirely outside our abilities.

He clears his throat and then steadies himself on his cane. "They should be back soon."

I nod. Over the last couple weeks, the General has sent me out on a few missions here and there, and apparently, he's been pleased enough to give me the promotion. Colonel Ghulam… not sure what I think of that. As a Navy man, it's a strange adjustment, but I'll get there. Unfortunately, the hardest adjustment now is sending troops out. Normally, I'm with them. Missions have always been where I shine, but now I have to train and equip others, giving them the orders I want to carry out.

The good news is, I'll get to lead the upcoming mission—the big one. The bad news is, the most competent officer I have to work with is standing beside me, using a cane to keep himself upright. I need him field ready, not limping through a bad knee. But at least he's alive. The Grek that kicked his leg out from under him is dead now… if only they'd taken it down a few seconds earlier.

A signal comes through from the soldiers manning the 50 cals at the gate. When word reaches Gordon and me, I smile. All four soldiers are on their way back. Didn't lose anyone.

I have focused the missions over the last while on collecting information. We need every detail we can about the mothership, getting there, entering it, clearing out the Greks, and maybe even the *Taken* if they're in there too.

One challenge is we really don't know where all the *Taken* are. There's obviously a lot of them in this area, and I assume it's the same across the planet, but this area had over a million people living here. It's hard to hide those kinds of numbers, but not only is there nothing we've seen so far to suggest the Greks are killing the *Taken*, but the largest group any of us have seen for a while is not much more than a few thousand.

The soldiers come into sight and jog through the gate unhindered, with Millar in the lead. I promoted him to Lieutenant just yesterday. I'm surprised they overlooked him when searching for officer material. The four men come right to me and Gordon, and stop before us, offering a salute.

I had wondered how the marines would accept me. There's often a lot of rivalry between the Marines and the Navy, but it turns out they got over that months ago. On this team of four, only two are Marines, the other two are Army and Air Force.

Returning the salute, I ask for a brief report. Typically, after a mission, everyone went straight to Doctor Liu for testing before giving a report. I changed that almost immediately. I want a report the minute they walk through the door, even if it's only a few words.

"Report, Lieutenant!"

"Sir, we scouted the area. We have three ways in, all of which are equally risky and dangerous."

I smile. "Risk and danger won't stop us."

"No, Sir!"

"Report to Doctor Liu. I want a full report in an hour."

"Yes, Sir!" the Lieutenant says, then barks at his team to get moving.

"Three ways in," Gordon says as he hobbles along beside me. "That's better than expected, assuming the risk he speaks of isn't too great."

"I expect it isn't. Millar's a smart guy. If the risk is far too great, he wouldn't call it a way in." I hear Gordon's a lot more pessimistic since his injury. I get that. The last thing you want is to be stuck in a desk job at a time like this.

"You think it'll work, Sir?"

I nod. "I do, Major. We've done our homework. We've scouted, researched, gone over our strategy repeatedly. Just need this final bit of information, and we're set to go."

We head to the briefing room and settle in. There's a lot of work to do, so we get at that while we wait for the soldiers to arrive.

When they finally arrive, I'm pleased to find the three routes in are good options. Despite the fact that they're well patrolled and heavily guarded, I believe we can slip inside the perimeter and make it into the ship. All the other details are falling into place.

"Do I need to remind you that you are not to speak of this with anyone, even each other?"

"No, Sir!" Millar says.

I look at each of the others in turn and await their response. When I'm satisfied, I inform them I have no problem throwing any of them in the brig if they break confidence, and they all reaffirm their commitment to secrecy before I dismiss them.

We've had to be extra careful. I haven't allowed any of the teams to speak of anything to anyone, and I've ensured there's a lot of crossover between the teams to minimize the chance of too many mouths capable of sharing plans. We've also given out information on a strictly need-to-know basis.

Still, I grind my teeth.

"What's on your mind, Sir?" Gordon asks.

"I just can't shake the feeling that something bad's coming, Major. I've read all the reports for the last couple months before I arrived, and the Grek attacks have dropped to next to nothing in recent weeks."

"You're thinking that's a bad thing, Sir?" Gordon laughs as he picks up his coffee.

"I don't think it's a bad thing that the Greks aren't attacking. I think it suggests they're up to something."

"What does the General think about it?"

I pick up my coffee and take a sip. Shaking my head, I say, "That's the problem. He agrees with me."

"Bang, Bang, Bang!"

I bolt up in my bed and reach for my weapon, but my hand comes up empty. I close my eyes for just a second and calm my heart before I climb out of bed.

"Bang, Bang, Bang!"

"I'm comin'!" Swinging open the door, I shield my eyes from the bright light to see Corporal Ligaya standing there. "Corporal, I was up all night. You think I can get a bit of sleep?"

"I'm sorry sir," she says, "the General's ordered you to report to the main hangar bay immediately."

"What's going on?"

She shakes her head, the concern clear on her face. "I'm sorry, Sir. I don't know. It looks like someone's knocking on our door."

I stare at her for a moment, then nod. "Just a moment."

I shut the door and scramble into my uniform, and in less than a minute, I'm jogging down the hall with the Private leading the way. Once we enter the busy hallways, she hollers for people to get out of the way and most do, allowing us a quick run to the hangar.

The place is a buzz of activity. Soldiers clear civilians out of the area, and a second defense is nearly constructed halfway back through the hangar. One thing about the General, he's organized and gets the job done.

I dismiss the Private, and she heads off toward the new defense line. From the looks of things, the forward defense still holds, which means we're facing something out there that's unexpected, and the General wants a solid fall back.

Jogging up to the center of the room, I salute the General, and he nods back at me. He issues an order to a Private and shakes his head. "We gotta get the command structure put in place better than this. A General should never order a Private to get more ammunition."

"We're working on it, Sir."

He nods. "You've made a big difference in that regard, Colonel, but I guess now's not the time to complain. We have a bigger issue on the table."

"What's going on, Sir?"

"The *Taken* avoid this place, mostly, as you know. But standing about five hundred feet from the 50 cals are five of them. Just standing there in the middle of the road, staring at our gates."

I nod. Not much else I can do while I take that in. "Orders?"

"Hmph! Orders? Aside from preparing to defend?"

I smile. This General is very different from any officer I've ever met. "What's your protocol if they approach the gate?"

"We let 'em in, but we keep 'em under guard."

I catch the eye of Lieutenant Millar. At the moment, he's my go-to guy. As Millar's coming toward me, I ask the General, "Where's Major Gordon?"

"He's on his way up. He was down on Level 12 when I sent for him. I expect he'll be a few more minutes."

Millar arrives, and I order him to set up an intentional guard to follow the *Taken* if they come in. He gathers his soldiers, and we wait. A few minutes pass, then ten, then fifteen. Finally, word comes back that there's movement.

I hold the radio to my ear and listen to the soldier spell it out. "They're moving, Sir. Nothing threatening, just walking toward the gate. Orders?"

"As long as they do nothing threatening, let them come."

A few minutes later, I see them. It's late enough in the day that the sun's setting behind them, so I can't make out much of what I'm looking at right now, but the soldiers at the gate don't see a threat. I have my 9mm, picked up from the arms room, strapped to my side. I don't expect any danger, but I really don't know what to expect.

"One thing's for sure," I say as Major Gordon finally arrives, "they sure change up their strategy often enough."

"That they do, but some things always remain the same," the General says. "If the pattern holds true, this should be a heavily emotional appeal of some sort."

I nod slowly. I'd been thinking the same thing. From my experience, the pressure had amped up a lot over the weeks and months.

When they step into the hangar, I can finally see them well enough to recognize their faces, and my heart races, my mouth goes dry, and my hands shake. I clasp them behind my back to hide the reaction and stand there as confident as I can.

With every step closer, it's all I can do to keep my feet rooted to the spot.

"Colonel," the General whispers to me, "what's going on? You know them?"

I open my mouth, but nothing comes out at first. Clearing my throat, then taking a deep breath, I whisper back, "The two men… I don't know them. Not sure I've ever seen them before."

"And the woman and the two children?"

"Mine," I say. "My wife. My kids."

Major Gordon shakes his head slowly. "So, it's you they're after this time."

Somehow, knowing that doesn't make it any easier.

Connie… she looks good. Healthier, I think, than the last time I saw her. Her hair's combed, clothes are new, clean, pressed. She doesn't look as thin and starved as she did last time. Alliah's grown a bit. She stands a bit taller next to her mom than she'd been when I lost her, and the look on her face… it tugs at my heart. And Aaron. He's smiling. Holding his mom's hand, almost skipping as he walks beside her as if he can't… as if he can't wait to get to me. The looks on their faces aren't far off from what I used to see all the time when I came home after a mission.

Gordon barks out, "That's far enough!" and they come to a stop about ten feet from us.

No one says anything at first. I'm not sure what to say, but Aaron smiles and waves at me.

And then… their eyes… they stop glowing. I see Connie's blue eyes, Alliah's dark browns, and Aaron's light browns.

"Hello, Xavier," Connie says. "I've… missed you. We've… missed you."

Alliah nods and tears pour down her face. "We have, daddy. Why did you run from us? I needed you."

Aaron just turns and buries his face in Connie's side, hugging her tight. She rubs his back and pulls Alliah in close. "We've only just been out there, Xavier. Why haven't you come to us? We've needed you."

Alliah's face turns sour, and she grinds her teeth before her voice fills with accusation. "All you had to do was come out there! But I guess you liked your new family more!"

I take a deep breath again and smile. "No, I love you, but I can't come to you. Maybe you should come to me."

Connie shakes her head and laughs, the softness of her voice gone for a moment. "Come to you? We tried that life, don't you remember? Living on scraps we could find, hiding in holes in the ground. Sure, you have a bit more comfort now, but you're all alone. All of you. You've got nothing. We live in comfort and have everything we want. We don't have to hide and live in fear." She steps forward but stops when Millar raises his weapon. "Xavier, what we have now is so much better. It's foolish to stick with these people. We know! We've tried both lives, and the life we have now is far better! What you have… it means nothing. You're wasting your life away when you could have everything!"

"Connie, you don't know what you're saying. You can't see how the Greks are controlling you."

She frowns at me as her voice grows quiet and cold. "These people… they don't know you, Xavier. Not like I know you. I know what you're capable of. I know the things you've done. Do you think they'd let you be here, wear that uniform, if they knew?"

"We know who he is, Ma'am," General Williams says, speaking up for the first time. "He wears that uniform. What he was before is unimportant compared with who he is now."

She shakes her head. "Marines? Do you know what he used to say about you? He loved the Navy… he hated the Marines. He thought you were all weak, afraid, incapable."

"I'm a Marine now," I say quietly. "If that makes me weak, I'm good with that."

"Daddy," Aaron says. "Come back with us."

Aaron and Alliah both look up at their mom, and she wraps her arms around them. Turning back to face me, she whispers, "You could have this too. We could be a family again."

"Enough," General Williams barks. "Why have you come?"

One of the men in the back steps forward. As he moves, his eyes flicker back and forth from glowing white to normal but then settle to a steady light brown. "We want peace. This fighting back and forth… it has to stop. We know you all seem to want nothing but war, but we just want it to end. We want to get along. The rest of the world… everyone has peace. Except you. We're willing to share it with you. No more fighting. You'd be welcome out there with us, and you could open your doors to us. A cultural exchange, if you will."

"What kind of peace do you expect?" the General asks. "We're not willing to become whatever you've become. Whatever makes your eyes glow like that."

The man offers an ingratiating smile and holds his hands out as if he's trying not to offend. "The eyes… don't worry about them. That's just one of those benefits of opening yourself up to the freedom and peace we have, but as you can see, we can hide that, if you're afraid. Not everyone wants to take advantage of all we have."

"And if we refuse?" General Williams asks.

The man's face turns sad. "I know how hard it is to let go of the safety you think you have. I found that hard, too, at first, and I feared change like you do, but the more I opened my eyes to what our friends offer, the more I saw how much I'd been wanting it all along!" He shakes his head. "Maybe you shouldn't take our word for it. Why don't you come and speak with those you call the Greks."

"They talk?" Williams asks.

All five of the visitors laugh. I'm trying my best to keep my focus on the conversation, but Connie and the kids… they're staring at me. Now and then Aaron waves again, and I smile and wave back. I miss them so much.

"They do, although not quite like we talk." The man takes a small step forward and offers, "Tell you what, why don't you come? We'll promise your safety. You won't be harmed; no one will force you to do anything you're afraid to do."

"And where would this meeting take place?" Williams asks with a frown.

"In a neutral location, about a quarter of a mile out."

I glance at the General and am happy to see he's not buying any of it, but Gordon speaks up. "General, perhaps we should take a moment and speak privately."

General Williams nods slowly, keeping his eye on our visitors. Finally, he says, "You'll have to excuse us for a moment." Glancing at Millar, he orders, "Don't let them go anywhere."

Once we're out of hearing range—as far as we know—the General looks at each of us. "Thoughts?"

I shake my head. "I think it's a trap, Sir."

Williams nods, then turns to the Major. "Gordon?"

He pauses for a long time, looking back at the five *Taken* once, then twice. Finally, he says, "If there's a chance of peace, I think we need to take it. How can we pass up the opportunity to end the hiding and the fear? We owe it to all the people in the base, the entire L-O—military and civilians."

Williams nods slowly. He doesn't like it any more than I do, but Gordon's got a point. "All right, I'll go with them and see…"

I shake my head. "No, Sir. It can't be you. If this is a trap, we lose our leader right in one shot."

"Well, I can't very well send some Private or Corporal, nor can I send a civilian into what is almost certainly a trap!"

"I'll go," Gordon says.

I bite my lip and shake my head. "This isn't a good idea. We know the *Taken* retain a fair amount of their memories, maybe all of them. You know too much about the L-O and our plans."

"I agree," Williams says slowly, "but I'm not sure we have another option. The civilians who stand out as potential leaders at this point are also the very ones we suspect as being *Taken* among us." He slowly shakes his head, looking back at the five visitors, then at Gordon. "You sure you're up for this, Major?"

"I am, Sir. But I'll have to take a vehicle. I can't walk that far."

"Take one of the golf carts," Williams growls. Shaking his head, he adds, "The kids will probably get a kick of riding in the back."

We return to my family and the two others. This time, I keep my eyes firmly on the guy who spoke earlier. It's taking everything I've got just to keep my feet where they are. I so badly want to wrap my arms around my kids and my wife. But if I do that, I'm not sure I'll ever let go.

"We'll send Major Gordon," Williams growls, "but here are the terms. You meet within sight of the 50 cals, and I'm sending a squad with him for backup."

The man smiles again, but this time his eyes drift to the floor. Taking a deep breath, he looks back up at General Williams as if he feels sorry for him. "General, you are all so violent, always looking to shoot and kill and destroy." He shakes his head before he goes on. "We can certainly meet within sight, as long as you don't harm us. We are no threat to you. But a squad of soldiers… that's not going to work. Those you call the Greks know how violent you are. You've killed a lot of them." With that statement, his eyes flash with indignation for a moment before he smiles again. "They don't trust you, since you've killed so many of their kind. We're asking you to take a leap of faith, to step out in trust as we are stepping out in trust that Major Gordon won't harm us."

"He goes armed," Williams barks. The man standing across from us shakes his head, but Williams cuts him off. "That's a deal breaker!"

The man pauses for a moment as if considering it, then slowly nods, smiling again. "Alright, then. He can come armed."

Gordon orders a nearby soldier to retrieve one of the golf carts used in the hangar bay. I watch the soldier as he goes, moving through the entire situation in my mind. Once Gordon's on his way, I'll be setting up some extra protection.

"Xavier…" I'm drawn back to Connie, and my heart nearly breaks as I see the tears in her eyes. Neither Alliah nor Aaron are looking at me. Both my children have their faces buried in their mom's shirt with their arms tightly around her. In a voice meant only for me, Connie says, "Come with us…"

I take a step toward her, but at that moment, her eyes flicker, just for a second, back to yellow… of all colors, her eyes shift to attack!

I take two big steps away and shake my head. "No." In a whisper, I add, "I'll get you out. Somehow… I'll get you out."

The soldier sent to get the golf cart rolls up at that moment and steps out so Gordon can hop in. Lieutenant Millar hands him his XM7, and Williams adds, "Major, your orders are to remain within sight of the 50 cals at all times. Is that clear?"

"Yes, Sir!"

I stay back while everyone piles on, and I make a point not to look at my wife and kids. My heart goes out to them, but it's not just the physical distance that separates us. Either I have to give up my life to the Greks, or they need to be broken free from the Grek's control.

Until one of those things happens, we'll never have what we had.

I watch them ride away. Aaron keeps waving at me, but Alliah just buries her face in her mom's shirt. I need to focus.

"Millar!"

"Yes, Colonel."

"I want two snipers, one next to each 50 cal in two minutes."

"Yes, Sir!"

While Millar scrambles to get the snipers in position, I turn to the General. He raises his eyebrows and asks, "What's on your mind, Colonel?"

"I don't think this is a good idea."

"I don't either, but Gordon's right. If there's a possibility of peace, we have to at least explore it."

I nod. "I know, but…" I take a step closer. "If this goes south, we're going to need to either ramp up our run for the mothership or scrap the plan altogether."

"Agreed, Colonel. How soon can you be on the move?"

"We're ready, Sir. I can be on the move in three hours."

"Make your preparations. I want to be ready to go the second anything feels off."

"Yes, Sir."

I wave for Millar and issue the orders, now that he's assigned the snipers. He knows everything has to be done quietly, and he's ready. He's leading one team. Corporal Ligaya has another. We're so short on officers, I'm putting a Corporal in charge of ten people! I'll lead the last team.

I shake my head and catch the eye of Ligaya as she runs by. "My office, Corporal! Now!"

She falls in step behind me. I'm sure Millar's given her orders she has to fill, but soldiers don't work well without a clear chain of command. I need to fix that little problem. When we reach my office, I head to my desk. "You have orders, Corporal?"

"Yes, Sir."

"What are they?"

"Lieutenant Millar ordered me to secure my team at the northern gate."

"Have you given your team their orders yet, Private?"

"Yes, Sir. I was on my way to the arms room to suit up."

"You need to take care of this first," I say as I toss her the new insignia. "Sew that on, Sergeant Major. I don't appreciate soldiers out of uniform!"

She looks at it in awe for a moment. Same look Millar gave when I made him a Lieutenant. "Thank you, Sir. I'll do my best."

"I know, Sergeant Major. You wouldn't have that if I thought for a second you'd let me down. Dismissed."

She salutes and heads out.

Rank… Corporals bumped up to Sergeant Major, NCOs becoming officers… we're putting a lot of trust in each other. Trust that hasn't been earned, but I still think it's well placed in Millar and Ligaya. Assuming we make it back, and she lives up to her potential, she'll be a Lieutenant shortly after we return. Which means I need some more Sergeants. More Captains. More of everything.

17

TIME TO MOVE

By the time I get back to the hangar, the snipers are in place, but Williams is mad. Really mad.

When I reach him, he's pacing back and forth. "Sir?"

"Colonel! The Major just stepped out of sight! He was standing there, talking to a group of *Taken*, then he just moved forward, down the hill. I sent a dozen soldiers to ascertain the situation."

My jaw begins to ache, and I have to force myself to unclench my teeth. I want to go out there myself, but I have to trust the troops. With a growl, I head out the hangar door. At least I can get a better view. When I reach the towers at the gate, I climb up the one on my left. At the top, I order, "Report!"

The woman on the 50 cal salutes but turns her attention right back to the gun while she speaks. "Sir, the Major stood within sight for about four minutes, right at the crest of that hill, there, then two people came and coaxed him forward. At first, they just spoke to him, but then they grew upset, judging from the hand-waving and jumping around, and he went with them. The soldiers should be there any moment."

A Jeep and a truck have nearly reached the Major's empty golf cart. No sign of Gordon. I grab a pair of binoculars from one of the hooks and scan the area, trying to catch some sign of him, but I see nothing. When the soldiers in the vehicles reach the crest of the hill, they come to a halt, and in seconds, they're out of the vehicles and spreading around the area, guns ready.

I still see nothing, but the soldiers aren't moving down the hill, nor are they firing. They're just waiting there. I listen to my radio as they report back to the General.

"Sir, we have eyes on the Major. He's down the road just far enough that he's out of sight of the L-O. He looks fine, Sir. He waved for us to remain back. Doesn't look harmed. He's there with a handful of *Taken* and three Greks. Orders?"

"Tell him his orders are to return immediately," General Williams replies.

"Yes, Sir."

I watch as they relay the orders, then hear, "Sir, he's coming back."

A few moments later, Gordon comes into view and climbs into the golf cart. One soldier joins him in the cart, and the other vehicles escort him back.

I can't stop myself from scowling. A simple meet and greet, and he steps out of sight in minutes! By the time I get down the ladder, the Jeep has reached the gates, and I stand to the side as it goes by, followed by the golf cart, and lastly, the truck.

Jogging to catch up, I get there about the time the General comes face to face with the Major. At first, I think the General is going to knock him down a few ranks right there on the spot, but he takes a moment to calm himself before saying, "I'm assuming, Major, you had a good reason for disobeying my orders."

"General, my apologies, but in the moment, I felt it was a good tactical decision."

"Explain it to me then, Major." The General waves the other soldiers away, and the Major waits while they clear out.

When we're out of hearing range of even the best ears, the Major whispers, "They were right, General. The Greks want peace."

"They really do speak?" I ask. I've taken up position behind the Major. Not sure what to expect, but the fact that he was out of sight for that long is concerning.

The Major glances back over his shoulder at me for a second, then addresses the General again. "Yes, they speak… or… well… not exactly. There was no sound, and I couldn't understand it completely, but I got bits and pieces. The man who spoke here translated it. I think they have some kind of telepathy."

"Mind readers," the General growls. "Perfect. At least that explains how they can send out family members and friends to meet our troops when they're out there."

"Absolutely, Sir," Gordon says enthusiastically. "They're… good… Sir. I mean, they're kinder and happier than a lot of the people here. We'd do well to either open our doors wide to them or go out there and join them." He glances back at me and then at the General again. "Do you notice something different about me?"

The General's hand goes to the weapon strapped at his waist, and I notice my 9mm is halfway out of its holster, my finger on the safety. "What's different?"

The Major shakes his head quickly. "No, Sir, nothing bad! Look!"

Gordon looks down and spreads his hands wide. At first, I don't see it, but then it hits me, although the General gets there first. "No cane."

"No! That's why I went down there, out of sight. I took a chance. There were two Greks there. Neither one threatened me, but they fixed my knee, my entire leg. I have to admit, I've never felt so good in my life!"

My mouth drops open. I saw the report. The doctor spelled it out to me. The Major would never heal without a complete knee replacement.

"We'll need Doctor Liu to take a look at that…" the General begins.

"Sir, we can certainly do all the tests you want, but I must relay the message."

"What message?"

"The Greks… they're not all that different from us, from what we have here. They're a strongly hierarchical society. The ones I met are actually the highest-ranking Greks on the continent. But the problem is, they don't want to discuss terms with me."

"And why not?" the General asks slowly.

"Because I'm just a Major. When they found out I was the third highest ranking officer in this base, and—we're the only ones digging in our heels on the entire western hemisphere, by the way—which again, I think we could welcome them in, Sir…"

"Focus, Major! What's this about rank?"

"They don't want to discuss anything with me, Sir. They want to talk to you, General. At the very least, they would consider the Colonel, but rank means everything to them."

"You learned all this in just those few moments, Major?" General Williams asks.

The Major hesitates for just a moment, but then he spreads his hands wide. "The man who spoke for the Greks spoke quickly. They are very focused and direct, Sir."

"What about other world leaders?" Williams asks. "If we're all that's left on this continent, what about other nations?"

"Most of them have been given the same offer and taken it. Many of the nations of the world are rebuilding their homes, their lives. They tell me the President and Prime Minister of India agreed to peace with the Greks a week ago, and already the people are mostly back to normal. Ukraine just joined them the week before. Here on this continent, the last few holdouts accepted the Grek's peace two months back. We're the only ones holding out. Anywhere!"

The General frowns and shakes his head. "We're going to have to think about this, Major."

Gordon steps forward, and my 9mm comes right out of its holster. "Sir," Gordon says, "they're eager to get this worked out. They might wait a day or two, but they're nervous. The two Grek leaders on this continent have taken quite a risk coming out like this."

General William's expression softens, and he actually smiles at Major Gordon, "Well, if they don't threaten us, we won't need to defend ourselves. Even so, we would like a couple of days."

"That's good to know, Sir. I don't think they're our enemies. Perhaps if they know they're not in danger from us, they'll be content to wait."

General Williams' smile grows, and he steps up to the Major. Putting his hand on Gordon's shoulder, he turns him back towards the center of the base. "Thank you, Major. I'll send someone out with our request for more time. For now, I'd like you to see Doctor Liu. I'd like that knee checked out."

As the Major steps away, the General gives me a quick nod, and I turn around and catch the eye of Lieutenant Millar. He and Ligaya stand casually next to one of the Jeeps, and Millar gives me the slightest nod back.

The mission's a go.

I stand before the thirty men and women.

On each team, we have four soldiers and six civilians. That's an absolutely terrible setup—it's like we're trying to fail. Typically, if I had to send two civilians into the field, I'd smother them in trained soldiers.

But that's not an option. We need speed. We need stealth. We need small groups. Small, focused teams. And the soldiers are really only going along to keep the civilians alive.

The civilians on each team have their strengths, for sure, but I selected each one because of their general knowledge of Grek technology. Not to fix it if it breaks, but to work it and figure out what they don't know. The six civilians on each team are capable, we believe, of piloting the spacecraft, working the onboard life support, weapons, and general operation of the ship. It would be best to have all eighteen civilians, with the twelve soldiers for security, but if only one team gets through, we should manage. In theory.

"Listen up!" I call out. "I'm not one for speeches, so don't expect some kind of rousing pep talk. We leave in five. Millar, Ligaya, make sure your teams are ready and report to me in three."

Turning to my team, I make eye contact with each of them in turn. I was hesitant to have Gerb on my team, but he's brilliant. There's no doubt about it. I would have thought someone with a chemistry focus would not be necessary for a mission like this, but he and Logan are naturals with the Grek technology. On top of their general ability, from what we understand of piloting the ship, they were each two of the better candidates to fly the thing.

Unfortunately, Gerb and Logan have shown themselves incapable of working together. Not that they fight or argue, but they get each other worked up and distracted. If we even let them stand too close while working on what they call the *Grektech*, they lose all discipline and focus.

"Gerb!" I bark at the boy. "Get back with your troop!"

"Uh, right…" he says, cautiously, remembering at the last moment to tag on the "Sir!" He isn't one for rank and formality, but he's managing. I don't mind, actually. He's not a soldier, and he's certainly needed on this team.

"Is everyone ready?"

The soldiers all respond with a "Yes, Sir!" and the civilians give everything from a nod to an awkward salute. Gerb actually sneezes his response and appears pleased that he could time it just right.

"We've been over this many times, but I can't stress this enough," I begin, addressing the six civilians before me. Among them, Gerb and Elizabeth stand near each other. I don't think the standing arrangement was Elizabeth's doing, by the look on her face. "I need to know that each of you will follow orders immediately. If I order you to hide, you hide. If I order you to run straight at a dozen Greks, you run with all you've got. You have to trust the soldiers to do their job. We're there to get you where you're going, which means you don't worry about us. Don't give our safety a moment's thought. You worry about following orders. Clear?"

They all nod their response this time. In times past, they looked confident, excited even. Today, they look like they're about to be sick. Everyone that is, unfortunately, aside from Gerb. I wish the kid would get how serious this is.

As we move out of the large storage room where we've assembled and into the emptied receiving bay where we're heading out, I begin to wish Fred were among us. If it weren't for his bad knees and back, he'd be on my team. The man's resourceful. I don't doubt that he'd be overwhelmed on the ship, and the tech boggles him, but I could use his steady voice and focus.

The soldiers at the gate have been chosen for their trustworthiness. The *Taken* seem able to hide their identity well, but there's been nothing to suggest these men and women are anything but free of Grek control. I hate having to wonder about our own soldiers. Sadly, it's the road we're on right now.

Slipping out the gate into the cool, dark night, we quickly move in among the rubble. Under the guise of extra security, we've set up cameras throughout this area, which means we know there's no one for the first leg of the journey.

We head north, as that's where the ship lies. Apparently, General Williams, back when he still had contact with others around the world, knew of another twenty-three ships here and there around the globe. Since this one hasn't moved, we suspect the others are still in the same places. The reason we're calling this the mothership is that from what we've learned, this is certainly one of the bigger ones around.

The Greks have a few smaller ships they use as well. At one point, we considered one of the smaller ones since they're less well guarded, but if Gordon's truly compromised, which we're pretty sure he has been, then our plans are revealed. He knew our interest was divided between the mothership and the smaller ship. The two advantages we have left now are the questions of timing and which ship. The third advantage is if Gordon's knowledge is in the hands of the Greks, we can use that against them.

When we reach the edge of the area covered by the cameras, I signal Millar and Ligaya, and they split off with their teams.

Three teams, three different directions.

Three different approaches to the same objective.

We rush into a small crevice, still within sight of the cameras, so I know it's clear, and we pull out the camo suits with the heat resistant layer. The night is warmer than I'd like, considering we're wearing such a heavy layer, but we can wash the sweat off. A shower won't wash away whatever the Greks do to people.

Confirming that everyone is all suited up properly, I nod to Corporal Adesina. She's impressed me in the short time I've worked with her. Everything she's taught, she learns the first time and applies it with enthusiasm. I'll promote her soon enough.

She nods back, and I'm reminded that her twin sister is out here somewhere. She told me she's run into her on missions out amongst the destroyed city on three occasions, and it's torn her apart each time. Yet, she stands strong. In fact, her strength has pushed me to carry on when I think of Connie, Alliah, and Aaron.

"Let's move."

The others follow me out, with Adesina bringing up the rear. We should arrive within six hours, if all goes well. On a straight run with soldiers and no obstacles, I'd expect to cover the ten miles in a little over an hour, even in the dark. But I'm concerned with this group. Six hours might be optimistic, but we can't push it beyond that. Any longer and the sun might make a showing. We need the cover of darkness to make our approach.

MOTHERSHIP

As the hours wear on, we move through the empty streets and dark alleys. Two of my soldiers have night vision goggles. We, unfortunately, have a limited supply back at the L-O, and since the civilians aren't equipped to wear them, I decided only select soldiers would.

At the moment, with the moon and stars, I prefer my own eyes.

"Grek, 11 o'clock!" Chavez hisses in the dark.

I lead our team off to the left and behind an old truck on its side with the flatbed nearly ripped off. With its position, it provides the perfect cover and the chance to observe the Grek. I peer up around the grill of the truck. The smell of old grease and oil are common smells, but the strong smell of radiator fluid tells me the truck was likely flipped recently. Sometimes, I've noticed the Greks get bored or whatever the Grek equivalent is and wreak a little extra havoc.

Chavez and Stewart will obviously have a better view than I have as they both have goggles, but I study the Grek in the dark, its outline clear against the night sky, now that I know it's there. The eyes of the Grek face east, which explains why it doesn't seem to know we're here. I can see slits with the green light casting an eerie glow on the hairy body. I've often wondered if they sleep during the night. Perhaps it's asleep right now, but it's too great a risk to take.

I signal to Stewart, and he confirms through his night vision goggles that the alley to my left is clear. A moment later, Corporal Adesina skirts around me and down the dark alleyway with Gerb right on her heels, followed by Elizabeth, then Stewart, then others. Lastly, I enter the alley and move along carefully. I fear we'll be seeing a lot of Greks from here on out.

————•——•——●——•——•————

Three hours later, we're just coming up on the area with the mothership.

The last time I was here was the day I chased the Greks carrying my wife and son to their doom. Now, months later, I won't stop a quarter of a mile out, abandoning two loved ones and hoping to find the one left. This time, I'm taking a risk. Risking my life and the lives of others, hoping to rescue not only my wife and children, but the wives and children and husbands and friends and parents and more of everyone we can.

"It's huge!" Gerb says. "I…"

"Quiet!" I snap. We're safe here, I believe, but the rule was Gerb can't speak until I give him permission. Once that kid starts, there's no stopping him. Turning to the Private closest to me, I order, "Chavez, confirm the other teams are in position."

While Chavez sends out the signal, I survey the area with my binoculars. As expected, the ground in this area is blanketed in Greks and the *Taken*. They've focused a lot of attention on this area of late. I suspect that's in response to information leaking out through the spies among us, but it changes nothing today.

I'd guess there's over two hundred Greks down there, and perhaps a thousand, maybe two thousand *Taken*—it's difficult to see for sure in the dark. The Greks stand out

192

somewhat, but the *Taken*, most of them are on the ground, likely sleeping.

On this side of the ship, and far to my left, sits that large structure through which Connie and Aaron were carried that day I lost them. I force myself to examine it. The large bay doors sit open—if there are even doors on that opening—and no light shines from within. It all seems as quiet as the rest of the valley.

The mothership sits in a bit of a valley in the center of all the Greks and *Taken*. It's huge. I expect thousands could enter it and still have plenty of room for… well, we don't know what else might be in a Grek mothership. The top and sides are round with a nose that comes to a point, and large oval exhausts, at least we think that's what they are, stick out the back.

So much guesswork here. We're having to rely on the geeks and scientists with us, hoping they can figure it out based on what they've learned of the Grek technology.

Gerb's beside me, inching closer by the second. His breathing is fast and not because of our six-hour journey. I'm sure he's exhausted from that, but the gasping, the shaking hands… he's excited. And when he gets excited…

I raise my index finger and put it to my lips, shaking my head. I know he wants to tell me everything he's thinking right now. Smart move to separate him from Logan.

He turns to head toward Elizabeth, but I grab the back of his pack and pull him away, shaking my head. This kid's a genius, no doubt about it, but he has a lot to learn about self-control. He'd have done well with some more of Fred's influence, or perhaps some military experience.

The primary door to enter the ship is facing us, but that's not where we expect to enter. It's large—big enough for forty or fifty people to march through, shoulder to shoulder. It's about half the height of the ship, and swings down from the side. The entrance we plan to use is on the far side of the ship, but we chose this approach as it offers a little more cover.

"Sir, everyone's in position," Chavez whispers.

A smile finds its way onto my face. The other teams are my responsibility. Knowing they've made it safely takes a weight off my shoulders.

Turning back to Chavez, I hiss, "Send the signal."

He nods and crouches down around his radio while I motion for everyone to gather around. By the time they reach me, Chavez has finished his task and has joined us. "Listen, don't speak," I say, knowing Gerb and maybe even Elizabeth might take this as an opening to talk. "From here on out, it's even more important to remain silent. The goal is to get through and onto the ship, not comment or discuss anything. Warnings are allowed, but even that has to be spoken as silently as possible and only in extreme situations."

I hate to stress this so much, but three out of the six civilians never seemed to grasp how dangerous this mission is. The closest we could get to it was Gerb telling us he thought it would be a fun adrenaline rush.

"We will move in a single file. I lead, Corporal Adesina will bring up the rear, and the rest of you have your assigned positions. Don't change the plan for anything without permission, but since you're not to speak unless there's an extreme emergency, I doubt you'll get permission. We will follow the outside of the field as much as possible. Do not signal to the other team. If we are captured, do not cry out for them to help us. If one team goes down, the others need to make it through, not stop to help. Understood?"

They all nod, and I give a stern look to Gerb when he opens his mouth.

"Chavez, what's the count?"

"Seventy-eight seconds, Sir."

"Good, form up!"

Adesina gets everyone in place, and I glance back at Chavez. "Fifty-Seven seconds, Sir."

Once we feared the Greks had compromised Major Gordon, the plan went through a quick revision. The original plan had favored capturing the smaller ship. We were going to use a diversion in the area around the ship to draw the Greks and *Taken* away, allowing us to slip in and board the ship. If we were to go after the mothership, we would use a similar tactic with a diversion in this region to pull the Greks and *Taken* away. So, the original plan required a diversion *near* the target ship.

Now that we're after the mothership, we've made a slight change. The plan is to cause the diversion around the smaller ship, even though that's far away from our position. Assuming Gordon's compromised, the Greks and *Taken* should believe we're carrying out the plan to take the small ship, just earlier than expected, and head right there, leaving us a clear run at the mothership.

We hope…

I watch the people below, and my heart goes out to Connie and the kids. Part of me wondered when I heard her talk, and the kids—Aaron waved at me, Alliah cried—are they really controlled by the Greks? Am I just being foolish and stubborn? Could I truly have the life I want with them alongside the Greks? Am I just paranoid? Shouldn't I just go join them?

I give the signal to Chavez, and a moment later he confirms the order has gone through. The diversion should happen sometime in the next few seconds. We won't hear it, of course, as the smaller ship is too far away, but the way the Greks communicate, word will spread quickly to this area.

Chavez gives me a thumbs up letting me know he's received confirmation that the diversion—an explosion mixed with the signal that attracts the Greks—has happened, and my mouth drops open as I watch the reaction in the valley below. All doubt of whether or not Connie is under Grek control slides from my mind. Every… single… Grek and every… single… *Taken* that I can see in the dark reacts immediately. The *Taken* and Greks on their feet turn as one toward the noise. Those on the ground—every last one of them—sit up at the exact same moment and turn toward the sound. In seconds, they're all running in that direction.

Greks move much faster, of course, their feet thudding on the open land. The *Taken* stampeding alongside them create a different sound. Not one of them yells or hollers or says a word. It's a silent running, only the sound of their feet on the ground makes any noise.

But as the Greks run, their giant legs crashing down among the *Taken*, not a single *human* is harmed. They miss one another. No one trips. No one bumps into another. They all run, faster, slower, larger, smaller, older, younger… every single Grek and every single *Taken* moves as though controlled by one voice.

That is *not* natural.

My Connie and my kids, no matter how much they sound like they used to, they are not free. Not anymore than anyone else down there.

"Follow me," I hiss.

We have a bit more freedom for noise right now as no one would hear us above the roar of the stampede, but we still keep silent. I lead the team down a small hill of rubble onto the grass below. The Greks and *Taken* race by about eighty feet to our left, but they move away from us and away from the assigned positions of the other teams.

Skirting around the outside of the giant field, I lead the team in the general direction of the mothership. At this point, we could probably go straight toward it as the Greks and *Taken* have covered quite a distance already, but we stick to the plan. Once they're gone, then we'll cut across the field, directly to our door. At that point, we'll have precious little time before they realize what we're up to.

We move, crouched over, as fast as we can. The soldiers among us make the occasional cricket sound to indicate that the civilians are slowing, and I bring my pace down a little, but despite that, we push on through the darkness.

The cricket sound changes, and I glance to my left to confirm. The area appears clear of Greks and *Taken*. Another cricket signal sounds to indicate that Chavez and Stewart, each with their night vision goggles, believe the area is entirely clear.

"Move!" I hiss.

We straighten and make a run directly for the door on the far side. At the pace we suspect the civilians can maintain by this point in the journey and over the thick grass, it'll be just over sixty seconds to the crest of the hill leading down into the valley, then another seventy-five seconds until we reach the door. After that point, it's difficult to know what to expect, only that each of the teams should arrive at roughly the same time.

Movement off to my left catches my eye. Sergeant Major Ligaya's team. I can't spare the concentration to count, just have to assume she's lost no one.

No sign yet of Millar's team.

We reach the crest of the hill and stop, crouching down. Chavez and Stewart give the signal again that it's all clear, and we race into the valley. There are no lights on or around the ship—we suspect the Greks can see fairly well in the dark— but we know where the landing gear for the ship comes down, and we can see well enough to move ahead.

I nearly growl aloud as I'm forced to slow down more than expected, however, because of the dark but a turned ankle now will slow us even more. The good news here is the ground in this area is well used, and since the ship has sat here for months, the grass is brown and flattened to the dirt. Reaching the doorway from behind, we come around and wait while Chavez and Stewart look up into the ship for signs of movement. Another weight comes off my shoulder as Chavez gives the signal that it's clear.

Ligaya's team comes around and goes through the same process. I insisted each team check, just in case, rather than trust the others at this stage. I wave the soldiers forward, and we wait until the "all clear" signal comes back again, then Ligaya and I lead the civilians into the ship.

"Sergeant!" I hiss. "Millar?"

"Coming, Sir. Just a bit behind."

I glance back to see him come into view. He goes through the same process yet again that each of our teams went through: confirm the way is clear, soldiers enter the ship, then civilians follow.

We're in complete darkness, but some of the tech we received gave a bit of a floor plan for a few ships. We believe that while this ship may be laid out differently, we're hoping it won't be too different.

"Ligaya, lead us on!" I whisper, loud enough for the others to hear.

We move through the ship in a clump. I can't see a thing which is a strategic mistake, but I have to trust my soldiers with the night vision goggles to lead well at this point. From the signals traveling back along the line of people, there's still no sign of Grek or *Taken*. We feared the ship could be packed full—we still don't know where all the missing people are—but an empty ship… that was our dream.

By my count, the Greks will have figured out we fooled them right about now, which means we have less than four minutes until they're back. That's not good news.

"This is it!" Ligaya hisses. "Lights!"

A loud clack rings out, the sound of the portable lights hitting the steel deck of the bridge, and I shield my eyes. A moment later, a blinding light fills the room.

"Everyone!" I order. "Take your stations!"

They all know what to do, but everyone stumbles for the first few seconds as our eyes adjust.

The room we're in is large—maybe sixty feet across, round with consoles everywhere. The civilians with us will have to figure out where their stations are and then work together to get everything up and running, but they don't take long to find what they're looking for. Based on the floor plans we had, the control centers followed similar layouts, so navigation, ship operations, weapons, and more should be easy to find. Should…

"Get those doors closed!" I order.

Gerb's on that team, and they're working fast. Gerb keeps trying to talk about how excited he is, but the two scientists with him keep telling him to be quiet. He doesn't seem to mind, nor does he seem to notice that the command "be quiet" isn't something that should have to be repeated every few seconds.

"Got it!" Gerb shouts, so loudly I instinctively go for my weapon.

"Quiet!" the man beside him hisses, but Gerb's shout is nothing compared to the sound the ship makes as it comes alive. Lights turn on, systems boot up, and the shake in the floor makes me think the engines have started.

"Outer doors closed," Gerb announces, and I relax a little.

Once the doors are shut, we believe we can keep the Greks out, although… there's more we don't know here than we do.

"Engines?" I ask.

"Getting it figured out, Xavier… um… Sir," Elizabeth calls back. "They're running… but… uh… I think… there! Got it!"

The ship lurches and everyone, including Elizabeth on the controls, falls to the deck. A moment later, she scrambles back to the console, and the ship levels out.

I turn to Millar and order, "Secure the ship."

"Yes, Sir!"

We're only going to do a partial securing of it now as the ship is far bigger than a small team can manage, but when we get back to the L-O and get more soldiers on board, that'll be the first task. The second task… well… we'll have to move fast.

Millar leaves two soldiers at the entrance to the control center… the Bridge… and then moves off down the lighted corridors. I turn up my radio so I can hear them as they sound off, announcing room after room, clear of any form of life. We have tranqs for the *Taken*, and tranqs for the Greks, but I'm hoping we won't have to use either.

"Can you fly this thing back to the L-O?" I call out. So much is riding on "if". We're all taking a chance here, and pretty much everything is riding on that one question.

"Working on it," a man at the same station as Elizabeth replies. "It's tricky figuring out directions with their interface." He mumbles something I don't quite catch to the others at his station, then someone at the station next to him hollers out, "I think I can help with that."

I go for my sidearm in reaction to what I see, but catch myself before I put a bullet through the hull. In front of the navigation section, a video screen... no... just the video, floating there, appears with just a sliver of light at first, then expands into a view of what's in front of us.

"Am I right in assuming that we're facing the ground right now?" I ask.

"Seems like it," Elizabeth says slowly. "We figured the ship had to have some kind of way to control gravity, so perhaps we just can't feel that we're on this angle."

"Can you fix it?" I growl.

She... shrugs.

I mean, she actually shrugs!

"Well, do something!" I order. "I don't want to fly to the L-O with our nose pointed at the ground. That won't inspire confidence, now will it?"

"No, Sir!" Elizabeth mumbles. "Maybe if we…"

I flip forward and slam into the side of an unoccupied station, then find myself dangling by my fingers a moment later, gripping the edge of the station.

"I think… that might… have been the gravity controls…" she says, grunting from the far end of the Bridge.

"I think you might be right, Elizabeth," I say sarcastically. "NOW FIX IT!"

I hit the ground a moment later, and by the time I get to my feet, Elizabeth has the entire ship right-way-up. Judging from the view of the ground whipping by below us, I'm guessing we're also traveling.

"Are we heading in the right direction?"

"Yyyy…esssss."

I frown. "That's the least confident 'yes' I've ever heard in my life, Elizabeth."

In a quiet voice, she says, "Sorry, Sir. I've never driven a spaceship before."

I pause, then smile. "Well, you now have more experience than any human I know, so we're counting on you!"

I take a moment and look around the room again, and I find myself nodding. Gerb and the others were right. I'm sure of it. They thought the Greks weren't the original owners or creators of the technology. Gerb based his theory considering both the design of the interfaces and a gut feeling, thinking the original designers were humanoid. The way my people fit the room so well and can work the controls so easily—what they can figure out, anyway—makes it pretty clear the Greks aren't likely comfortable in here. Add to that the height of the ceilings—they're around nine feet, maybe nine and a half—this entire ship must have been a real squeeze for them on the journey here.

It also explains why the Greks don't often enter the ship.

I continue to listen to Millar and the others sound off on room after room. Somehow, they managed to survive the *gravity issue* a moment ago. As hoped, the ship appears empty. I hope it truly is.

"Colonel Xavier, Sir," Gerb says, "I have a button I want to press."

I look at the others standing with him. I'm sure my expression must communicate what I would assume everyone in the world also would think in response to a statement like that at a time and place like this.

"Uh," one of the women says, "I… think it might be a good button to press."

I roll my eyes. "Give me more."

"If I'm reading this right," Gerb says slowly, "I think it'll give us a whack of view screens."

Shaking my head, I order, "Then press it!"

"Okay," he says. As he reaches for it, I'm sure he mumbles, "or it'll fire a rocket…"

"What's that about a…" but I'm cut off by a series of screens appearing here and there around the Bridge. A smile works its way up onto my face, but only for a second. "Wait… what's that on the third view screen to the left?"

Elizabeth looks up and says, "I think that's the rear view."

I jog over to that area to get a better view and then quickly order, "Elizabeth, maintain your speed but turn us to the west! Do not stop at the L-O!"

"But, Sir…"

"You have your orders!"

I watch one of the side screens as we come within about half a mile of the base and then leave it behind. At this speed, I think in an hour we'll be far away from the Last Outpost.

"Sir?" Elizabeth asks.

"From what I'm seeing behind us, the Greks are following us. We knew that was a possibility, but we didn't expect that many. I think just about every Grek in the region is on our tail. That'll make settling back in at the base a terrible idea. There's no telling what they'll do, but there's as good a chance as any that they'll attack."

"Won't they know we're just trying to lead them away?" Hennessey asks from beside Elizabeth. "I mean… they could attack the L-O anyway."

"They could," I say slowly. Shaking my head, I add, "We'll have to hope they don't."

Williams and I discussed this possibility briefly. If there were a lot of Greks on our tail, and they appeared threatening, we were to take the chance of heading off on our own, just for a bit. Williams was going to signal me if they attacked the L-O so we could return, but neither of us believe they'll do that.

We continue for another hour, and I radio down to Millar to keep going on his search of the ship. The original plan was to search out the area around the Bridge, but now we might be on our own for a while. Maybe we can even get a couple floors done. The more the better. I want to know what's on my ship!

I watch the four people on the weapons console. That was the one station we were most concerned about. We had little to no information on that technology, so the four of them just studied everything we had, hoping they could apply what they knew. I haven't yet asked, as I can see they've been deep in thought and quiet conversation, shaking their heads and growing more frustrated by the moment. But as I watch, something changes, so I call out, "Weapons status!"

"Sir!" Adeline Messier calls back. She leads that team as she has an outstanding track record of solid guesses when it comes to Grek technology. "We think we have access to everything now; we just don't know what everything is."

"Explain!"

"For the last hour or so, we've been trying to gain access to the weapons—getting nowhere, actually. Finally, we chanced upon a switch that needed to be turned sideways…"

"Not interested in learning how to operate it, Messier! Just need an update." Civilians always struggle to work in these kinds of situations.

"Sorry, Sir," she says, and I hear the frustration in her voice. "All that to say, we now know how to fire and control everything. We just don't know what each of these weapons does. This one here, for instance, could fire a single bullet, some kind of energy weapon, a bomb, a nuke… who knows!"

"Fire something you suspect is small into space."

"Okay," she says with a laugh, shaking her head. "Firing… now."

I watch her view screen as an orange light shoots off into the sky.

"Do you know what that did?" I ask.

"No… oh… wait…"

Messier and the four men with her crowd around the console, talking quickly and quietly together. When nothing seems to come my way, I bark, "I need an update!"

"Oh," she says with a laugh, all frustration gone from her voice. "After we fired it, a report flashed up on a screen. If we're interpreting this right, that was some kind of stun. We… think… it's not for people, but for ships."

"That's handy. Does this give you information on anything else?"

"Maybe, Sir, we need to check something else we didn't understand before, but might now…"

I leave them to their work while they go back to their excited whispers, and I turn to navigation. "Elizabeth. I want you to find an area that seems relatively clear of people and Greks and other ships. A place where you can practice landing. If we have the time, we might as well use it."

She nods slowly, and her team moves around the navigation panel. Unlike the other consoles, it looks like they can access navigation from every side. Seems disorienting to me, but then again, whoever these people were who made this ship, they weren't us.

"Millar! Give me an update!" I wait, listening for the squawk of the radio. Nothing at first, so I radio him again. Still nothing.

I'm about to order one of the soldiers stuck guarding the Bridge to head down there when I hear something. Millar's voice comes through the radio, but I can barely hear him. I turn up the volume as loud as I can and order him to repeat the message. "Sir, Millar here, we're two decks down. No Greks, nothing, until now. We just came across a large room, maybe three hundred feet across and sixty feet high. It's packed full of Greks, Sir. Hundreds of them. Sleeping or hibernating or something. Not sure."

I grind my teeth and shake my head. Here I was, hoping we'd found the ship empty. "If there's no sign of movement, leave a soldier there—OUTSIDE the door… he's not to enter without a direct order. Let him keep an eye on 'em. You continue the search."

"Yes, Sir."

That complicates things. "Gerb!"

"Yes, Xav… Colonel."

"Locate a room, two decks down, approximately three hundred feet wide by sixty feet high."

He goes at the panel in front of him, focusing hard on figuring it all out. I wanted him on the console overseeing the general operation of the ship, not weapons, not navigation, but general operation. Less distraction for learning how to do a flip in the air or shoot a comet or asteroid if we make it into space. Besides, the boy does well with multitasking and operations should give him enough to keep him from distractions.

I hope.

"Got it!" he says and then gives himself a fist bump.

Shaking my head, I order, "Give me everything you know about that room."

"Well," he begins, "the size is about right. The door the Lieutenant likely used to get in there is maybe six by eight feet, and I think I can lock it securely from here, so they're not likely a threat to us—at least right away. I don't think they can get out if I lock it, but if they can, that doorway's small enough it'll slow them down if they break through."

"How did they get into that room? I doubt hundreds of Greks squeezed their way through the hallways and then through that door, just so they could sleep."

He nods, slowly. One of the others at his console leans over to give him a hand, but without taking his eyes off the screen, he puts his finger on the man's forehead and slowly pushes him back.

I nearly tell him off, but he speaks before I can. "I think there's something on the outside wall."

The ship lurches and shakes, nearly knocking us all to the floor.

My radio squawks and I hear Millar shout, "Sir, Chavez just radioed me. An outside door just opened in the room with the Greks."

"Millar, tell Chavez to hold, and you get back there." Grabbing hold of the edge of a console amidst the shaking of the ship, I growl, "GERB!"

"Sorry, Colonel, I… I thought there was some kind of… scanner or something on the wall, but it turns out it's a large loading ramp."

Through the radio, I holler, "Millar. I need confirmation. Are the Greks still hibernating?"

"I'll confirm, Sir."

I wait while Millar gets a hold of Chavez, then I finally hear, "They're waking, Sir, but they're not fast about it. Chavez says none of them are even on their feet yet."

"I need options, Gerb!"

"Uh, we could dump them, Sir."

I take a moment to let that settle in. "Explain!"

"Maybe we could… angle the ship… you know… with the doors open. Gravity might solve our problem for us."

"Gerb, seal the door leading into the Greks' room."

Over the radio, I holler, "Millar, radio me the moment you reach the room and confirm Chavez is safe, then secure yourself. We're going to flip the ship on its side." To the Bridge crew, I begin handing out orders. "Navigation, I want the ship brought to a stop, a minimum of three hundred feet in the air. Once we're at a complete standstill, flip the ship on its side, ready to dump the Greks. Operations, I want your finger on the gravity plating or whatever the system is that keeps us thinking the floor is down. The moment I give the order, and not a second before, I want the synthetic gravity turned off."

They go into action, and I see the land on the view screen turn sideways. "Everyone, secure yourself so you don't fall." Into the radio, I holler, "Millar, we've flipped ninety degrees to port. We'll be turning off the synthetic gravity in just a second. Confirm you're ready."

"Just coming up on Chavez, Sir!" Millar replies. "Okay, we've got him." There's a moment's pause, followed by, "We're ready, Sir."

I position myself on the starboard side of a control panel, then visually check everyone on the Bridge including the two security guards. As best as I can tell, we're ready too, although it's hard to wrap my mind around gravity switching like this.

Gerb's got his finger on the button, and I give him the order.

SHIFT

The world flips to one side so quickly it takes me a good five seconds before I can figure out where I am. I give it another ten seconds, then shout, "Turn it back on, Gerb, and then close those outer doors."

Our world flips yet again, and a moment later I'm back on my feet. The flip back seems easier. Through the radio, I holler, "Report, Millar!"

"Sir, the door's sealed. I can't confirm anything."

"Open the small door, Gerb."

I wait until Millar reports, "Sir, all but two Greks are gone."

"Clean 'em up, then get back to searching the ship." I return the radio to my belt, then turn my attention back to the Bridge. "Gerb! I want you to search the schematics of the ship for any rooms similar to that one which held the Greks. I want to know what we might be facing. Elizabeth, what's the word on a possible location?"

"Having a hard time finding one. There's so many Greks down there."

"How fast can we go?"

"Uh… I'd say somewhere around… well… really fast. I can't help but think we could circle the globe in about… five to seven minutes."

That gets my attention. We'd have to be fast to get off the planet, that's for sure, but that's faster than I expected to fly while in the atmosphere. "Find us a spot in Antarctica. Let's see if the Greks like the cold."

Elizabeth hesitates for only a moment before she replies. "Antarctica it is."

I shift on my feet, wishing for the tenth time that the Bridge had a seat for the Captain, but it looks like I'm stuck going without. Gotta fix that problem, eventually. Without it, that could make for a long interstellar journey.

I watch the view screen near the navigation console while trying to keep an eye on everyone else. Logan's off in a corner at the moment. He's been pretty quiet since we got here. I know he's excited, yet scared out of his wits to be on the Grek ship. We assigned him to a floater position, despite my concern he'd *float* over to Gerb. Logan has a knack for quickly collecting loads of information and putting it all together. His job is to figure out, generally, what all the other stuff on the Bridge does. That's a heavy load for anyone to carry, but Logan has a better chance than most of doing it well.

I wander over to one of the empty consoles. Logan's been over this one already. It has a piece of tape stuck to it that says, "Dunno." Unfortunately, a lot of my confidence slides away at the sight of that. The next console, however, says, "Food stuff." I nearly snap at him, but then I hesitate. On one hand, I'd like more detail, but on the other, I expect the label means this console deals with food. If that's the case, there's not much more I can ask of him than "Food stuff".

The next console says, "Life support and games." That one makes me smile. Maybe humans aren't the only ones in the universe who like to play. The console next to the one he's working on at the moment has a piece of tape that reads, "Command... or... not."

"What's 'Command or not', Logan?"

His head jerks up as though I just scared him. From the look on his face, it's not far from the truth.

"It's… uh… um…" His eyes keep flicking to the doorway.

"Don't worry, Logan. We have guards at the door. I'm keeping tabs on Millar. He's now three decks down and still no sign of anyone." I nod my head back at the console in front of me, and he takes the hint.

"Oh, that… I think that might be a command console, but I'm not sure."

"Is there a seat?"

"I don't think the aliens that built this ship sit down. Maybe they had no knees." He hesitates, and his eyes drift off as they lose focus. "Or… maybe no butts."

If he were a soldier, I'd just stare at him with an unimpressed look, but Logan will never pick up on that. "Forget the seats. We can figure that out later. What does the Command Console do?" Shaking my head, I add, "Aside from a console from which to command."

"Hmm… well… Sir… I'm just guessing, but I think the commands go out to the entire ship through there. There's also access to comms, and if I'm reading it right, whoever sits here… or stands… can take over navigation or weapons or life support."

"But it's facing the wall!"

"Oh, that shouldn't be a problem," he says quickly. "Here… stand in this spot."

He pushes me into position in front of the console and tells me to place my hand on the little screen, palm down. I do, and a light shines quickly on my hand. A moment later, the alien language, which a lot of this bridge crew has figured out on a basic level, fills four screens down on the console.

"Okay, so… you see that thing over there? The thing that looks like a stepped-on Twinkie?"

I shake my head and am about to tell him to describe things better, but then my eyes land on it. It looks exactly what I think a stepped-on Twinkie would look like. "Yeah, what about it?"

"Grab it."

The moment I touch it, the entire console spins around, not too quickly, but fast enough to turn me back toward the crew in just over a second. "Okay, that helps."

"I don't know what this is, though," he says, pointing to a small, round object in front of me.

It's in the shape of a cylinder no thicker than my thumb, all matte black around the sides, and the top seems to be black glass. When I touch it, it turns, and when I grab it, it pulls out of the console, attached by some kind of retracting cord. Without thinking, I pull it up to my mouth and say, "Hello?"

"Tried that already," Logan says. "It's not a microphone, as far as I can tell."

The glass on top of it is shiny and deeply black, yet I feel like I can see something inside. Raising it higher so I can inspect it, I find myself frozen in place, unable to move while a bright light flashes in my eye! The pain drives me to want to scream as it's worse than anything I've ever felt in my life, but I can't breathe or move, let alone make any sound!

The agony, the pain, the terror I feel… it goes on for minutes… maybe hours. I can't see anyone else past the bright light in my eye, but I don't care. All I want is out of this place. Can't scream. Can't breathe. I'd choose death in an instant over even another second of this.

"…so, I think we'll have to take our time to figure that out, but I'm wondering if it's some kind of reader or something. Maybe you use it to scan information or… even translate… I don't know."

I stare at Logan, then look around the Bridge. Everyone's hard at work, and it sounds like Elizabeth has found a place to land. When I look down, I see I've dropped the little black cylinder, and it's retracted back to its spot. "Did… uh… ahem… Logan, how much time would you say has passed since I pulled out that little thing?"

Logan raises his eyes to look at me and both his eyebrows climb up his forehead for a second before he says, "Sorry, sometimes I get talking and don't know when to quit."

"Answer the question."

He drops his head and says, "Maybe... fifteen seconds. Not long. Twenty, tops."

I shake my head. "Something happened. I thought I was gone for hours. I saw a bright flash come out of the end of this thing, and I felt pain like I'd never felt before."

Logan chuckles like he thinks I'm making a joke, then his face grows serious. "You don't normally joke, do you?"

I shake my head. "Not these days. Something happened. It was excruciating. I..."

"Hey!" one of the men at the ops station hollers out. "Hey... uh... everything's changed!"

The ship lurches to the side for a moment before Elizabeth regains control, and then the entire Bridge seems to warp and slide sideways again before it settles. Once things clear, Gerb says, "Oops, that last one was my fault."

"Report!" I holler out.

"Sir," Elizabeth says, "Everything's in English now. And when it switched over, the controls all changed order. That's what made me hit the wrong button."

"And what did you do, Gerb?"

"I... well... I tried to lower the temperature a degree since it felt warm in here, but it switched at that moment, and I hit a button that says, 'Shift'. So... I guess we shifted."

"Find out what that means!" I order. "Everyone, figure out what happened."

I look down at my console and see the main screen has changed.

Commander Engaged.
Colonel Ghulam identified, evaluated, adjustments enacted.
Language: English.
Cultural adjustment: Human Technology, 21st Century.

"Logan," I begin, "is it possible that cylinder I put to my eye scanned my brain and adjusted everything to fit… me?"

Logan shrugs and leans over my console. "Well, let's take a look." He swipes across my screen, but nothing happens, then tries again. "Looks like it's locked us out. It's not allowing us to do anything anymore."

I try it myself. The screen slides easily to the next one.

"Ohhh… I get it!" he says, his voice filled with excitement. "You're the Commander! I mean, of the ship! The Command console will only respond to you now."

"But we can change that with a new eye scan?"

He shrugs. "Maybe. But it sounds pretty painful." He stares at the console for a moment before smiling. "Can I try?"

Stepping back, I wave my hand over it. "Be my guest."

While Logan moves in, Elizabeth calls out, "Found a suitable spot. No sign of anyone around at all—no life aside from penguins, from what I can see, and the closest one of those is over a mile away. Having everything in English is going to speed this up a lot!"

"All right, let's try this…" Logan says with a big smile.

I put my hand on his arm for a moment, reconsidering matters, then order, "Elizabeth, set the ship down." Turning back to Logan, I order, "Wait till we're secure. I don't need a shift in controls while Elizabeth is learning to land this thing."

He waits, kind of, but I keep my hand on his arm. The guy's pulling like he thinks he can get there regardless of what I say.

The ship doesn't even shake when we land. Instead, I hear Elizabeth say, "We're down. That was easy!"

"Gerb! Tell me what you've figured out about that shift-thing."

"Well, Xavier…" I give a sharp look, and it causes him to rethink his approach. I've already explained this is a military operation. "Sorry, Colonel, I don't really know. I have a guess, though…"

"Tell me your guess."

"From what I'm seeing here, we *shifted* somehow. I know that's obvious from the name, but I don't mean something shifted. I think *we* shifted. Like... the ship itself shifted along with all of us and everything inside. At first, I thought maybe we jumped from one location to another, but nothing changed in our surroundings or speed or anything. Then I thought the ship changed shape, but from what I see, it's the same."

"Any other ideas, then?"

"Only one, Colonel."

"Spit it out, Gerb."

"I think somehow we shifted in a way that... makes us invisible."

I let that sink in for a moment. "Logan, get back to what you were doing and steer clear of the Command Console." While he scurries to where he was before, I order, "No one's allowed near this console without a direct order from me. It appears to be the Command Console. We'll experiment with it more soon, but at the moment, it's tied to me. I want to know what we're dealing with here with a few things before I switch things up again."

I grab the radio and call out, "Millar!"

"Here, Sir."

"Report."

"Sir, something happened a few minutes ago. Everything blurred for a moment. We all saw it."

"Yes, we're trying to figure that out. Where are you?"

"Fourth deck down. Most of the area is easy to move through. Open doors, large rooms. We just don't know what everything we're seeing is."

"What are you seeing?"

"Lot of tech, Sir. Strange machines, consoles, boxes of stuff. It's all secured down, not going anywhere, but we have no idea what it is. Most of it's on this deck."

"Hold on, Millar. Remain on that deck until I tell you otherwise." Glancing up, I ask, "Gerb, can you seal off the lower decks? Everything below Millar's team, so anything on those decks can't get up here?"

"For sure! It's easy now! The whole thing is rearranged… like it's more intuitive now. Easier to find stuff, move through their system."

"Seal it all off, Gerb."

"All right… done."

"Millar!"

"Yes, Sir."

"Finish the deck you're on. Once it's confirmed secure, inform me and head to the door we entered. I need you to look outside."

"Yes, Sir."

"Gerb. I want those doors to the lower decks locked, if you can. Don't open them for anything without a direct order. Understood?"

"Yep, Colonel."

"And the door leading outside?" I ask.

"You want it open."

"Absolutely not, Gerb. We follow orders here, not listen in on conversations and make guesses about what the Colonel wants. I'll tell you what I want, and I want it closed until I give the order." To the rest of the Bridge, I ask, "Anyone's console have a weather update?"

No one replies, but I see Logan point at my console. I return to it, and when I get there, I'm pleased to find I can easily move through the menus and information. A moment later, I'm looking at a temperature of -14F and winds of over thirty miles an hour. Not going to be a fun one for Millar. Not by any stretch of the imagination.

"Elizabeth! Can you confirm we're stopped? Do we need to turn off the engines, or can they run while we sit here?"

She looks down at her panel, then up at me, then down at her panel again. Obviously, that thought had never crossed her mind. "I think… well… yes, we are stopped, but… as for the engine thing… I think we can just let it run. But if we have to shut down at some point, it didn't take long to start up the first time, so we can get going again easily."

The radio squawks. "Colonel?"

"Go ahead, Millar."

"We've secured this deck. We're on our way to the door."

"All right, Millar, here are your orders. I won't be saying anything you expect me to say, so pay attention. We're parked right now, somewhere on the South Pole. Somehow, the ship has gone through a kind of adjustment. That was the blur you felt a short while ago. Gerb suspects this is a form of cloaking technology, but far more advanced than we've known. We may actually be invisible. I need you to get outside quickly, look back at the ship, then get right back inside. You should wear your Grek camo and put on gloves and cover your face. It's cold out there, and there's a nasty wind."

I wait for a moment while he takes it all in. Finally, I hear, "You're right, Sir, I didn't really expect much of that. Orders understood. We'll be at the door in five minutes."

"Ms. Messier," I call out to the woman leading the weapons team. "Have you been able to decipher all the weapons?"

"Yes, Sir!" she says cheerfully. "Having everything in English helps. The beam we fired is a stun, of sorts, for ships. I believe it also works on people. On ships, it appears to set them back a few seconds—maybe overload the circuits for just a bit. For people and Greks, we think it knocks them right out but doesn't hurt them. Aside from that, we have missiles, something big like a nuke, some kind of laser weapon that we believe does a precise cut through metal, and a weapon that shoots some kind of projectile, maybe bullets, and some kind of sonic weapon."

"Sonic?"

"Yes… Sir. As best we figure, it'll shake up a ship pretty badly. I don't really know its purpose, but that seems to be what it does."

"Okay. Good work, Messier. Logan! Learn anything new?"

"Nothing that helps us at the moment, although I found an engineering console. I think it's for monitoring everything, but I believe limited repairs can also be done from it."

"Gerb! Stay at your station!"

Gerb stops only a few steps from his own station with his eyes on the engineering console. When he turns back, I see the saddest face I've ever seen.

"If you think that look will get me to change my mind, Gerb, think again."

"Sir?" Millar's voice calls out over the radio.

"Go ahead."

"We're at the door, Sir, and I'm all suited up along with Chavez. I'm taking a second with me. We also have another four suited up and ready to go, but they'll remain on board unless needed."

"Good thinking, Lieutenant. As soon as the door's open, you have a go. I want the Sergeant Major giving me constant updates."

"Confirmed," Adesina says.

"Open it, Gerb."

I half expect to hear some kind of rumble, but the door's far enough away that there's no sound or even vibration felt. However, I feel a rush of cold air from the doorway leading to the Bridge a moment after Gerb confirms it's open.

"Sir," Ligaya shouts through the radio, "Millar and Chavez are making their way down the ramp. It's windy out there; they're having trouble staying on their feet." The radio cuts out, then I hear, "They've reached the bottom of the ramp, Sir, and they're making their way out into the snow." Again, a pause. "They're about twenty feet from the ramp. They keep looking back. They're going out farther… Sir, they've stopped about forty feet from the bottom of the ramp. I can barely see them. They're moving kind of funny. Orders?"

I'm about to order her to send out the four prepared to follow them, hoping they can bring in the two out there, when her voice comes through again. "Sir, they're returning. They're running… they've reached the bottom of the ramp… they're in, Sir."

"Close it, Gerb!" Through the radio, I order, "Millar, report to the Bridge."

As I walk to the Bridge entrance, I look back now and then to make sure Logan's not sneaking over to take another look at the Command Console. I don't need him playing around with that right now. A few moments later, I see Millar and his team coming down the hall and meet him partway.

"Report, Lieutenant!"

He salutes but then rubs his hands as he speaks. I can tell the cold got to him quickly. "Sir, we could see the ship fine from the bottom of the ramp, and then out for a little way. I'd say somehow just past forty feet… maybe forty-one or forty-two… just a guess, Sir, somewhere around there, the ship winked out of sight. We stepped back and forth a few times, coming across that point and stepping back out, and the ship appeared, disappeared, each time. I'd say if that holds true for farther out, we're pretty much invisible unless something's right on top of us."

"That would help explain how the Greks got to all the world's military bases so easily," I say absently, then focus in. "Good work. We're going to return to the L-O now. We'll have to move quickly once there, Lieutenant."

"Yes, Sir. May I ask what we're doing once we arrive? I expect the Greks will want their ship back."

A smile breaks out on my face. "That they will, Lieutenant. I wish I could give you more, but everything's need-to-know right now. Everything. So, sit tight, follow orders, and we'll all be good."

"Yes, Sir! Do you want us to continue with the lower decks?"

Shaking my head, I tell him, "No. I want you at the main door, not the one we came in, but the big one on the starboard side. I'll give you your orders soon enough. Until then, radio silence, except with me."

He salutes and leads the team away while I return to the Bridge. When I arrive, I find everyone's still hard at work, which I'm pleased to see. Even when I'm not giving out orders, it doesn't mean there's nothing to do. They'll likely have no end of stuff to learn in the coming weeks and months. But for me, I have something else on my mind. I have to send a message to the General, but we didn't work out a code for "ship turns invisible."

I'm so focused on crafting the message that nothing seems out of the ordinary as I take a seat at my Command Console. Everyone's distracted by their work, all except Logan, who's staring at me with a big grin on his face.

"What's on your mind, Logan?"

He says nothing. Instead, he just looks down at my chair, then back up at me, then down at the chair again. "You notice anything new, Colonel?"

I bolt out of the chair and spin around. The seat I'd just been sitting in looks like it's been there forever. Secured to the floor, about the right size and shape for me, and it turns around to allow me a view of the Bridge.

"Where did this come from?"

Logan laughs and shrugs. "Just after you left the room, I heard a buzz, and it just kind of… formed there. Like it was built, tiny piece by tiny piece. I think the system knew you wanted a chair."

That makes me frown. To be honest, setting aside the convenience of that kind of thing, it doesn't seem good to have a computer system that can read my thoughts. "Can we turn off the system's ability to just do stuff without permission?"

He shrugs again. "Maybe. It might take a while to figure out how."

Dropping into the seat, I wave for him to get back to work and focus my thoughts again. The code was to be a series of digits and letters, which, based on their order, would communicate the situation. So far, most details are easy to put together. Mission is a success, team is safe, time we are returning, whether or not the L-O should be on alert… but no way to communicate that we're invisible. Not without compromising the code, anyway.

In the end, I have to admit to myself that the invisibility will have to be a surprise. We don't know what the Greks are monitoring, so there's no wisdom in taking a risk.

"Elizabeth, if we were to head directly back to the L-O, how long would it take us to get there, including takeoff, landing, everything?"

She smiles at the request and quickly punches a few things into the console in front of her. "That's an easy one. The system figures it all out for us. That'll take…" She smiles again like she's really proud of it and announces, "Four minutes, twelve and a half seconds."

"That's precise."

She laughs. "I don't know if my landing or controlling the ship will slow things down, but it's all pretty simple, to be honest, so at most, we might add a few seconds onto that estimate."

"That's good enough for me. Prep the ship. We leave in five minutes. Remain invisible… hmm… let's call it the *Shift*. We'll remain with the Shift engaged through the entire journey, and it's not to come off until I give the order."

Four or five nod, and a few grunt a response.

I definitely prefer working with soldiers.

Once I pull off my pack, I quickly grab the SAT phone I have stored in there. There are a few dozen satellites left up there, some are ours, the others belong to a few other nations such as North Korea or Russia. We haven't been able to make use of the others yet, but Williams has been regularly sending fake codes through ours for months now, so if the Greks pick up a genuine code, they might think nothing of it.

The code goes in just fine, and I fire it off. Then I wait… ten seconds… twenty… I know Williams has his phone with him, but if Gordon's right there, he might need to excuse himself so as not to give us away.

Thirty seconds… a full minute. Not a good sign.

THE LOST OUTPOST

At two full minutes, I finally get a response… a simple error code. A proper code would give me information, likely instructions. A long string of fake code means stay away. An error code means he's received my message, and I have a go.

"Elizabeth, we leave in less than three minutes." Through the radio, I order, "Millar, keep everyone together. No one uses a radio or contacts anyone, except for you or Ligaya, and you are only to contact me. Return to the hallway just outside the Bridge for now."

From my chair, I watch everyone like a hawk. I hate to be so suspicious, and everyone here has remained above suspicion, but the next few steps are too crucial to take any risks. If we can remain invisible, perhaps we can accelerate the plan. No one appears to be acting strangely, and we put multiple people on each station for security's sake, not just to enable them to pool their resources.

"Logan!"

"Uh, yeah, Colonel?"

"Why don't you give that a break for a few moments and come over here?"

He saunters over to me with a look on his face like he expects he's in trouble. When he reaches me, I just signal for him to wait. I don't need him for anything, I just need him not to touch anything for a bit.

"Time to go, Elizabeth. Get us back to the L-O and give me step-by-step updates of what you're doing."

"On it!"

She moves through a dozen steps to launch and punches in the course, but I wait until we get in the air… and… there it is.

"Elizabeth, when we arrive, I want to remain with the Shift engaged, and you are to get us to the north bay doors."

"There's barely room to land there, Sir."

I get up from my seat and wander over to her station. "You think you can manage it?"

She smiles. One thing about Elizabeth is if she's under pressure, her stress goes through the roof, and she grows irritable. But give her a challenge… and she shines and never disappoints. "I think it's going to be tight, but…" The smile grows larger. "Don't worry, I think I've got it."

Returning to my seat at the Command Console, I watch everyone carefully as they go about their business. When Elizabeth announces we're thirty seconds out, I send through an error code to Williams to let him know we're just about to complete the code I originally sent.

Calling out to the team at the Scanning Console, I ask, "Any sign of Greks or *Taken* in the area?"

"Sir," Mateo Sanchez replies slowly, "If we're reading this right… it's hard to understand since it appears to be designed for outer space where the sensors read everything on a XYZ Axis, not just for relatively flat land like we have here…"

"I'd forgotten you were Canadian," I say with a laugh.

"Getting me to say that is a good way to identify that, Sir," he says, returning the smile. "As far as I can tell, we're clear. There are a few Greks to the south of us and about forty

Taken moving along about a mile to the east, but I think… I think we're clear."

"Millar! Get your team in here!"

A moment later, Millar enters the Bridge along with his soldiers as I confirm with Elizabeth that she's landed the ship. Addressing everyone, I lay out the plan. "All right, here's how this is going to work. We will all maintain radio silence with everyone. The only exception is Millar through his radio to me. Lieutenant, any conversations we have over the radio will include nothing that might give any hint as to the ship. You will speak as though you and your team are out among the ruins on a scouting mission. No hints, no hesitations in your voice, nothing to suggest anything's out of the ordinary. When I signal you and tell you I'm about to enter the L-O, you will lift off and hover approximately five hundred feet above the ground. I will contact you regularly, every five minutes." I take a deep breath. He's not going to like the next part. "Millar, if the intervals between the points I contact you are greater than fifteen minutes, Logan will show you how to take command of the ship, and you will take everyone here and find a safe location. Try to find other humans who haven't been *Taken*, and your task will be to follow the signal where it leads and destroy whatever is sending it. Understood?"

Millar just stares at me for a moment. I've seen this in soldiers before. Sometimes orders like this have to be given, and the soldier is left torn between abandoning their commanding officer and obeying orders. He shakes his head slowly before he finally says, "Yes, Sir. Understood."

"The Bridge is yours, Lieutenant."

"Aye, Sir."

Everyone remains silent as I walk out. I don't know what they're so worked up about. I've no intention of dying or anything. I'd just never want to leave them waiting for me to return if I walk into the L-O to find everyone under Grek control.

I head down the long hallway and along the turns until I reach the doors, at which point I radio back to Millar. "Lieutenant, open the door."

A moment later, the door opens, and I head down the ramp. I've seen the Grek ships fly overhead before—rarely—but they never make a sound. I'm assuming it's also the case with this ship.

When I reach the bottom of the ramp and step out onto the ground, I'm within sight of the walls, but I'm assuming they won't see me until I get to that point around forty feet from the ship. A lot of assumptions here, but the guards at the gate don't seem to notice anything out of the ordinary.

I turn away from the base and wander around behind a rubble pile just a few feet from the bottom of the ramp, then pull out my radio. "Millar, I'm about to enter the L-O."

"Confirmed."

The door closes, and the ship begins its ascent. A few seconds later, it winks out of sight, and I step out from behind the pile of rubble.

The guards jump into action, and I raise my empty hands to put them at ease. Within a few seconds, I hear them call, "It's the Colonel!"

The soldier manning one of the 50 cals on this side of the L-O sends someone back through the big hangar doors as I walk forward.

Two soldiers on each tower… hands on their weapons… another dozen guards within sight, all armed to the teeth… The entire L-O is on alert.

When I reach the gate, a soldier calls down from above. "Sir, it's good to see you. We were all concerned."

He suspects me. That's a good thing. It likely means he's not *Taken*. If he were, he'd know where I stand.

"Glad to hear it. I need to speak with the General right away. Send word."

"Already did, Sir."

Four soldiers come back through the gate, and when they reach me, the Corporal salutes. "Sir, will you please come with us? We will escort you to the General."

I nod and as we walk, I ask, "Where is Major Gordon?"

"The General has him on assignment in the lower levels overseeing long term food supply and storage."

I keep the smile from my face. Both wise and strategic… another good sign.

They lead me through the large bay doors and straight to the General's office. Once there, the guards remain while Doctor Liu does a quick physical, focusing mainly on my eyes, of course.

When she's finished, she gives a quick nod to the General, and she and the soldiers leave the room, but the soldiers remain outside the door with the door open just a crack.

"Report!"

Keeping my voice low, I say just the bare minimum. The General knows from the code that we have the ship. "Sir, we had to avoid the L-O after taking the ship as the Greks were chasing us. I feared with the number of Greks, they'd overrun us."

He nods his response. This is how the Greks initially defeated the military. The creatures came in fast, relentless, aggressive attacks. "And now?"

"We've found the ship has a form of cloaking technology. We call it the Shift. Somehow, the ship is not only silent, but it can hide itself. The ship's hovering above the L-O at this moment."

His eyebrows shoot up, and he smiles, but then he asks, "And how do I know you aren't *Taken*, Colonel. Doctor Liu's scans of you are not entirely conclusive."

I shake my head. "Sorry, Sir. I've no way to prove it. You're going to have to take a risk."

My radio squawks, and I grab it. "Go ahead."

"Sorry to contact you, Sir. There's a large group of Greks approaching our position." Millar sounds concerned, but he's choosing his words carefully.

"What direction?"

"South, Sir."

"What's your evaluation of the threat?"

"Overwhelming, Sir."

I look back to the General, and he's frowning. "We picked up a large group of them on a satellite image just half an hour ago."

"They must have been planning this before we started back, but they'll know we're here now. Even if they can't see us, whatever causes them to know to send out my wife and kids is likely alerting them to our presence." To Millar, I ask, "ETA?"

"We figure fourteen minutes, Sir."

The General's mouth drops open, and he shakes his head. "I guess it's face the Greks or take that risk you're talking about. Order an evacuation."

I nod and send out word to the L-O. We've prepared for this. The people will think it's still just a drill, but they've learned to move fast. We'll start filing them into the northeastern hangar.

"Millar!"

"Yes, Sir."

"Set down at the northern entrance. Open the doors and prepare to receive people. Lead them down a few decks and get the other doors open for loading supplies. Have soldiers in place to direct everyone. Radio silence continues, except for communications between you, me, and the General."

"Yes, Sir."

"And Millar, send me three soldiers who understand a little about the Shift so they can tell the civilians what to expect."

"Yes, Sir!"

The radio clips back on my belt, and Williams starts talking right away. "I have the soldiers in the northern bay all ready to load. How long till they land?"

"Likely a few seconds from now. Not long."

"Get down to the northern hangar and take command. I'll make sure we're good to go with Gordon."

Running out of the General's office, I head down to the hangar. The Sergeant in charge of this area is shouting out orders, but I wave him over.

"Sir! We'll be ready to load as soon as the trucks arrive."

I shake my head. "No trucks arriving, Sergeant. We're loading a spaceship. Any loaded trucks go right on the ship and park, and fork trucks will move back and forth with loads. Radio silence, no matter what. You catch anyone on the radio, aside from General Williams, Lieutenant Millar, or me, you arrest them on the spot, regardless of who they are. Understood?"

"Yes, Sir."

"The ship's out there now. You can't see it, but it's there. Soldiers will meet you at the doors to direct you. It's parked about a hundred feet from the 50 cals. It'll wink into view when you're just about upon it. Clear?"

"Not really, Sir, but we'll make do."

"See that you do, Sergeant. You have three minutes to get everything you can onto that ship. After that, I can't guarantee a single second. Now RUN!"

He turns and bolts towards the soldiers working in the hangar, and within twenty seconds, a half dozen fork trucks are on the go, along with three trucks already loaded. I've no idea how much time we need, but we'll take what we can.

Three soldiers run up to me from Millar's troop, and I give them their orders. They run over to the door where the civilians will come through in a few minutes, ready to prepare the civilians for the shock of seeing the ship—as best they can in the few seconds they have.

The seconds tick by, and I watch the Sergeant like a hawk. He's moving fast and not wasting any time. That's good. When the three minutes are about up, I grab my radio. "Millar! Update on the Grek force?"

"It's growing, Sir. It should hit us in about eight and a half minutes."

"Any changes in the suspected outcome?"

"None, Sir, other than to say what's coming is even more overwhelming, if that's possible."

"Understood."

With my SAT phone, I call Williams, and a moment later, he picks up. "Williams here."

"Sir, the ETA is approximately eight minutes."

"How are the supplies coming?"

"Good, we can continue this for as long as you need."

"We'll come now. Williams out."

I wave down the Sergeant, and he hurries to me. "Sergeant, keep loading, but keep your trucks to the west side of the doors. The people will come through the main east doors to load onto the ship. They are the priority. When I give the order, whatever fork trucks are on the ship are to remain there. Everyone else is to make it onto the ship, whether they drive something or are on foot. Understood?"

"Yes, Sir!" He salutes and begins passing out orders immediately.

I hope this has given enough time for the people to assemble and still think it's a drill. If Gordon is *Taken*, the moment he knows what's up is the moment any Greks in the area will converge on this place. Hard to know for sure, but the large group of Greks might even pick up speed.

Every second counts.

22

LAUNCH

A crowd of people pour through the large set of doors, civilians and soldiers alike, not quite running, but moving fast. Two soldiers lead the way, and they look as confused as the people behind them. They'll understand soon enough. Millar's soldiers immediately start hollering a brief explanation and telling people to run.

I watch the crowd jog along and shake my head. I don't know if it's all in my imagination or not, but I see the occasional flash of glowing yellow eyes. Yellow… that's attack.

They now know something's up.

"Millar," I say through the radio, "we may have just lost all secrecy. Hurry the people along and keep them all contained and away from the Bridge."

"Yes, Sir."

At the speed the people move, we'll get them all loaded, but we won't have time to search the base for anyone left behind. I holler at the civilians to pick up speed, but I suspect the fact that they're heading out of the safety of the L-O into the unknown will only make them drag their feet more. "Millar?"

"Yes, Sir?"

"I want a countdown on the ETA. Every minute."

"Yes, Sir. We're at four minutes."

I watch the crowds stream by. The Sergeant overseeing loading continues to run back and forth, issuing orders and hollering at his soldiers when they make a wrong move. Every second counts.

"Three minutes, Sir."

I shake my head. This is going to be close. I holler at the soldiers directing the crowds, "Pick up the speed, soldiers! We need everyone loaded NOW!"

"Two minutes, Sir."

The SAT phone comes out. "Sir, how many more?"

"Just about done, Colonel. Can the ship hold everyone?"

"Yes, Sir. No worries there. We have approximately ninety seconds."

"That's cutting it close, Colonel."

Millar's voice comes through again. "One minute, Sir."

Shaking my head, I holler out for the Sergeant to call it quits as I run to the side wall. The Sergeant immediately orders anyone not in the process of loading something to get on the ship, and soldiers bolt for the hangar door. When I reach the wall, I grab the handset and punch in my code, then hit the intercom for the entire base. "Attention all soldiers and civilians. This is Colonel Ghulam. Abandon your post immediately and head for the northern hangar. You have thirty seconds. This is not a drill. I repeat, abandon your post immediately and head for the northern hangar. You have thirty seconds. Colonel Ghulam out."

I keep out of the way of the civilians streaming through, but a look down the hallway used for the evacuation leaves me shaking my head. I can see the end of the line, but they're moving slowly. Far too slowly. General Williams and Major Gordon are both at the back hollering at the civilians to move, but no one seems to get the urgency.

Civilians always think soldiers are too uptight.

"Move, move, move!" I shout. "This is NOT a drill!"

The radio squawks, and Millar shouts, "Thirty seconds, Sir."

I scowl and shake my head. We still don't know about Gordon's loyalty, but Williams, Gordon, and me… we're the only Senior Officers. If Williams doesn't make it, I have to be on that ship.

I run for the ramp.

The moment the people see me run, it puts a bit of fear in them, and some panic. We don't need a panic, but at this point, maybe that'll get them moving a little faster. Through the hangar doors and past the abandoned 50 cals, I run on with the civilians running behind. I can't see anything yet, aside from some of Millar's soldiers. They stand just this side of the Shift and try their best to explain once again to the civilians what'll happen as people run by.

I step through and find I'm just as shocked as the civilians when they come through. It takes a lot to get used to something like this. A quick look around shows me all the doors used for loading supplies are closing or closed already.

"Move!" I holler. "We'll be under attack in about ten seconds!" To the soldiers, I order, "Take up position! Defend the civilians until the second you're ordered to retreat."

When the civilians hear that, they break into an all-out run, and many scream. I guess they just assumed we'd never stop loading. Truthfully, I don't know at what point we would, but we can't compromise the ship's security.

The thudding of Grek feet grows in intensity, like a steady roar of thunder, growing louder by the second. I've never heard what this many Greks sound like, but they're moving fast!

I race up the ramp. There's plenty of room. The civilians have spread out a lot and many of them slow down on the ramp, but this ramp is about seventy-five or eighty feet wide. I see two elderly people struggling. After the run, now the ramp, they look like they're about to fall over.

I know there's no dignity in it, but they're both thin and small, so I pick up both of them, one under each arm, and get them to the top of the ramp. Their flustered faces fill with gratitude, but I leave them there and bolt for the Bridge. When I arrive, "I holler, Millar, I'm taking command of the Bridge. Get to the ramp and keep your soldiers in defensive positions until I give the order. We're about to lift off!"

He bolts out of the Bridge, and I take in what's going on around me. The people on the Bridge are nearly in a panic, and there's a large view screen—bigger than anything we had before—showing the view of the L-O. From this height, we can see the Greks. It's like a sea of brown and black mixed with the gray of the legs swarming toward the L-O. The front of the wave has hit the far side, and concrete and building materials fly every which way. I doubt the 50 cals would have done anything to slow that down, were they still manned.

"Ms. Messier!" I holler. Shoot that stun weapon at the front line. "Do it now!"

"Sir, we…"

"Now!"

A shot goes out, and the front line of the Greks falls back. Hard to tell with that swarm, but I'd say over a hundred Greks fell in one shot.

"That barely made a difference," Elizabeth says, her voice coming out in near panic.

"Keep firing! That's an order! You shoot at the closest Grek each shot." Into the radio I holler, "Millar! How long till we're loaded?"

"Twenty or thirty seconds, Sir!" As his voice comes across, I hear the roar of gunfire. It's a wonder he heard me over the radio.

"The second we can close that door, you tell me, Lieutenant!"

"Yes, Sir!"

"Gerb, your finger better be hovering over that button!"

"It is…" he says, his voice shaking. "I…"

"Elizabeth! You be ready to get us into the sky. I want us up a hundred feet and out of range of the Greks."

"Okay… I…

"I know you're all scared!" I shout. "Your fear is not a problem for me. Don't let it be a problem for you!"

"We're in, Sir!" Millar shouts.

"Close the door, Gerb! Elizabeth, get us up there!"

Without Millar's soldiers firing, the wave of Greks pour over the top of the L-O into the north gates. The 50 cals disappear under the swarm, and Grek after Grek leaps through the air, slamming against the side of the ship.

"Two hundred feet, Elizabeth!"

"Okay… just about there!"

I watch the Greks, still leaping toward us, but coming up short. I'm hoping none have managed to hold on to anything.

"*Humans* to the north of us, outside the L-O," the man at the scanning station announces.

"Get me a visual on them," I order. I'd hate to find we've left a few soldiers behind to face the swarm.

The camera flicks back to just behind us. I see them. Standing there.

"Zooming in now," the man says, but I don't need the zoom. I know who they are.

The camera centers in on them, filling the screen. Connie stands in the middle of the street. Others stand around her, but she's there, right in the middle, the center of everything. I can't hear her words, but I see her lips move, and there's no question what she's saying. Over… and over… She's calling me… begging… "Please, Xavier… please. Come back to me." Her face is distraught… her lips quiver and tears stream down her cheeks, but her eyes… they're full of one thing and only one thing. Accusation. She shakes her head at the man abandoning his wife and children.

I feel the pressure of a hand on my shoulder, and I almost pull away and order Elizabeth to land the ship. The voice that speaks in my ear is rough, old, scratchy, but wise. Kind, even. "Xavier… son… this is the only way we can get them back."

I turn to face the man behind me. He's short with thin white hair on top and a lot of wrinkles all over his face. "Fred… I…"

"We all pay a price, son. This is yours."

I clench my jaw and take a deep breath through my teeth. "Elizabeth! Two thousand feet. Someone shut off that view screen. And Gerb! I want a report on the supplies and the people!"

"Oh, the people are good."

"Gerb!"

"Oh… sorry, Colonel. Uh, the people are all on the two decks below us. The supplies are on the two decks below that. Everything seems fine, but the people are scared."

I turn back to Fred and nod at him. "Thanks."

In a quiet voice, he says with a smile, "Good thing I made a wrong turn and ended up here."

"You're welcome to give Logan a hand, Fred, but you'll have to stay out of the way of most of the stations."

"Yes, Sir," he says with a smile as he wanders over to Logan.

"Anyone have eyes on the General?"

No one answers. Just a bunch of heads shaking. Into the radio, I bark, "Millar! Find General Williams and get him to the Bridge."

A few moments later, I hear Millar reply, "Yes, Sir. Just having a bit of trouble keeping everyone contained. A lot of scared people, Sir."

"I get that, Millar. I'll see what I can do." The radio slips back easily onto my belt, and I pull my thoughts together. "Gerb, do we have a ship-wide intercom?"

"I… uh… think so. That's one of those things that's labeled weird, even with the English translation."

"What's it labeled?"

"Uh… 'So all may hear,'" he says. "I figure that's for ship-wide announcements.

"Let's try it."

He presses the button, and a moment later I hit the ground, my hands over my ears. I try to scream for him to shut it off, but nothing comes out… or maybe it's coming out, but I can't hear it.

I try again, but at first there's nothing, then, "…URN IT OFF NOW!"

My hand grips the closest console as I pull myself to my feet, the room spinning just a little. My voice cracks as I manage to say, "What was that, Gerb?"

"I… I don't know. I think it might have been their form of entertainment."

"Never, ever, ever press that again, Gerb, or I might entertain myself by shooting you."

He laughs but then stops when he sees my face. "Okay. Uh… Sir." He gets back to his console and mumbles to himself while he searches through everything he has.

I check on Fred, but he has a dazed look in his eyes, and I just leave him. No one likely fared well with that. I drop into the seat at my console, and the panels in front of me come to life immediately. Searching through the options before me, I find one that says, "Cross-deck communication."

"All right, everyone, I have one here that might work. Brace yourselves."

I hit the button, every muscle in my body tense, but nothing happens until I let out the breath I'd been holding. The moment I do, I hear my breath as through a megaphone echoing down the hallway.

"That's probably it," Gerb adds unhelpfully.

"Attention everyone on board," I say. "This is Colonel Xavier Ghulam. We're sorry to have to move everyone so quickly, but for those of you to board last, you know we were in danger of being overrun by the Greks. It'll take us a bit to get everyone situated, but we ask for your patience. We're still learning some of the controls for the ship. Please be patient with us. Stay with your family or close friends, and we will hopefully find everyone a room soon enough. The ship's large. We just have to figure out the details first. Please await further instructions."

I lean back and take my finger off the button, then clear my throat. I hear the cough down the hallway and jump back to the console. Hitting the button a second time doesn't help. Pushing it harder doesn't turn it off. Finally, I swipe it, and the color of the words change back to green, which seems to indicate the control is "off".

"If the name's not to your liking, you can rename it," Elizabeth says. "Press it and hold it for three seconds, then swipe it."

I try that, and a moment later a keyboard pops up, laid out in a circle. Once I get my mind around the arrangement of the letters, I slowly punch in "Ship-wide Intercom." When I'm finished, I notice the button is right next to another button labeled, "Purge All Decks" which seems like not only dangerous, but poor placement. "Is there a way to lock any of these buttons so I don't accidentally press the wrong one?"

"Yeah," Gerb says, "I just did it for that scary button on my console. Press it, hold it for three seconds, swipe it, just like you're changing the name, and there's a little option at the side with something that looks like a cross between an X and a cat. Press that and it'll lock it. You can unlock it again by following that same pattern."

I can't believe I have to press a button labeled "Purge All Decks," so that I can avoid pressing it, but I press and hold it, go through the process, and a moment later, it's locked. I have a feeling I'll be locking out a lot of controls.

Through the radio, I call, "Millar! What's the word on the General?"

"Got him, Sir. We're on our way to the Bridge now. Should be there in less than a minute."

I hear them jogging down the hallway, and the soldiers at the door salute as the General comes running in. "Sorry to take so long to get here, but I nearly had my eardrums blown out. Was that some kind of Grek weapon?"

"No, Sir," I say. I notice everyone else suddenly sees the need to focus on their consoles. "Just proof that we still have a lot to learn about this ship."

He nods, but I see he's not impressed. I'm not either, but there's not much we can do about it. We're bound to make mistakes. Instead, I take the time to bring him up to speed on what we've done with the ship, where all the people are, and where everything's stored.

"Recommendations, Colonel?"

"I recommend, Sir, that we set the ship down in an isolated spot while we get everyone situated."

"Any place in mind?"

"As a matter of fact, Sir, I know exactly the place."

23

SETTLING

Ten minutes later, we settle in Antarctica again, about six hundred miles from where we landed the last time. I don't want to set up a pattern, just in case the Greks can figure out a way to track us.

Even if we're here for a few weeks or longer, the cold shouldn't be a problem for the ship. If it is, we'll never survive in the vacuum of space.

Mateo Sanchez, the lead on the Scanning Console, gives me a thumbs up, letting me know we're clear of Greks. In time, they'll all have to learn how to interact on the Bridge of a ship. Thumbs up won't do, but for now…

"Mr. Sanchez, I want continuous scans. Let me know if you find anything other than a penguin or an animal native to this area. If a Grek ship flies through the sky in this general area, I want to know."

Another thumbs up. I'll deal with that soon enough.

I turn to see a smiling General. He sees how sloppy we're operating, and he's amused!

"General, the Command Console seems to adopt an individual. At the moment, I'm listed as the commander of the ship. It's a painful process to switch it to someone new, but it only takes a second."

He raises his hands. "No, Colonel, you seem to have a certain order you've figured out here. Let's leave things as they are for now. Do we have an office nearby, or some room we can use as a command center?"

I laugh at that. "General, we've only just figured out how to fly the thing. Lieutenant Millar has explored a lot of the ship, but I don't know what he's found, yet. His focus was ensuring there were no Greks or *Taken* aboard."

"There's something back there," Logan says from the other side of the room, where he's in the process of sticking a piece of tape on a new console. "I took a look at some of the rooms around when I got bored with this."

"Bored…?" I begin but then stop myself from saying what's on the tip of my tongue. Instead, I shake my head and let it go. Another issue to deal with later.

We head toward the door Logan pointed out. When we reach it, it slides up, and we step into a well-lit room. A few tables, secured to the floor, sit here and there, along with chairs, also secured to the floor. Three desks line the far wall.

"This is suspiciously similar to our command center back at the L-O," the General growls.

I nod. "When the command console latched onto me, it translated all the consoles into English. It also gave me a chair. Before that, we had seen no chairs on the ship. I suspect the ship adjusts the rooms somewhat to need."

"That's good news!" the General says with a laugh. "When I left all the civilians and soldiers below, we'd set aside a few rooms with dozens of buckets for toilets. No one was happy with it, but if we can get some toilets and showers, that'll be a good thing. Make it happen, Colonel!"

I shake my head slowly. "That's the problem, General. I don't know how to make it happen. I don't know how this command center happened, either."

General Williams frowns, but takes a seat and waves for me to sit in another. "All right, then, we need to establish priorities. What do you think is the Grek threat?"

"I think we're invisible, but anyone among us who is *Taken* will alert the Greks to at least our general location, if not exactly where we are. I think we might have far less time than we need."

"Priorities?"

"The two immediate priorities are civilians and crew. The civilians and soldiers need to be given rooms. We'll need to establish everything from food distribution to toilets to barracks to shift rotations and more. Second, we need to establish and train a rotating Bridge crew. At the moment, we have enough to maintain three, twenty-four-hour shifts, but that doesn't account for any days off, sickness, or anything unexpected. It also requires that each station be manned by only one person at a time. We need to train extra crew members." I smile and add, "And I'll need to establish a Bridge protocol. At the moment, I'm called everything from Colonel, to Sir, to Xavier, to 'hey you'."

"After that?" Williams asks.

"Well, sometimes, if I don't react, they call me 'Yo, boss-man!'"

"No, Colonel, after Bridge protocol," he says with a laugh.

I take a deep breath. Typically, I would expect the General to lay out priorities, but he fully expects a constant attitude of training and pushing one another. "Not so much after, but as we work through all this, we need teams learning more about the ship's systems. There may be need of repairs at some point, and we don't know how to do any of that. Our teams need to be organized and moving through the ship, developing their skill and familiarizing themselves with everything. We've sealed off all the lower decks as Millar has only checked this deck and the four below it. I would say it's a priority to secure more decks, moving down through the ship's levels. There could be dozens or hundreds of Greks in the lower sections of the ship. Or there could be weapons we could use to defend ourselves, or any number of things."

Williams frowns. "There could even be hundreds or thousands of the *Taken* down there."

There's nothing I can do other than nod. It was a thought I'd considered.

"All right, Colonel, here's the plan. You have the Bridge, and you will maintain command. Aside from showing me how to take over the command console, it's yours. You are welcome to build your Bridge crew however you see fit, and command of the ship is yours. I will oversee the setting up of teams below to get everyone situated as well as continue securing decks as I can spare soldiers. My focus will primarily be the civilians and oversight of all military operations below this deck." He pauses for a moment and leans back in his chair. A smile creeps up on his face. "Xavier, I read your file. You're an excellent leader, and you've seen more combat than anyone else in our ranks. But you never read my file."

"It's not my place, General."

"No, it's not, but let me tell you what you'd find if you were to read my file. Sure, I've been a military man since I finished at Quantico, but aside from a few years out in the field, most of what I've done is more administrative than anything. I'm good at it, I know, but command decisions on the fly is not something I've done in a long time."

"I've enjoyed serving under you, General."

He laughs. "I'm not giving up, Colonel! I just want to play to my strengths, and you to yours. We need you to lead us through this. Get your Bridge in order and organize your Marines."

"Yes, Sir. And Major Gordon?"

Williams taps his fingers on the table, and I see grief in his eyes. "Gordon…" His eyes drop for a moment, and he takes a deep breath. Letting it out slowly, he shakes his head. "Shortly after we landed, Gordon tried to take command of the soldiers—all of them. I had him arrested, and he's in a room, along with the soldiers who joined him."

"How many?"

"About four dozen. Most were under suspicion already."

"We knew they'd show their hand, eventually."

"We did, but it's no less a loss." He shakes his head again and asks, "What else?"

"As for moving forward, we're handing out promotions like they're candy on Halloween." I smile and a laugh slips out. "Millar's our guy. He's out of his league as a senior officer—he's great in the field and organizing small groups—but we're going to have to train him up. I recommend you pull Corporal Adesina in to work with you. She's got a lot to offer."

"Make it happen, Colonel," Williams says as he stands up. "I'll be down below, organizing the civilians and assigning quarters and barracks. Send me my officers when you've prepped them."

He walks out, and I examine a small console near my hand on the table. It offers some of the same options as my Command Console… which means… the computer is tracking me. If it's tracking me, maybe it can track everyone…

I flip through and find an option called "Locator," and a moment later, it asks me who I want. A smile crosses my lips. I wonder… Out loud, I say, "I want Lieutenant Millar, Sergeant Major Ligaya, and Corporal Adesina to report here to this room, which I'm now naming the Command Center."

The word "Confirmed" pops up on my screen, and I get up to head to the Bridge. When I get there, Adesina's already on her way onto the Bridge with a surprised look on her face.

"Corporal. I told the system I wanted you. I gather this means it found you?"

"Yes, Sir, I was just down the hall, and a voice told me to come here. Was that the ship speaking?"

"Hope so, Corporal, or we're haunted. My Command Center is just through that door. Head inside. I'll be in shortly."

I ask for a report from each of the stations. So far, they're figuring out more by the minute. But Logan's the most excited.

"Yo! Boss-man! Watch this. There's a button on every console that looks like a round circle inside another circle. If you hit it, you can speak, and the computer listens to you!"

At my console, I locate the button and hit it. "Computer, we need bathrooms down on the lower levels that can accommodate humans, including toilets, sinks, and showers, along with all appropriate plumbing. We need enough bathrooms for all the people below. We also need bathrooms up here, and we need kitchens and eating areas for all the people."

Nothing happens, so I just shake my head, and wave for Millar and Ligaya, who have just shown up, to follow me.

When I step into the Command Center, I notice a new door on the far wall. A quick peek inside reveals a room with a toilet, a sink, and even a shower.

Not bad.

"All right, listen up. This is the Command Center, and I'm maintaining command of the Bridge. General Williams is overseeing the civilian population and the larger Marine force. Now, under normal circumstances, there'd be an order and process for everything, but not so anymore. Things have to change, and I'm promoting all of you. None of you set out to be officers, but we don't need more Sergeants."

All three react with various displays of shock, but I don't give them a chance to say anything. Instead, I just lay it out. "Millar, you're promoted to Major, and you are in command of the Marines. You report directly to me. At the moment, your primary focus will be to get everything organized below under General William's lead. Soon after, you'll be organizing search teams into the lower decks, but not until the order is given. Any questions?"

"No, Sir." His smile nearly splits his face in two, and he stands a lot straighter.

"Ligaya. Just like Millar, you're jumping a lot of ranks, but your role will be different. I'm promoting you to Major as well, but you're my second on the Bridge. Your immediate task is to familiarize yourself with the Bridge operations, help establish a Bridge protocol for a bunch of civilians, identify and train new Bridge officers, and run this ship when I'm not in the chair."

The look on her face says it all. I just dumped way more on her than on Millar, and he's had a few more years of experience than her. I put my hands up. "We don't have the luxury of turning down promotions. Not right now. However, just because you're my second doesn't mean you carry the Bridge all by yourself. It means I carry the Bridge, and you back me up. We'll be walking this road together, Major."

She relaxes a bit, but I still see the worry. Truth is, she doesn't really even know me yet.

"Adesina, I apologize that there are no more promotions to Major today, but perhaps Captain will do."

Her mouth drops open, and she almost takes a step toward me. She looks like she wants to give me a hug, but obviously knows better.

"Your initial assignment will be to work with the General as his aide. He'll keep you hopping, but I won't have you facing pushback from the Sergeants, so Captain Adesina it is."

Addressing all of them, I say, "Your promotions are necessary for the proper running of our forces. However, I did not choose you at random. You've stood out and proven yourselves. Well done. I'll get you your insignias soon enough, but I expect you not to stand for any pushback, and I also expect you to stand up for the others. If someone questions the authority of one of the other officers, you make them understand. If they don't accept it, send them to me. However, I doubt any of you will face any problems in this area. Millar, you won't have any problem because you ranked higher than all the soldiers before this promotion. Adesina, you'll be working with the General. You won't have a problem. And Ligaya, it's just the Bridge crew you have to worry about. The pushback they give won't be because of rank, but because they don't really understand the concept of protocol."

I take a deep breath and shake my head. "Just to be clear, since you, Millar, and you, Ligaya, have been promoted at the same time, neither of you outranks one another. Matters of the Bridge and its reach fall under Ligaya, matters of the larger military force fall under Millar. Any questions?"

All three shake their heads. "Good. Each of you are also to keep your eye out for potential officers. We need a lot more. I'm not interested in favoritism. I want quality. Millar, take command of the soldiers. Adesina, report to the General. Dismissed."

The two officers salute, then walk out of the command center, leaving me alone with Ligaya. "You up for this?"

She nods.

"You worried?"

"A little, Sir."

"Good. I like an officer with some humility. It'll serve you well under my command. Especially when you're going to be commanding a bunch of civilians."

"Yes, Sir."

"I know you won't enjoy this first part, but I'm going to throw you in the deep end."

She looks at me questioningly, but I just ignore it and wave for her to follow.

Out on the Bridge, I call for everyone's attention. "Listen up. We're going to settle in here for a little while. Perhaps days. Perhaps weeks. It'll all depend on how things turn out. During that time, we're going to figure out a few things such as Bridge protocol. That involves how we act on the Bridge, how we speak to one another, how we address the commanding officer, and how and when we arrive and leave." The expressions on most of the faces tell me they understand. Logan, however, looks worried, and Gerb looks scared.

"We are also going to create a schedule of Bridge officers. Those who work hard and can follow protocol will continue to be on the list. Those who do not… will not."

Gerb's definitely confused. I suspect he's never understood the concept of 'no'.

"This here is Major Ligaya. I am in command of the Bridge, and the Major is my second. When I am not here, her word is law. Understood?"

I see a few nods, but Gerb's eye is doing that thing it does when he thinks everyone around him has gone nuts. "What it is, Gerb?"

"You really expect me to show up on time?"

I wait, hoping he will hear how ridiculous that question was. When nothing clicks, I ask, "Out of everything I said, that's what you have a problem with, Gerb?"

"Yes… uh…"

"You'll call me Sir."

"What do we call Ligaya?"

"*Major* Ligaya!"

"What do we call Major Ligaya?"

"That's something you'll ask her when she takes command of the Bridge in a moment. What's your question, Gerb?"

"If I don't show up on time, I still get to play with the console, right?"

I shake my head. "No, we'll find someone we can count on. These days, everything we face might be a matter of life or death. If we can't rely on someone, the cost could be far too high to pay."

Gerb opens his mouth to say something, but then stops, closes it, and nods. I wouldn't be so harsh with them, but Ligaya's going to have a difficult time if they act like they've been acting over the last few hours.

I pause. Has it really only been hours?

"If there are no more questions," I say before turning to Ligaya, "the Bridge is yours, Major."

I see a flash of irritation in her eyes. I know this is an annoying thing to do, but I need to get down to see how everything's coming together below—especially to see if the ship really does create things like bathrooms and kitchens upon request, beyond just the small one off my Command Center.

24

SIGNAL

Four days later, we're getting everything under control.

General Williams is right about one thing, administration is his thing. He has the entire civilian population living, eating, and surviving. Everything's running smoothly with the new bathrooms and kitchens and dining areas. We've made good use of the ship's ability to transform rooms, and we even have plans to set up a school, some entertainment, and more. He's also managed to secure more decks, and as of now, we have eight decks in total.

I have to admit though, with the creation of bathrooms all around the ship, the thing that worries me most is that no one seems to have any idea where the wastewater is going. Not even a decent guess. I fear the day will come when we find out, and, as Gerb has so eloquently stated, "…it will be a dark day indeed."

Captain Adesina has settled in well to her role, and just this morning, we transferred her back to Millar's command. Many of the soldiers have already worked under her in recent days, so it won't be a problem for her.

What thrills me most, however, is that Major Ligaya has found her niche. She works wonders on that Bridge. She has everyone working hard, focused, and enjoying themselves. Even Gerb shows up on time. Or has the last three days. He still doesn't understand that he can't just wander off whenever he wants, but we'll get there.

Major Ligaya also picked a name for the ship: *The Pagasa*.

Her parents are… were… We know nothing about where they are or if they survived. They had immigrated from the Philippines before Ligaya was born, and she grew up speaking both English and Tagalog. She suggested "pagasa" as it means "hope". It wasn't hard to agree to a name like that.

The *Pagasa*. Hope.

We now have hope… now that we might have a way to free the *Taken*.

My quarters are only a thirty-second walk from the Bridge, and the ship produces a coffee for me just inside the door leading out to the hall every single morning. It's a great way to start the day. We also have a small kitchen for the Bridge crew, just a short walk from everyone's quarters, and Fred takes care of breakfast every morning.

As I walk down the hall, something feels off. I'm not sure what it is at first, but I pick up the pace, and a moment later, my coffee spills as I break into a run.

I run through the open door of the Bridge past the two soldiers standing guard. Inside, there's screaming, hollering, running back and forth… the Bridge is in chaos. Ligaya's hollering for details about something, but everyone else is yelling at one another, or crying, or panicking. Altogether, we appear to have lost all the discipline we'd gained in recent days.

"HEY!" I holler, and the Bridge goes quiet. Gerb tries to speak, but I put my index finger up and shake my head. Turning to Ligaya, I order in a calm voice, "Report, Major."

"Sir, about three minutes ago, we picked up a signal. It's messing with our computers, but aside from that, I apologize, I don't seem able to get answers out of anyone."

"Who received the message?"

"Mr. Stanley."

I give a scolding look to Gerb to remind him to be quiet and then turn to Eric Stanley. He looks like he's about to fall over. "Be direct, Stanley. I want to know what's going on quickly."

"We received a communication, Sir. It was from somewhere to the north of us."

"Everything's to the north of us. Can you be more specific?"

"No, Sir. I think it was from the Greks."

"You know what it says?"

He shakes his head.

"Who can tell me why everyone is so worked up?"

I'm grateful Gerb's not manning the Operations Console right now. I'm not up for one of those battles. Instead, the Head Operations Officer, Sarah Connelly, speaks up. "Sir, I don't know what's going on, exactly, but it's activated something on the ship. I think."

"You think? Certainly we have more than that to go on! Tell me what's gotten everyone so upset!"

She shakes her head. "I think it's some kind of sabotage from the Greks. A lot of my readings are going haywire. So is everyone else's. We've lost control of a few areas such as life support and I believe navigation."

A quick glance at Elizabeth, and she nods back at me before she remembers. "Confirmed, Sir."

Back to Connelly, I order, "Continue."

"Sir, it's not that we've *lost* life support or any of the other systems. We just no longer have control over any of it. It looks like if we even want to change the temperature, we can't."

"I want a full list of everything of which we've lost control in Major Ligaya's hands in five minutes. However, I want to know what caused everyone to throw out Bridge protocol."

She shivers. "It's the lower decks, Sir."

"What's going on down there? Spit it out, Connelly!"

"Sir, I think the signal activated something. Or a lot of things."

"Mateo, turn the scanners in toward the ship. Tell me what we're facing."

"Sir, while everyone was screaming and arguing, I tried that. I don't have control of all the scanners right now, but from what I have… as far as I can tell… there's nothing alive down there. Unless it's hibernating."

"Then what's the problem?" I growl.

He shakes his head. "Sir, Connelly's right. There's a lot of something down there. It's just… again, Sir… none of its alive. Whatever it is… whatever *they* are, they're moving fast. I don't know if it can get through the sealed doors, but whatever it is, it's moving up from the lowest levels through the decks towards us. Sir, I'm not really sure, but from what I see here… we're in trouble. I think whatever it is… it's coming after us!"

CONTINUE READING IN
GREKS: DESCENT

Book Two in The Grek Invasion series!

Are you craving more sci-fi?

Grab ADA (a sci-fi novella) for FREE and get a bonus fantasy read from The Ridge Series!

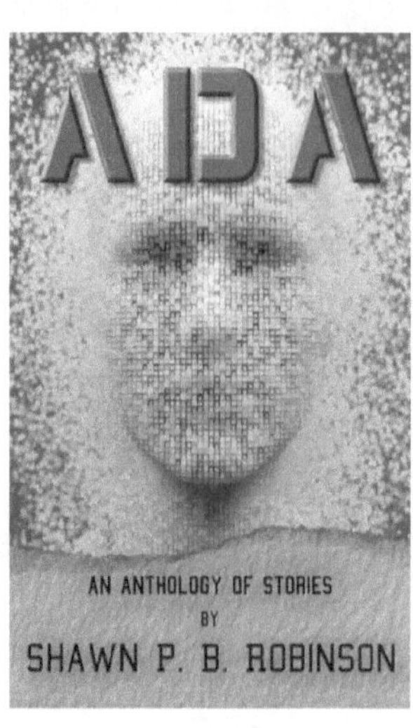

MEANINGS OF NAMES

Aaron

Aaron means "Mountain of Strength, Exalted, Strong," which is what he can be if he finds freedom from the Greks.

Abaya Ligaya

Abaya means "Refuge" and Ligaya means "Happiness". Her name means "Refuge of Happiness or Joy". Her first and last name are of Filipino origin.

Adesina

Adesina is a Nigerian name meaning "the crown avenges my suffering" or "royalty has made a way". Adesina had lost her twin sister to the Greks. On a few missions, she sees her sister, but while she does her duty, it tears her apart. She lives in hope of a brighter future, a *way* without suffering.

Alliah

Alliah means "Rising". The hope for her is that she can rise beyond what she has fallen to.

Connie

Connie means "Steadfast and Reliable". This is what Xavier needs from her the most in these painful times.

Elijah Williams

Elijah means "Yahweh is my God" (of Hebrew origin), and Williams means "Helmet of protection, resolute protector" (old German). His last name fits him well in his role as a resolute protector of the people.

Elizabeth

Elizabeth means "God's promise" or "God is my hope". Elizabeth, like so many others, has lost so much, but her hope is in a brighter future.

Geoff

Geoff means "God's peace". This peace is something that is lost to him along the way. His stubbornness led him away from a life that could be his own.

Gordon

Gordon means "Spacious, Fort" (Scottish) and "Beloved" (Irish). He lives as someone who stepped up to be what those around needed, but even a well-defended fort can fall, if care is not taken.

Logan

Logan is a Scottish name which has two meanings. The first is "Little Hollow". The beauty of this name is that Logan appears to be a somewhat "hollow" person at first (shallow, scared, and not what we hope for in a time when we need heroes). But as time goes on, we find strength in him. The weak truly is strong, and his name takes on its second meaning, which is "Strong and Resilient".

Maverick (Gerb)

Maverick, as strange as this sounds, means "an independent man who avoids conformity, a free spirit." Maverick (nicknamed Gerb) is someone who truly lives this out, so much so that his nickname means he's a big baby, and he's quite content with the name.

Millar

Millar is a Scottish name referring to "one who grinds grain", but what is unique is that the Millar clan had this as their motto: "The best things await us in heaven." Someone who grinds grain does it day after day, enduring the monotony of it, and remaining faithful to the task, without which, no one will eat. Major Millar is very much this man: a man who faithfully pushes through the monotony, but looks forward to a better hope in heaven. Millar is a resolute, reliable soldier.

Xavier Ghulam

Xavier and Ghulam are both names of an Arabic origin. Xavier means "New House", and Ghulam means "Servant". Together, this name points to a New House of Servants, a people who will love and serve one another.

CHECK OUT THESE BOOKS BY
Shawn P. B. Robinson

Adult Fiction (Sci-fi & Fantasy)

The Ridge Series (3 books)
ADA: An Anthology of Short Stories
The Grek Invasion (3 books)
Modder's Run (Coming Soon)

YA Fiction (Fantasy)

The Sevordine Chronicles (5 Books)

Books for Younger Readers

Annalynn the Canadian Spy Series (6 Books)
Jerry the Squirrel (5 Books)
Arestana Series (3 Books)
Activity Books (2 Books)

www.shawnpbrobinson.com/books

9 781989 296783